I0760717

PRAISE FOR EXPIRED HOPE

"What do you get when you combine a fire chief and a mental health counselor who find themselves in a deadly game of cat and mouse with a killer? A slow burn romantic suspense packed with bombs, bullets, and burning buildings. With its expertly crafted plot, complex characters, and sweet romance, it's sure to keep you up late into the night."

LYNETTE EASON, BESTSELLING, AWARD-WINNING AUTHOR OF THE EXTREME MEASURES SERIES

"What a ride! *Expired Hope* gripped me from page one and didn't let go. With intriguing characters, hard-hitting action, a tender romance, and danger on all sides, this story of a struggling fire chief and the burdened therapist he's forced to work with will burn brightly in readers' minds long after they close the last page."

KERRY JOHNSON, PUBLISHERS WEEKLY BESTSELLING AUTHOR OF *SNOWSTORM SABOTAGE*

"Teeming with rich characters and stirring tension that rises with each turn of the page, Besing's latest suspense is beautifully rooted in redemption and hope—a heartfelt romance that just won't let you go. Highly recommended!"

ABIGAIL WILSON, AUTHOR OF *WITHIN THESE GILDED HALLS*

EXPIRED HOPE

LAST CHANCE FIRE AND RESCUE | BOOK 2

LISA PHILLIPS
MEGAN BESING

To my husband.
You are so much better than any fictional hero,
and I'm so blessed to have you as my real life
happily-ever-after. Thank you for cherishing
me and all my weirdness.
I love you.

"But now, Lord, what do I look for?
My HOPE is in You."
PSALM 39:7 NIV

A NOTE FROM LISA

Dear Reader

It's hard to believe a tiny germ of an idea for *Expired Hope* has come this far. One of the things I love about writing novels is the community I can create within the books. Those tight-knit friendships, relationships, and families drive the stories I write, and I hope there are many more to come.

Expired Hope is a heartfelt story about two broken people and a whole lot of danger! You'll be as glued to the pages as I was waiting to see what happens next. But underneath it all is a God story that is written in all of us when He takes the hurt and pain of the past and makes all things new. Only He can bring the hope that sustains us, no matter what happens in our lives.

I'll keep saying it with each book – but I love these characters!

Bringing the Last Chance County Fire Department to life in the Fire and Rescue series has been a blast. All the characters feel like friends, and getting to know them as they came to life has been so fun.

What came as a surprise to me was the community I would find with other authors! The Sunrise family is a blessing to work with. It's been an absolute pleasure riding the ups and downs of the past year or so and getting to know other authors. I've grown so much as we've wrestled stories onto the page, collaborated, shared, and prayed with each other as a team. All those behind-the-scenes things that go into getting a great story out so readers can enjoy it.

Megan, you've been a blessing to work with, tackling everything that was thrown at you with grace (and lots of coffee). I'm looking forward to all the stories to come and watching you grow with each one. It's so fun, right?!

Creating a community of readers is something every author wants to do. My readers are amazing people who are so friendly and supportive. Chatting with each person lets me know I've been doing my job, and I will keep striving to grow and improve with each new story I write. Every book is for you guys. It's why I do this.

So, as always, Happy Reading!

Lisa

1

"Peter, you are not at war. Look for Joey in your backseat. Do you see him?" Natalie Atkinson gripped the steering wheel of her Volkswagen Beetle and put on her hazards. If only counselors had emergency lights.

"Stand down." She spoke loud and clear over the phone connection. "There's no enemy."

Not one they could see.

Trash bags whipped past her window and her mouth fell open. Clearly, the highway department had left sacks on the side of the road all over town. To a veteran who'd served where IEDs were concealed in anything from garbage to ditches to animal carcasses, those discarded bags could have sparked a memory of an explosion—the one that had flipped Peter's Humvee and killed everyone inside except him.

A trigger Natalie should have anticipated. For him, and for herself.

"Peter, I want you to pull over. I'm—"

"I-I'm not at war," Peter rasped. "I'm no longer a soldier."

"That's right." He needed to be grounded by the truth. Being a soldier was only a thing of both their pasts. Not their futures. "Do you see Joey?" His six-year-old had noticed something wasn't right and called her on speaker. "Joey, are you still with us?"

"I'm here, Ms. Natalie." Unlike his father, his voice was as steady as a sharpshooter. "We're pulled over."

"Good." The stoplight turned red before her, and Natalie slammed on her brakes. She brushed her bangs back in place, covering her scarred forehead. "Do you know what exit you last passed or what store you're by? I'm heading toward you, but I need your location."

Based on their normal schedule, Peter would have picked up Joey from school and they'd be on their way home. But an errand might have gotten them off the primary route.

"Umm..." A beep echoed over the phone. "Ms. Natalie? The phone's making noises."

"Just stay with me, Joey." Whoever was calling Peter would have to wait. "Can you tell me where—"

"We're by the best french fry place."

That didn't exactly help. "Okay, I'm almost there." Sort of. If it was the mom-and-pop restaurant nearest their house, they were close to home. Almost to safety.

Another beep interrupted the silence.

"Ms. Atkinson?" Peter sounded less dazed.

"Still here, Peter. What are you looking at right now?" Natalie needed to keep Peter talking. Keep him in the present and away from the past. If only she could do the same.

According to the file she had studied when she first got hired at the Ridgeman Center, it had been months since his last episode, and Joey needed him now more than ever. "Do you see any—"

Another beep. Which meant it wasn't someone trying to reach Peter. It was worse.

"Joey, does your dad have a charger for his phone?"

But it wasn't Joey who answered. "I-I can make it home. Have to make it home for my son. I promised to protect him."

She pictured him squeezing the bridge of his nose like he did when a difficult topic arose during their sessions.

"There's no rush, Peter, there's—"

Her earpiece clicked off, and the hum of the tires on the road was anything except comforting. She'd been about to remind Peter there was no rushing the healing process, but now was the exact moment to hurry.

She pressed her accelerator and whipped around the curves.

Peter and Joey's house sat at the end of the cul-de-sac, giving the appearance of a man handling his new full-time, single fatherhood well. Between him and his ex-wife, Angie, Peter had seemed like the most stable to care for Joey. Her boss, Dean Cartwright, and even CPS agreed with Natalie.

But what if she'd misread someone again...

A silver car with a *My student is on the honor roll* bumper sticker was already parked in the driveway. A deep breath in and out slowed her nerves. They had made it home. She hadn't let anyone else down.

Natalie parked and grabbed her briefcase from the seat beside her. The hope of decompressing with a horse trail ride tonight at her cousin's house would have to be postponed, but she was thankful she'd slipped away from the office. Since she had been home, she'd grabbed one of Joey's favorite treats from her pantry. Peter's file had already been in her briefcase in prep for their scheduled meeting at the end of the week.

As she hustled for the front door, her navy pencil skirt restricted her speed and her low-heel pumps pinched her toes.

Peter wasn't pacing or wringing his hands on the porch. Joey wasn't sitting on the steps either. How fast had Peter driven? Only the smell of something buttery being cooked somewhere in the neighborhood welcomed her. Until her foot hit the last step and the door swung open.

"Wel-come ho-ome." Peter's ex-wife stood in the doorframe like she belonged there.

Unlike the first time Natalie had met Angie, the woman didn't have a lick of makeup on, and her hair had fallen out of what, at one point, might have been a bun. Her stained apron was upside down. Apparently, she'd lost even more unnecessary weight since their last meeting.

Natalie squared her shoulders. The day did not need to get any worse for her patient. "Ms. Johnson, does Peter know—"

"Don't you dare call me that," Angie spat.

Right. Well, she was no longer a Mrs., and by court mandate, she wasn't supposed to see Joey outside of set visiting hours. Ones that would be approved *after* her rehab completion.

A slam of a car door had Natalie spinning back toward the street.

Peter ran toward them. Natalie did a quick scan. His face was pale, yet his eyes were focused. First on Natalie, then onto Angie, and finally the open front door. Life wasn't often kind. It had plunged him from one massive problem to another. "How did you get inside?"

Angie narrowed her eyes, not at Peter but at Natalie. "I knew she was the reason we're not together. She's got you believing her lies. I told you, I don't need help. Especially not hers." Angie puffed out her bottom lip. "That's the real reason you both sent me to rehab."

Did Creekside Therapy know she'd left? If only she had agreed to go to the Ridgeman Center where Natalie worked.

Peter extended his palm to his ex. It was steadier than Natalie's heart rate. "Hand over the hidden key."

"Momma?" Joey's freckled face peeked out from behind his father.

"Oh, baby." Angie flung open her arms. "Come here."

Joey looked up at his father. Peter squeezed the bridge of his nose. "Make it quick and then go up to your room."

While Angie hugged and whispered promises to Joey, Natalie stepped closer to the door and set her briefcase inside. She flipped her phone over in her hand. If Angie didn't leave soon, she'd have to call the police.

"Joey. It's time," Peter murmured. "You can play your video game until I come and get you."

Joey wiggled free from his weeping mother and raced inside. His footsteps thundered up the staircase.

"How could you?" Angie brought her hands to her neck. Her face was splotched red and tear-stained, while her gaze filled with what resembled regret.

Natalie fisted her hands and reexamined Peter's expression and body language. Color had returned to his cheeks. His shoulders weren't drooped. The IED trigger had passed. He had gotten himself calmly home and was processing the problem before him in a healthy way. As a father, ready to fight for what was right for his son.

Which meant, patient or not, Peter wasn't the one who required Natalie the most at the moment. She lifted her chin and turned toward Angie. "Why don't I give you a ride back—"

"No." Angie ran her hand through her matted hair. "I'm not the one who must leave."

"Ange, she has to do her job. I need some help or Joey—"

"Don't you dare let her take Joey from you too." Angie pushed her pointer finger against Peter's chest. "You promised me you'd always take care of him. Promised!"

Peter clenched his jaw and rubbed at his chest. "I'm not the one breaking any promises. All you have to do is get sober and stay clean. Then the court said they'd give back your rights."

"They never should have taken him away from me." Angie pressed her lips together. "I'd never hurt my Joey."

Peter's gaze swung to the open door behind Natalie and back. "Our son found you on the floor with a needle still in your arm."

By the flash of rage on Angie's face, Natalie knew there would be no horse riding tonight with her cousin. No moment to decompress after a long day. Not when others' needs were more important.

Natalie stepped in between the stare-off. "Let's take a moment to—"

"I'm tired of your moments." Angie picked up a flowerpot painted with little thumbprint butterflies. "Drugs helped me because you broke my heart. It's your fault I don't have my son. *My* son!" As her voice rose, she thrust the plant at Peter's feet.

Peter jumped out of the way, and the pot shattered on the concrete. The scattered soil and drooped flower served as a recap of how well Natalie was helping. But she could fix this. Had to fix this.

"Get out of my house." Peter's voice was low, and it carried a punch.

Angie moved. But in the wrong direction. She twisted past Natalie and dashed for the staircase. "Joey! Honey!"

As Peter sprinted after Angie, Natalie dialed nine before he reached for his ex-wife and hoisted her up.

She kicked her legs. "Put me down!"

Natalie pressed the one and scanned the stairs. Still no Joey. There had never been a more perfect time for a child to be playing video games.

Angie whimpered and went limp in Peter's arms.

If Natalie finished the call, would it help or hurt Angie's recovery process?

In the driveway, Peter marched her down to the silver car Natalie had thought was his.

Peter planted Angie on her feet. "Don't come back until you complete your therapy. Then we'll talk. Not before. We can't keep our promise to care for Joey if you keep breaking the rules."

Natalie was all for Angie leaving the boys in peace, but did she need to drive? "Angie, when was your last hit? Your last drink?"

Instead of another angry outburst, watery-eyed Angie wilted against her car. "Two days. I promise. I just—I miss Joey. Pete, I'm sorry—"

He shook his head. "If you love Joey, finish the course." Peter gently placed his palm on her shoulder. "If you keep showing up, they might take him from me too. Is that what you want?"

Angie shook her head as a tear rolled off her chin like a last goodbye. "You gotta keep him safe." She hiccupped. "You promised."

At Peter's nod, Angie got into her car. Natalie hung up the phone without completing the call to emergency services.

Peter rubbed his chest again, watching the back of Angie's car as she drove away.

Natalie took in the sweat lining his forehead. His hand rested flat on his chest instead of clenching in rage. Defeat might be written all over his sweat-stained shirt and swimming through his eyes, however, his response in this heated situation showed the hope of growth. He'd thought through the problem instead of reacting. Stayed in the present. He was the right parent to keep Joey in a stable home.

She offered him a smile. "I'm proud of you."

"Yeah, well, I pay you to say those kinds of things."

"You most certainly do not. You pay the Ridgeman Center to help you process life."

He kicked at a rock in his driveway. "I hope you don't plan on raising your rates after seeing how broken I am."

If he only knew who he was speaking to. "Hate to break it to you, but we're all a little broken. Some just hide it better."

Like she had to.

"Maybe." He motioned for the front door and froze.

A cloud of smoke rolled out the door and filled the ceiling of the porch. Peter bolted. Natalie raced on his heels.

Inside, the living room was already hazy. It made her eyes water.

The stove top and cabinets were engulfed in flames. Angie had been wearing an apron. Why hadn't Natalie noticed?

Peter reached into the cabinet under the sink and pulled out a fire extinguisher.

Natalie blinked at the angry flames. She wanted to help. Needed to. Except her arms and legs were heavier than the Kevlar she used to wear.

The heat and the flames...

Instead of being in Peter's kitchen, her mind jumped to her last duty station.

"Clear the area!" the MP yelled.

Natalie jumped the barricade. Something sliced her leg right through her ACUs, but she couldn't stop. She couldn't leave her friend with a bomb strapped to his chair.

"Ms. Atkinson!" Peter held the canister against his chest. His breaths peppered as fast as her own. "Joey..." Sweat oiled his forehead as his gaze danced around the room to each flame. "You—"

Natalie didn't wait for orders. She sprinted for the stairs.

Her shoes disappeared off her feet on the third step. She opened the first upstairs door. A toilet. Sink. No Joey. The next bedroom was empty. She flung open the last door. A twin bed. Dresser and a basketball. Still no Joey.

Had he somehow left the house? A line of lyrics she recognized floated from close by, and she remembered where Joey's favorite place was—his closet.

She hopped over the bed and opened the closet. Shoes. Clothes. A baseball bat. No freckle-faced boy.

"Joey!" She shoved the hangers of jeans and hoodies aside and found a half door at the far left.

Natalie fell to a squat and opened the latch. A lantern and Joey were surrounded by pillows. He held his portable video game, headset on.

"Joey, we've got to go." She gulped as darkness feathered on the outside of her vision. "There's a fire."

"Hold on a sec."

She leaned into the storage compartment that was longer than any normal closet. "No, now. Fire—"

He did a fist pump. "Gold level! Take that, Simon." He stuck the edge of his tongue along his cheek. "Dad usually has a fire when he cooks. He burned nuggets in the microwave once. That's why we order takeout. Is that where we're going? I'd rather have your pretzels."

Natalie didn't wait to explain. She crawled in farther and grabbed his earphones and the gaming device.

"Hey!"

"We've got to get out. There's an actual fire in the kitchen. Your dad needs our help."

Joey blinked at Natalie and then nodded. Natalie had a harder time moving backward in a skirt and the cramped space. She reached the closet door and was hit with another wave of heat.

Joey yanked on his gaming system, and it fell from Natalie's fingers.

She gaped. Joey's curtains were on fire. So was the basketball goal. The posters on his door curled and turned to ash. Flames flickered up from his trashcan.

She threaded her fingers through Joey's. "We need to get out of here." But the door and window were blocked by hot flames. *Please, God, not again.*

Joey gripped her hand. "What do we do?"

2

Fire Chief Macon James turned his command vehicle into the parking lot. The last student question from his classroom visit still rang in his head.

Are all firefighters heroes?

He jumped out of his truck and headed for the open bay door of Eastside Firehouse. Two members of Truck 14, Zack Stephens and Ridge Foster, were lined up in front of their lieutenant, Amelia Patterson. Their turnout gear and equipment placed on the ground had been sectioned out like a relay race.

"Wait. Wait." Zack Stephens, their youngest Truck firefighter, raised his hand, a smirk on his face. "What do I get if I win?"

Amelia held up the stopwatch, her expression almost pulled as tight as her blonde ponytail. "The satisfaction of doing your job correctly."

Ridge Foster picked up his helmet with a grunt. "This is a complete waste of time. We'd be better off checking our regulators again."

"You're just mad I beat you."

Ridge swiped his gloves off the floor. “I got my gear on in under ninety seconds, didn’t I?”

Zack kept a neutral expression as he hooked his thumb in Ridge’s direction. “You also got beat by a girl.” When he spotted Macon, he waved. “Hey, Chief. How was the classroom visit? Wait...what do I get if I beat the chief?”

Amelia folded her arms without a glance at Macon. “He has more important tasks to do than race you. Stay focused, Stephens.”

Ridge shuffled the equipment in his arms. “So, you do agree with me? This exercise is a waste of time. Ladies and Gentlemen—or should I say, Lady and Gentlemen—there’s a first for everything.”

Before Amelia ground out a reply through her noticeably locked jaw, Macon jogged over. His boots thumped against the concrete, and the scent of the orange cleaning solution they used overpowered the lingering smoke smell that was a permanent resident.

“Hold up.” He stepped between Ridge and Amelia. “Let me grab my gear, and I’ll get in on this training.”

“Yeah, suckers.” Zack pumped his fist. “I bet you both I’ll beat the chief by seven seconds.”

Amelia rolled her eyes. “Just be faster than ninety or you’re doing my toilet duty.” The lieutenant pressed her lips together. Macon wasn’t sure why his agreement to participate in the training had somehow made her even more unhappy. She didn’t wait for Macon to spread out his gear on the ground.

She clicked the stopwatch. “Go.”

“Hey, now,” Zack screeched.

Macon knew better than to waste seconds complaining. Even if Amelia’s methods could be less drill sergeant-like, she had a point. Always be prepared. Fire waited for no one.

“Twenty seconds.”

Macon already had his boots, turnout pants, and jacket on.

When he grabbed his self-contained breathing apparatus, or SCBA, the fire alarm went off.

A voice crackled through the PA speakers. “Truck 14, Ambulance 21, residential fire.”

Zack paused and lowered his brows. “Is this training or for real?”

Ridge slapped him on the shoulder and handed him his TIC, a thermal imaging camera. “I thought you weren’t a rookie anymore.”

The bunkroom door flew open. Trace Bently and Izan Collins rushed over to Ambo 21. They would be ready if there were any medical emergencies. Rescue Squad 5 would meet them there if need be. But that didn’t explain why Truck 14 was one man short.

Macon glanced around. “Where’s Greene?”

Ridge slammed the driver’s side door closed and leaned out the open window. “Ghost gets gastrointestinal distress when Amelia starts drills.”

The newest firefighter had been with them almost for a month. Four weeks, and Mickey’s death was still a shock wave rumbling through his crew. It hadn’t helped that Dave Greene had yet to fill his predecessor’s shoes, earning the nickname “Ghost” because of his skill at being invisible inside the firehouse. Nor did it help that Dave’s grandfather, George Greene, was on the city hall oversight committee.

Amelia sprinted to her side of the truck. Gear on, the only thing they required was their fourth person. Which wasn’t supposed to be the chief.

“Greene?” Amelia hollered.

The hallway was clear, and Dave wasn’t running or yelling for them to wait.

Macon hopped in the truck beside Zack. “Let’s go, Ridge.”

Ridge obeyed, but Amelia spun around in the front seat. “Sir, I got this. We don’t need you.”

Macon didn't miss how Amelia never used his chief title. "A lieutenant has to know where their people are. As chief, I will not let any of my trucks go out undermanned."

"Someone's crabby that she won't be the highest rank on scene now." Ridge glanced at Macon in the rearview mirror.

Technically, she was right. It was Macon's day off. Attending the classroom career day had been a favor to Macon's old high school baseball coach. It'd been the least Macon could do for quitting when the team had needed him.

Amelia fixed him with her stern gaze. "Even you can't disobey protocol. Regulations state you cannot be on duty for more than—"

"I have until Friday to take my day off." Not counting the hours of paperwork he would forget to log when he arrived back at the firehouse. "Keep to your job, Lieutenant."

Amelia huffed and turned back around. Ridge sailed through the traffic with ease. Office buildings and shopping areas dotted the streets, yet nothing completely blocked the mountains that nestled the city. A familiar baseball diamond flew by his window, and Macon rested his head against the seat.

They turned by a purple building and whirled into a subdivision. A muted rainbow of siding where every third house had an identical porch design. Ridge whittled his way down the tight roads. Rescue radioed in that they were across town and fifteen minutes out.

Smoke saturated the air. Macon leaned forward. "Looks like we've got smoke coming out the open front door."

"Blocked fireplace?" Zack spoke into his walkie, despite everyone being able to hear him.

"Negative," Amelia said. "No visible chimney."

"I call the kitchen." Zack leaned forward and squinted out the windshield. "My money's on a burnt grilled cheese."

"There's no betting allowed when lives are at stake."

True, but Amelia didn't have to scowl to get her point across.

The truck stopped, and Macon was the first one out the door. "I'll perform my three-sixty. Foster, get the hose stretched. Stephens and Patterson—"

Amelia launched from the spot where she'd taken a knee to pull on her SCBA. "Heading through the front door to assess internal damage."

Stephens blinked at the rolling smoke and adjusted his helmet.

Two steps away from the house, Patterson turned. "Stay on my heels, Stephens!"

His crew needed a three-sixty too. It hadn't been a smooth adjustment since he'd taken command and lost one of their crew-members on his first day. But right now, the house and fire assessment had priority.

Macon rounded the corner of the house. Still no visible fire from the front, but flames had to be somewhere. Smoke thundered from the open front door.

Neighbors congregated on their own porches and front lawns. As long as they stayed away, he wouldn't have to worry about blocking the road. Yet people rarely remained where they should.

A woman in purple pajama pants and a shirt that said *I love bunnies* ran toward him. She pointed at the blue car parked on the road in front of the house. "That's Peter's car." She shook her head at the white car in the drive. "Never seen that one before."

Macon radioed his crew. "It's possible we've got multiple civilians inside."

He motioned the woman back. Rescue would have to handle barriers and roadblocks when they arrived from their earlier call. There was no threat of oncoming traffic, just nosy neighbors and scanner junkies.

Trace parked the ambulance right behind them. Macon relayed to Rescue the condition of the narrow roads even though their driver, Jayson Owens, should be able to handle them.

The left side of the house had a gate to the backyard. Still no visible flames. Macon hoped it was only a burnt grilled cheese. They were overdue for something simple—and for one single day of being the chief at Eastside Firehouse to go smoothly.

The almost fifty pounds of gear didn't slow Macon down. Training and experience had taught him how to appreciate and work with the lifesaving equipment. At the farthest window, Macon spotted what ruined Zack's bet and Macon's wish. Flames and smoke were both visible between the window blinds.

Macon grabbed his walkie. "Ridge, get the hose back to left lower. I've got flames."

"Kitchen fire. Hundred times worse than a seared grilled cheese," Zack said.

"Getting one civilian out." Amelia's voice crackled. "Bently, heading your way. Unconscious male."

Another quick scan of the area using his TIC. The thermal energy reading proved it would not be an easy day. The siding melted like an ice-cream cone at the beach. "Fire's pushing upward into second story. ETA on that hose?"

"Hydrant's giving me fits," Ridge yelled. "Thirty seconds!"

Macon pushed through the fence gate and fell over a discarded bicycle. His walkie crashed onto the ground, and the TIC got stuck on the handlebars. He jerked the tangled mess free and got to his feet.

He grabbed his thermal imaging camera and scanned the second story. Either the fire was moving quick, or there were people upstairs.

People who may not have thirty seconds.

Macon raced to the back door on the opposite side of the fire. *Please be unlocked.* The door opened as if God still listened to Macon's prayers.

Inside, the smoke was dense but thankfully gray, not brown. The untreated wood hadn't been hit yet by the flames, which meant the structure was still as stable as possible.

He hunched over and dragged his hand along a wall for guidance. When he pushed a chair out of the way, his gloved fingers felt only air. Finally, the staircase.

Smoke waved past him as if it couldn't decide where it wanted to go first. He squinted in the haze. Was that a woman's shoe on the steps? "Heading upstairs. Possible civilians. Passing command to you, Lieutenant."

Macon scanned the rooms with his TIC as he moved along the upstairs hallway. The farthest area had the most heat, which would be his best guess for any civilians.

A scream stopped his path. He swirled around, and his TIC showed someone in the opposite room. He followed his screen to a small door inside a closet—something he never would have found without his thermal imaging camera.

Except a bookcase in the closet blocked their exit.

"I'm Fire Chief James." He grunted and lifted the edge of the bookcase. "I'm going to get you out!" With the shelves stacked with books, it would take too long to push it out of the way.

Banging came from the other side, and Macon's heart rate soared.

He squeezed behind the bookcase and knocked it over. Once the books tumbled out, he shoved the bookcase out of the way and flung open the hidden door.

A boy flew into his arms. As much as Macon wanted to offer comfort, he needed to know two things. "Are you hurt? Is there anyone else in—"

The boy pointed at a woman behind him.

She crawled out of the tiny closet wearing a gray shirt and a wrinkled skirt that would hang past her knees but had wedged higher than she probably preferred. The woman stumbled to her bare feet, looked at the boy in Macon's hands, and then her eyes rolled backward.

"Whoa there!" Macon caught the woman with his shoulder against the wall. He would radio for more hands, but he didn't have any to spare.

"I can walk," the boy offered.

Macon released him and gathered the woman into his arms. She mumbled and tucked her head against his chest.

With a quick scan of their smoky exit, Macon yelled to the boy, "Hold on to my jacket."

Flames in the hallway ate up the opposite end. One step at a time, they made it down the stairs. The boy coughed, and Macon wished he could offer him his air. But if he did, he'd struggle to carry the woman. Strength and training had less to do with it than breathable air did.

Her grip tightened around him.

"We're almost out, ma'am. I've still got you." Macon felt the tug of the boy behind him. "You too, buddy."

Up ahead he spotted a break in the smoke and picked up his pace. They were almost to the exit when Macon ran into one of his crew members.

Through her mask, Amelia's eyes narrowed. She grabbed the boy's hand, and Macon followed her shadow.

Out in the fresh air, he allowed himself to smile at the woman he cradled. "You okay?"

A cough rattled through her. "Where's Joey? Peter?" She squirmed in his arms.

He eased her to her feet. "Go slow, ma'am."

But as soon as the woman turned, the boy wrapped his arms around her waist. As Macon steadied them both, he took in the fire. Flames had popped out through a caved in section of the roof. However, the hose made the flames hiss under the water's power. At least Ridge had won the hydrant battle.

Was the rest of his crew safe? The other civilian?

Izan rushed over to the woman and knelt in front of the boy. "Does anything hurt?"

By the corner of the house, Zack grabbed on to the hose behind Ridge. Where had Amelia gone? And why hadn't Rescue shown up yet? He hit his walkie button. "Patterson?"

Nothing but the roar of the fire and the whoosh of the hose filled the pause. He aimed his TIC back at the house. Surely she hadn't gone back in without telling anyone.

Movement by the fire truck caught Macon's attention.

Amelia stood at the rear of the truck, struggling with their second hose. Macon dropped his TIC. As he hustled toward Amelia, he spotted the rescue squad truck parked behind the ambulance. Charlie Benning and Eddie Rice ran over with their hose.

"Patterson."

She glanced over at Macon but continued to attach the hose to the truck.

"Wait on this hose." Macon stopped beside her. "Rescue is here. But when I radio you, make sure you answer. I thought you had—"

His other lieutenant from Rescue, Bryce Crawford, radioed in. Except Macon only heard it on Amelia's walkie. Not his own.

Amelia answered Bryce. "Copy that." She frowned at Macon's chest. "Guess Foster was right." She flicked Macon's severed walkie cords. "My training was a waste. Or perhaps the right chief for us would have double-checked his own equipment instead of trying to buddy up with his crew."

Macon James isn't the committee's first choice for chief.

No matter what good Macon had achieved today, he couldn't unhear the committee. Amelia showed her agreement in their daily interactions, especially after she claimed Mickey's death was Macon's fault.

He folded his arms. "Patterson, I won't—"

"Dad!"

Macon jerked his head toward the cry and away from Amelia's judgment of his leadership. Away from the brief victory he'd had rescuing two lives.

The doors to the ambulance slipped open to reveal Trace performing CPR on a guy Macon assumed to be the homeowner.

Memories of Macon's own brother receiving CPR in an ambulance snaked through his mind.

He dropped his helmet and ran for the boy. The teacher had been right today. Being the firefighter chief was a costly burden.

But there was no other option.

3

Even if hospitals smelled like freshly baked cookies, it would still never make the wait more bearable. Two vending machines lined the opposite wall, but Natalie couldn't even offer Joey a distraction in the form of food. Her purse was still under the seat in her car, and her briefcase and pretzels had likely burned in the house.

The way she and Joey almost had.

She slid her fingers under her leg. She should have responded to the chaos like she used to when she first joined the army. Instead, she had frozen. Failed the mission.

Joey had his socked feet tucked up on the supposedly cushioned chair. His arms wrapped around his legs, resembling the way the firefighter had carried her out of the house. Away from the flames. Away from the past.

For a brief moment when the firefighter had smiled at her, there had been something she hadn't allowed to blossom in a long time.

Hope.

But it had flatlined after seeing Peter's lifeless body. Too much death followed her.

Lord, please save him.

Joey sniffed once. Twice. "Is Dad going to be okay?" He kept his gaze glued to the doors on the right. His dad was somewhere back there, fighting for his life.

She climbed over to the chair beside him, and he leaned against her shoulder. With each tear that dropped onto her blouse, she begged God for healing.

How could she trust God if He never listened?

Her phone chimed. One of the two things she'd had in her pockets. Her boss, Dean, had sent a text.

DEAN

You okay?

Natalie swallowed. Her throat burned as hot as the flames that had reached Joey's bedroom. She was glad Dean wasn't here to study her.

She texted back with one hand so as not to disturb Joey.

NATALIE

I'm more worried about Joey and Peter.

His next reply made her stomach twist.

DEAN

CPS should be almost there.

She hadn't been much older than Joey when she had waited for news about her father. She touched her bangs. The curl of her hair had gone flat hours ago, but at least her old burn scars along her hairline remained covered. The last thing Joey needed was to get scared by the wounds from her mistakes.

Another text vibrated her phone.

DEAN

Tosha's great at her job. If you need me there,
I'll rearrange my schedule.

Natalie had been hired to help Dean and Kelsey Scott at the Ridgeman Center, not become a liability.

"Excuse me, are you Natalie Atkinson?" A woman Natalie hadn't heard come down the hall stood beside them.

She wore a pink sweater with a gold heart in the middle that somehow matched her khaki pants. With a closed-mouth smile, she stuck out her hand. Enough copper bracelets to supply the town with pennies for a year swung around her wrist. "I'm Tosha."

Natalie accepted her welcome. "Under the circumstances, it's nice to meet you."

The side door opened.

Joey flew off his seat and sprinted toward the man in green scrubs. "Where's my dad? When can we go home?"

The surgeon placed his hands behind his back. His haggard gaze skipped over Joey and darted around the room. Other than a raised brow, nothing hinted at the type of news. The doctor didn't even blink.

As they met up with Joey, the floor was chilled beneath Natalie's bare feet. She stretched out her hand for Joey. "How is he?"

The surgeon widened his stance. "Is one of you his relative?"

"Social worker." Tosha displayed her identification.

"Counselor." Except Natalie's ID had been in her briefcase. Although it would only take a phone call to confirm her identity, Joey couldn't wait.

The surgeon crossed his arms. "Until you or the patient provide proof, I don't feel comfortable—"

Natalie held up her hand. She knew what following orders was like. And he was only doing his job by obeying HIPAA.

She squatted beside Joey. "I'll be right over there by the chairs. Tosha will be here with you."

Tosha stepped closer to Joey.

Joey squeezed her fingers once and let go. As she walked away, she prayed his father breathed down the hall. Still alive to share the future.

Once Natalie was seated out of earshot, the doctor spoke to Joey and Tosha.

Joey's face turned the color of the bleach permeating the flooring.

Natalie gripped the armrests. As the surgeon made eye contact with her, her heart burned in her chest. Natalie rose onto her numb feet.

Why did God keep taking people in her life away?

Joey spun around and ran to her. Inside her embrace, he wiped his arm along his face, smearing his tears. "Why won't they let me see him?"

Natalie squeezed her eyes shut. "*It's a blessing to remember those you love in the best way.*" The empty words a soldier had said to her after her mother was killed wouldn't make it out of her mouth.

God, where are You?

"Joey..." Tosha's voice was full of compassion.

Joey sniffed. "It's a stupid rule. Dad would want to see me in the I-see-you. See you too. Why would they name the room that if—"

The *ICU*. "He's okay?" Natalie blurted.

Tosha reached for her. "Yes! Oh, goodness. Sorry. I thought Joey told you. Peter had a heart attack during the fire. The surgeon had to do an emergency bypass surgery. A few minor complications, but overall it went as well as can be expected. However, Peter's going to need to stay awhile in the ICU."

Peter was alive. But Joey would need a place to stay until his father got well. His mother wasn't an option.

Tosha frowned as if reading Natalie's mind. "Joey, don't you think some quiet would be good so your dad can get his strength back?"

Joey edged closer to Natalie. "I can be quiet. I promise I won't make a sound. When Mom used to want to be alone, I remembered to be extra quiet. I only disobeyed once, and Dad said it was a good thing."

Natalie met Tosha's gaze.

"I'm sure you'd be a big help for your father." Tosha lowered until she was eye level with Joey. "However, ICU rooms means no overnight visitors."

"That's a worse rule than you can't earn double bonus in the *Cloud Alien* game." As he wiped a tear off his cheek, he smeared a trail of soot. "Can I go home with Ms. Natalie?"

Tosha shook her head.

Natalie dropped to her knees beside Joey. "I wish you could, buddy. But that's not how things work."

Tosha stood and adjusted her purse strap. "I've got a backpack full of clothes and a few toys for you. How about we go check them out?"

Joey slowly lifted his face, but not Tosha's way.

Natalie wiped a tear off Joey's cheek. "Since your dad needs some healing, Tosha's going to take you to a house where you can get a good night's sleep too. Just while—"

"Please don't take me away from my dad." Joey's lips trembled, and he shook his head. His hair flopped around. "Dad never did drugs, and if it's the fire, we'll get pizza out every night. Or Ms. Natalie, you can bring us pretzels."

Tosha twisted her lips to the side as if thinking about Joey's suggestions. "How about I'll take you to the Cunninghams'? They have a boy a little younger than you, and he's been wanting to have a buddy to play with. You can stay until your father is well enough to come home from the hospital."

His shoulders sagged. He leaned against Natalie and finally whispered, "Can I see my dad first?"

Tosha squinted. "It may not be possible tonight. But it can't hurt to ask."

After an hour of waiting, a nurse finally said Joey could do a quick peek at his father from outside his ICU room.

Joey followed the nurse, and Tosha took out her phone. "Joey seems attached to you. Do you mind if I get your cell number in case we run into any issues?"

"Sure." Natalie rattled off her number and kept her attention on the doors Joey went through. "Thanks for staying longer. He's a great kid."

Tosha spun one of her bangles on her wrist. "Trauma rarely brings out the best in people. I find it's better to be prepared. And if I was in his shoes—or rather, socked feet—I'd want to see my dad. Even only for a second."

Natalie would too. And Tosha was right. Shock and distress presented differently in each person. Joey had been a very brave six-year-old. He'd faced so much since the fire, and with the previous events concerning his mom.

A chill ran down her back, and Natalie crossed her arms. "Honestly, I wish Dean didn't have to call you and I could have brought Joey home with me."

"The Cunninghams are great people. I wish I could bring every kid in need to them. And it actually wasn't Dean who let us know about Joey's situation. A friend of the family alerted our office and offered to care for the boy. But the call was disconnected during the emergency background check process. So, unfortunately, until he calls back and we can verify who it is, Joey will stay with the Cunninghams. The family lives in the same school district as Joey's elementary, so nothing else will be disrupted."

Natalie touched the ends of her bangs again. Nothing else out of the ordinary except Joey having seen his father receiving CPR, being stuck in a closet with the threat of fire destroying their house, and having no other personal items than the smoky clothes on his body.

Tosha touched Natalie's arm. "I'll give you all the updates I can."

The nurse returned, and Natalie walked beside Joey as Tosha explained the plan for the next few days. All too soon, they were outside where Tosha unlocked her vehicle for Joey to get in.

Natalie painted on a smile. "I'll see you soon, okay?"

Instead of answering, Joey hugged her. "Thanks for getting me off my video game. And I'm glad the firefighter was there to catch you."

Tosha sent her a look over the hood, but Natalie ignored her and fixated on the breath that caught in her chest. "I'm glad the firefighters rescued all of us."

In all the chaos of trying to get Joey to the hospital to find news on Peter's condition, the fire almost felt a lifetime ago. But the memory of reaching fresh air made her take in a deep breath. When the firefighter had flipped up his facemask, his smile had lit up with joy. His deep brown eyes had searched hers.

Joey laid his head against her stomach, whisking her back to the present. "Will you bring chocolate-covered pretzels when you come pick me up?"

She combed the boy's hair to the side. His skin, thankfully, wouldn't have to endure the burns she had. "I sure can."

At least he didn't ask when that would be.

Natalie's ride home was filled with a combination of flashbacks from standing in Joey's fire-blocked room to the explosion that had caused her scars and taken her friend Jeremiah's life.

Her road was far narrower in the evenings, with her neighbors parked along the street. Her rental didn't have a garage, but she had one of the few driveways.

She put her car in Park and her stomach growled. If only she could eat a bowl of cereal and fall asleep in a sugar haze watching some cheesy show that made her laugh. Laughter sounded like the best kind of medicine tonight.

The thumbnail moon made her sidewalk and landscaping blur together. One day she'd make time to buy a replacement bulb for the porch. It had burned out the first week she moved in. Habit allowed her to remember the uneven grade of the concrete and where her plants were without tripping.

She pulled out her keys and felt for the latch. The doorknob twisted in her grasp. Why was her door unlocked?

Natalie pushed her purse higher on her arm and turned her keys around in her hand with the points ready to jab or thrust. More than likely, she'd left it ajar when she'd rushed out to help Peter. However, military training had taught her not to let her guard down.

She crept inside and flipped on the entry lamp.

The living room clock ticked as loudly as Natalie's heart. She squinted, but there were no unordinary shadows in the half-lit room. That didn't mean someone wasn't hiding. Just last week, there had been break-ins three roads over. Someone could have picked her lock.

She typed nine-one-one into her phone for the second time that day. Her finger hovered over the Send button while she tiptoed down the dark hall.

Outside her bedroom, she slid her hand along the wall. Then turned on the light.

Dresser drawers weren't sprung open. No damage to her hidden safe in her closet. Her ruffled bedcover and robe were exactly where she'd flung them in the morning's rush.

However, she knew life wasn't always what it seemed. Her job was to see the hidden.

Natalie inched down the hallway. Checked each room. With all lights on and every closet cleared, she inspected the front door once more. The only abnormal things were the unlocked door and the smell of smoke in her hair.

She flipped the deadbolt, then set her purse and keys on the entryway table before heading for the kitchen.

She pushed the healthier box of cereal out of the way and went for the sugary one. But as she closed the cabinet, she knocked over the extra bag of chocolate-covered pretzels she stocked for Joey.

Natalie leaned against the counter. The unlocked door from her quick exit was the least of her worries. What if Peter hadn't seen the trash bags on his way home and Joey hadn't called Natalie? Would Joey have been able to get out of his fiery room in time? Would Peter have had a heart attack anyway?

She closed her eyes and took a deep breath. Even with her training, her anxiety fought for control. She had to be the dependable one. She had to process the logic. The truths.

If Natalie hadn't been at Peter's house, Angie may not have gotten upset. Either way, Natalie should have acted more like her mother, the medal of honor recipient, would have.

With trembling fingers, she opened the cereal and took a much-needed bite of food. Her phone rang. Her cousin's photo popped up on her screen. Below it, his name. *Allen Frees.*

A tight-lipped hello and a sigh. "Hey, cuz, I hope your day was better than mine, because I'm going to need a favor."

She swallowed slowly and did what she'd sworn as a counselor she'd never do.

She lied.

4

Macon closed the blinds on his office door. Becoming chief meant he had to tackle the *S*'s: safety, solutions, and sacrifice. And apparently, on occasion, sneaking.

He grabbed his clipboard and rolled his chair close enough to his desk that he could reach his morning coffee while taking advantage of the sunlight. Today was technically his day off, which meant if Amelia caught him here doing paperwork, she wouldn't let it go.

However, there was no point in staying home. He needed to go over his report on yesterday's fire. Amelia had him second-guessing his decisions. She hadn't liked that Dave's absence from yesterday's last run had been her responsibility. Yet more important was how they'd all failed to work together. Again.

Macon rubbed his eyes and took another swig of his coffee. He glanced at the tower of paperwork that, if he had to guess, Amelia had added to.

If Macon could somehow get everyone to stop nitpicking everything, the firehouse would become more like a family. The brother-and-sister banter flowed naturally, yet the safety and forever bond of having each other's backs was nowhere near the trusted comradery Macon had been a part of on other fire teams. Their current state reminded him of his relationship with his own brother.

A knock came at the door. Macon laid down his pen. So much for calling today his time off.

"Come on in." He didn't know who he'd expected, but it wasn't Allen Frees.

The fire department's community liaison officer rolled his wheelchair through the door, the width of his shoulders almost brushing the doorframe.

Allen's frown deepened as he lifted his chin toward the ceiling. "Why are you sitting in the dark?"

Macon flipped on his desk lamp. He couldn't tell the guy who'd hired him he was hiding because he wasn't technically supposed to be there yet. "Waking up slowly, I guess." Which was partially true.

"Bad night?"

Sleep hadn't been his friend for years. The woman's eyes had kept showing up when he'd finally drifted off last night. A part of him wanted to check if Amelia had recorded the woman's name in her report. "Something like that."

Allen rolled right up beside Macon. "Did your rough night have anything to do with yesterday's call?"

The fire, his radio disconnection, his crews, his responsibilities, his past. The woman he'd carried out in his arms. The one who'd looked at him like he was her hero.

Macon clutched the armrests instead of kneading his temples. It always seemed like all of life's burdens waited until he lay down and then they'd all start screaming. "It wasn't that bad. Might need to break down and buy a new pillow or something."

Allen stared at him for a moment and then shook his head. "You're going to have to work with me, Macon. Same team.

Remember that. But also…" He held up his finger before waving it between them. "We have to learn to communicate. It's not necessarily my strong suit either, but we owe it to our hometown to be ready to help when they call. And in our positions, that means making tough decisions."

Usually "tough decisions" had to do with letting someone go. Was it Dave? Macon was all for that, but he wasn't sure if he was ready to make the mayor or the committee even more unhappy before his trial period ended.

Returning to Last Chance County wasn't going as smoothly as hoped.

Allen wheeled over to the window and glanced outside. "We should have figured this out back when I was first hired. Then lately I was busy trying to find the right chief. And then with Mickey's death…"

Macon tipped his coffee cup too far, and coffee dripped onto his hand. He sucked in a breath and set the cup down. Despite it being ruled an accident, did Allen secretly blame him too?

"You all right?"

Macon wiped his wrist on his pants. "Yeah, I've survived hotter."

His first day as chief had been the worst in all of his firefighter career. He'd never had to tell a mother she'd lost her son before. A call for a warehouse fire and a collapsed wall and his damaged air regulator. Mickey never saw it coming. None of them had.

Allen nodded. "That's another reason I've decided that the crews need counseling."

If Macon had still been holding his coffee, he would have dropped it completely.

"A mental health evaluation will give the oversight committee peace of mind, so to speak. Especially with all that's been going on the past few months. Years, really. You guys deal with all sorts of trauma. Some on your crews were around when Steven Hilden was here, and they somehow survived that horrible disaster. We need to make sure everyone can handle what this job throws at them."

Instead of pacing, Macon crossed his ankles under his chair. "I'll interview everyone and make certain I don't see any—"

"Nope. You'll need to go too."

Macon glared at Allen. "Me?" Was this how Amelia felt when she didn't agree with what Macon commanded?

"A chief isn't immune to the burdens this job brings. In fact, your position is the reason why a checkup was brought up to begin with."

His position or him personally? Even though Allen hadn't been the voices on the committee saying how Macon wasn't their top choice for the chief position, he represented them.

Macon gave in and allowed his thumb to press along his pounding head. "I know I have a lot of work to do to get this fire station up to par, but counseling will be a waste of our time." It had been pointless for his family. Nothing about their family had been the same since that counselor had torn them apart.

He fisted his fingers. "With all due respect—"

Allen held up his hands. "There was a recent complaint filed against you. It's either get everyone checked out and signed off on—and I mean *everyone*—or I'll have to get a chief in here who knows what's best for the Eastside Firehouse."

A fiery arrow hit Macon's soul. He'd lain in bed last night wondering if he was doing enough to be chief, and Allen's words now confirmed that he wasn't. Macon swallowed. He needed to prove to this town that he was more than what they expected him to be.

Macon's phone vibrated on his desk. His brother.

He hit ignore. "I don't trust counselors." Allen wanted communication. Maybe if he knew Macon's background, he'd understand why it was better not to trust outside help. "My family met with a counselor when I was younger. He destroyed our family. I won't let that happen here."

Allen nodded. "I understand your hesitation. However, this is beyond me. The mayor has decided. A therapist must sign off on you and the crew by the next committee meeting, or you won't be officially sworn in as chief. But I've called in the best this town has to offer. Trust me, my cousin's the best there is."

Macon squeezed his fingers into fists. The counselor being Allen's family member didn't guarantee anything. It would be up to Macon to protect his crew. "Can the sessions be completed here? That way, my guys won't use up any personal time or miss any fire runs."

Allen scratched his chin. "I'll let you know. Hopefully, we can get this ball rolling as early as today."

His stomach grumbled, and it wasn't because he hadn't eaten breakfast.

After Allen left, Macon opened his door blinds. There was no time to lay low. He'd already had a meeting with his boss, and now there was an upcoming counseling session to survive.

No fire calls came in, but Ambo went out twice and Rescue had a construction worker trapped, so paperwork filled his morning. A text from Allen confirmed the therapist would arrive from the Ridgeman Center at noon.

With hardly an opportunity to break the news to his crew, Macon slipped his phone back into his pocket. He spotted Zack in the weight room.

Macon opened the door and motioned for Zack to take out his earphones. "Round everyone up. Conference room. Meeting in five minutes."

Zack did one more bicep curl. "Got it, Chief."

"And make sure you find Greene."

Zack grunted and put the weights back on the rack. "If I'm searching for Ghost, we'll both be late."

"Just find him. Sit outside the toilet if you have to. If he really does have a medical condition, I need to know." Otherwise, the guy was going to get a written reprimand in his personnel file.

Zack grimaced and hustled out. Macon readied the conference room.

He didn't miss the way Amelia and Ridge sat on opposite sides. Then again, no one ended up close to Amelia. She held her nose in the air as if she smelled whatever Jayson was probably red-faced and chuckling about. Too often the firehouse was like a high-school classroom, filled with a class clown, the teacher's pet, and the rebel. Or in the case of their only female on his crew, the wannabe leader.

Ten minutes later, Dave strolled in with his hands in his pockets. Zack whipped around him and grabbed a seat in the front. Would it be wrong to wish for a fire call so they could get out of the therapy session?

Macon uncrossed his arms. "Listen up. A mandatory mental health evaluation has been issued."

The room echoed the groans Macon felt like making.

"For everyone?" Amelia opened her mouth to say more, but Macon raised his palm.

There was no point in arguing, especially since, for once, they were on the same side. "To make it easier on us, the therapist will arrive here. At noon."

"Today?"

"But Charlie made his famous spicy gumbo," Dave whined.

Macon lifted his brows. "I'm sure it will reheat if your session is during lunch. It would be in the station's best interest to cooperate. Let's get through this together. As always, if a call comes in, I expect you to be on the trucks." He eyed Dave. "Pronto. In a session or not."

Before Macon could request the group to give him a "yes, sir," the intercom system crackled overhead.

"Chief?" someone from the front office asked.

He strode to the door and pressed the intercom button. "I'm here."

"Looks like the therapist just pulled up. Do you want me to bring her on back?"

"Her?" Eddie's dark eyes grew the size of the Oreos someone had failed to hide in the top kitchen cabinet. "It's not Dean? Is it Kelsey, or the new chick? I heard she's—"

Macon gave Eddie the glare. No one needed to call their therapist a chick. Or whatever else was about to flow from his mouth. "No one is to hit on, flirt with, or fall for our therapist, understood? Let's keep this professional."

"Chief?" The intercom beeped again.

He pressed the button. "I'll meet her at the front office." On his way out, he pointed at Bryce. "Your squad will go first. Keep Eddie in view while he's doing his session."

Bryce stood and pushed in his chair. "No problem."

Eddie tipped his chair back. "I'm not twelve. I know how to behave."

"Then show me." Macon hoped this speed bump would be as painless as possible.

He paused before opening the main office door and glanced at the counselor through the glass window. She was seated in a chair, looking down at her phone. Her blonde hair was in a loose bun on the back of her head, and a thick pile of bangs covered most of her forehead. She had on a navy silk shirt and black pants.

Her foot bounced up and down as she scrolled on her phone. If she was nervous, that could be encouraging. Possibly cut down on the questions she might ask. Get her to sign off on their evaluation quickly.

Macon opened the door, and the woman glanced up.

It was like he was in a smoke funnel. His knees locked beneath him as he blinked at the same blue eyes that had hung around in his dreams. They belonged to the woman he'd rescued out of the fire.

As if they'd never met, she stood and extended her hand. "Good afternoon, I'm Natalie Atkinson from the Ridgeman Center. I'll be the counselor assessing you and your firefighters."

His lungs ached at the memory of her collapsing and him cradling her. *Natalie.* The name suited her, but this was not how he'd imagined them meeting.

He wrapped his hand around hers and, for a moment, they stared at each other, until she slipped her hand away. She'd been beautiful yesterday, but with her hair up and the spark in her eye, he wished they were introducing themselves during dinner at Backdraft Bar and Grill instead of a professional meeting.

Macon cleared his throat. "I'm Chief Macon James."

She studied him, yet said nothing about yesterday. Not that he expected a thank-you when he rescued someone, but it was strange she didn't even bring it up. Maybe she was self-conscious about how she'd fainted.

She glanced left and right before picking up the notebook from the chair beside her. She hugged it to her chest. "Do we have a more private place for your session?" Her voice had a raspier tone than earlier.

"I'll lead you to the conference room. We'll address all the crew there. Rescue will go first with their individual sessions." When he turned for the door, her hand landed on his arm. Her touch was like the strike of a match.

She jolted away, rubbing her fingertips together as if she'd felt the spark too. With her lips pressed together, she glanced at Meredith behind the front desk, who was not at all hiding her attention from them. Neither of his receptionists would.

"Actually..." Natalie said, "I find it helpful to start with the leadership."

He eyed her and opened the door. She finally met his gaze, searching past the stern expression he wore.

Macon clenched his jaw. What was helpful to her was not what his crew needed. "Right this way."

Their footsteps kept in sync as they marched down the halls. Did she want him to go first because she actually found it helpful, or was it because she needed to talk to him about yesterday?

"I'm afraid I've already informed my crew of the schedule." Macon needed Eddie to hurry and get his session completed so he couldn't get creative in the ways he might ask out their therapist. Not one of them needed her getting upset. She was there to sign off on his crew, and the quicker she did her thing, the quicker Macon could get them working as a team.

At the conference door, she tilted her head. "I'll follow your lead..." She paused as she stepped past him. The fruity smell of her perfume or shampoo did not match her chilled tone. "For now."

Macon stiffened at her abrupt sternness. As a leader, he thought over his words before they blurted from his mouth. Something made this woman closed off to him after rescuing her. Just because he didn't want to have the first session? She was lucky he wasn't complaining about going at all. Having a therapist here was pointless. Unless...

He watched as she introduced herself to his crew without waiting for him. Her eyes found his as if she knew what he was thinking. All the fear that had surrounded her yesterday was gone. Perhaps she was embarrassed he'd had to rescue her out of the fire and that was why she hadn't brought it up.

Macon's pulse kicked up. Wait. What if... The thought turned him cold.

What if she was the one who'd filed a complaint against him?

5

Natalie tapped her pen on the open firefighter's file on her desk and stared at her office wall. After having a white office in the army for years, she'd finally gotten a chance to choose a real color. In the fluorescent lighting it looked like "cloudless blue" leaned more toward gray, but either way, it was a hue that suggested this was a tranquil and inviting space. Yet her knotted shoulders didn't get that memo.

Fellow Ridgeman Center therapist, Kelsey Scott, leaned against the filing cabinet. The air vent over her head blew her auburn hair, making it swish around her shoulders. As she faced Natalie, she wrinkled her nose, and her freckles creased together. "Which one's Eddie again?"

Poor Kelsey. She'd only stopped by to borrow a stapler.

Natalie blew out a breath. "I'm sorry. You've got your own workload. You don't have to—"

Kelsey slipped into one of Natalie's client chairs. "Remember, we're a team. That's why I love it here at Ridgeman. Two are better than one. Now, run through them one more time."

Natalie twisted her chair from side to side. "Eddie's on

Rescue. Not Truck. And he's the one with the foster care background. He was pretty open about that. But there was still something he wasn't sharing."

"Oh." Kelsey pointed her stapled papers toward Natalie. "I think I had him mixed up with Ridge, who is on Truck, right?"

"Yes, Ridge Foster is on Truck." Natalie set down her pen. "He hides behind his sarcastic banter. He's either upset that he's not lieutenant or has a crush on the lone female firefighter. I can't tell which yet. And Amelia..."

"Sounds like she needs a friend," Kelsey added. "I remember her. And none of them mentioned the recent death in their crew?"

"Nope." Natalie popped the *p*. "Not even the chief."

Natalie rested her face in her palm and sighed. She had promised both her cousin and her boss, Dean, that she was up for the task of evaluating Eastside Firehouse. Except the last thing she'd expected was to interview the man who had saved her life.

She hadn't recognized him at first. The chief's strong jawline had been hidden by his helmet. Nor had the way his shoulders tapered down into a narrow waist been evident in his turnout gear. Then when she had recognized the way he'd looked at her, it had been too late to start over. She'd barely kept her face blank during their session. Her demeanor professional. But that hadn't opened him up to her at all.

Natalie leaned forward in the chair in front of the chief's desk. The sunlight from his office window shined against Macon's back. It didn't take away from his stern expression. "Do you enjoy being Eastside Firehouse's chief?"

"I do." At least he'd finally made it up to a two-word answer.

The tick of the clock on the wall echoed across his office. His desk held no picture frames. No personalized items. Only stacks of paperwork and files. And one pen.

Macon resembled his desk. Dressed for service. But what was stored on the inside?

When the silence stretched, Natalie cleared her throat. "How is your crew as an overall unit? Is there someone working through a burden that is affecting the entire team? Perhaps putting everyone in jeopardy?"

He pointed to his office door. "Each one of them puts their lives on the line to save people."

His arms were relaxed on the armrests, but by his tone it would have made more sense if he'd crossed them over his chest. "I have a difficult time answering questions from a therapist who seems to be more interested in tearing my team down than letting us get to our job."

Kelsey tapped her paperwork against Natalie's desk, bringing Natalie back from her thoughts. "Now you have the basics down. The next sessions should go deeper."

Should being the key word. Yet it wasn't a guarantee.

Natalie wrote down a note about Mickey on the top of Macon's file and underlined it twice. If only Allen had told her about Macon's distrust of counselors *before* their session. Not on her way back to the office. She might have approached things differently.

A ding chimed, and Kelsey pulled out her phone. She frowned at the screen. "Looks like I'm going to have an emergency appointment here in a moment. But I'm available later for more talk-throughs if you want."

Kelsey answered her phone and waved as she left Natalie's office.

What Natalie wanted to do was hit the horse trails. Something to take her mind off the unproductive time at the fire station. Allen's request for a favor—that she evaluate the fire department—coming the same night she had been rescued had caught her off guard, but she believed it would help her process her reaction to the house fire. She had coached herself on the way over to the firehouse today, and she'd still made a fool of herself in front of the chief. The one who'd seen her at her worst—and of course was the most handsome in the entire conference room.

Natalie reread Macon's file. If only he hadn't been on the evaluate list—then she wouldn't have had to explain to her boss how Macon had been the responding firefighter yesterday. It had been so hard to think when he was near. She kept picturing his smile when he'd rescued her and Joey.

He'd been the strong one when she'd been weak.

But at least she could do her job, and help the firehouse, and thereby repay the favor he'd done saving her life.

The firefighter sessions had revealed a wide range of characters. From stubbornness to flirts to practically mimes, it was a full house of personalities. But the least helpful part of the sessions had been Macon's gaze. Did he not believe she was qualified to help them?

Determined footsteps clicked in the hallway. Had Kelsey returned already? If Natalie could finalize a few more summaries, she'd allow herself to be finished for the day.

The footsteps stopped. "There you are." The voice of Ridgeman Center's receptionist filled the room. Wren, the petite, round-nosed brunette, only knew one volume: bright sunshine. "I didn't think you had left yet."

"Hey, Wren."

Wren stepped farther into Natalie's office. "Have you been really busy?"

Natalie dropped her gaze to the file on her desk. Thicker than the one on her computer because there was just something about putting ink to a page that helped her process things quicker. "A bit more than normal, but nothing I can't squeeze in if you need me."

"It's just, you didn't answer any of my calls."

Natalie checked the unlit message light on the phone on

her desk. Wren was known to check in with those she had messages for, but typically if she couldn't reach them, she'd have the clients leave a message. "I was gone for about three or four hours, but otherwise, I've been here."

"I buzzed you at least three times this morning and once this afternoon."

Natalie grabbed her desk phone and pressed it against her ear. "There's no dial tone."

"That makes more sense."

Wren took a pen from the mug on Natalie's desk. The one Allen had gotten for her when she had been hired on at the Ridgeman Center. It read *Born for this* and had a picture of a horse with glasses sitting and reading a book.

After the Leon disaster at her last job, her cousin had helped her get this one. She didn't want to let him down. She still wasn't sure he knew how involved she'd been with the fire at Peter's—only Dean knew all of it, and why she was determined it wouldn't cause a conflict in her doing her job.

If Allen had known, he may not have called her for that favor.

Wren grabbed a piece of scratch paper and scribbled down a note, her polished nails sparkling in the light. "I'll get someone in here to fix your phone."

"You can always reach me on my cell. Just don't offer it to any clients." She was slower to give it out to her patients these days.

"That's why I came down here. A Leon Polmes called three times. And the last time, he asked for your personal number. Said it was urgent."

Natalie sucked in her breath. How had Leon found her? "Did you give him my number?"

Wren shook her head. "There was something in my gut telling me to wait and ask you. I provided him with the emergency counsel line, but he didn't seem...happy."

As much as Natalie wanted to close her eyes and imagine this conversation away, she wouldn't let her clients ignore the heavy topics, so she couldn't either. She lifted her candy dish off her desk. She stood and held it out to Wren.

Wren hesitated. "It must be bad if you're offering treats."

She was the perfect receptionist for a therapy center. Natalie smiled. "Have you ever thought about becoming a counselor?"

With a shrug, Wren unwrapped a candy and popped it into her mouth quicker than Joey had on his last trip here.

Natalie sat on the corner of her desk. "Your gut was right about Leon. Never give him my information."

Dean had been informed of the restraining order against Leon when she'd been hired. "After I left active duty, I worked at an off-base clinic. Leon was an ex-soldier I helped evaluate—he struggled to understand boundaries. It progressed until I was encouraged to get a restraining order."

Natalie set the candy bowl down and picked up the file on her desk. "I don't know how he found me, but if he's trying to be treated here, we'll need to refer him to another facility. Or at least let me know if he's going to be in the building. And I'll make other plans."

Wren's eyes widened. "Goodness, I—"

A knock interrupted and Macon stood at her door. His gaze locked on to Natalie's. Determination set in his eyes.

Natalie clung tight to the firefighter's folder in her hands.

Macon cleared his throat. "Kelsey pointed out your office."

"Oh," was all that made it out of Natalie's mouth. So professional. She groaned and finished putting the file into her bag. "Was there something you wanted to add to your session, Chief?"

He eyed Wren and shifted his feet. "I came to bring you the approved evaluation form for my crew."

She took the paper and set it on her desk.

Macon sized up Natalie before his gaze dropped once again to Wren and then back. "Can I have a private word with you?"

A smiling Wren stood and pointed over her shoulder. "Let me just—"

Natalie held up a finger, and Wren sank back into the chair. If Wren left, it was likely to take longer with the chief than if Natalie surrendered to his request to feel in control. She couldn't make any assumptions yet. However, the man was bossy. He had no way of knowing Wren wasn't a patient. But he was correct; he had every right to want to keep whatever he desired to tell Natalie private. It was her job to hear him out.

"This will only take a second." Natalie gestured for Macon to lead the way out into the hallway. Then she'd clear up any questions Wren might have concerning Leon.

Outside in the hall, he was close enough for her to wonder if the hint of cedar and spice was his cologne or soap. He folded his arms. His muscles stretched the arms of his uniform.

Natalie jerked her eyes up where they belonged.

Macon glanced over. "I've already reviewed the evaluation and signed it. It only needs your signature."

She took a step back. "I'm still reviewing my initial notes. Our time together was a good start." Did that sound breathy? She cleared her throat. "But at this time, I can't sign the evaluation."

Something flashed in his eyes, and for a second, the chief's gaze looked like Jeremiah's had before the end.

Oh.

Her fingers inched to check the position of her bangs covering her scars. "In fact, I will probably need more time with your crews. And with you."

He rolled his shoulders back. "About that..."

Before any other words left his lips, a boom rumbled through the building. A painting tumbled off the wall and fell onto the chair by Kelsey's door. The window at the end of the hall rattled. Something in Natalie's office shattered and Wren squealed.

The blast rocked Natalie forward.

Into the chief's arms.

He grabbed her. Steadied her.

Shielded her as if her life mattered more than his.

"What was that?" Wren's voice sounded close. She must have stepped out of the office. But Natalie couldn't move, and Macon didn't let go. Instead, his head came down, next to her ear.

"You okay?" His voice was husky.

She nodded, but he didn't release her for three thundering heartbeats. He was warm and solid, and when she lifted her head and met his eyes, she couldn't think.

Just...yes. Right now, she was okay. Confused. But okay.

"I've never been in an earthquake before," Wren said.

"That was no earthquake. Stay here." Macon raced down the hall.

Natalie shook her head, breaking the trance Macon had on her. Kelsey! She jogged across the hall. A quick bang on Kelsey's door, then she twisted the knob. "You okay?"

Kelsey turned from shutting her blinds. A forced smile on her face. "You are safe, Mr. King. Why don't I get you a water?"

The client on the chaise had his knees pulled up on the cushion and his face tucked.

Natalie pulled opened Kelsey's minifridge and handed Kelsey a water bottle. She whispered, "Do you know what happened?"

"Something exploded outside," Kelsey whispered back. "Here you are, Mr. King."

No way could Natalie stay here if someone out there needed her. She spun around—thankfully, she hadn't worn heels today. However, Macon was heading back inside when she reached the exit.

He veered in front of her. "Call 911. I'm going to go check—"

She glanced out the glass doorway and spotted flames in the parking lot. The exact location she'd parked.

She shuddered. "That's my car."

She sprinted for the door. She had to reach her glovebox before it was too late.

Natalie made it outside into the smoke-filled air, but before she reached the parking lot, someone caught her around the waist.

"I don't think so."

She clawed at Macon's uniform shirt. "Let me go!"

He tightened his hold around her waist, her back hugged up against his chest. "Not on your life. I don't want to have to pull you from a fire again."

She twisted around and blinked at him. Then stared at her burning car. "How did this happen?"

Wren ran up beside her, panting. "I've called 911. Everyone's safe at the PT annex. Kelsey and Dean are settling the residents. You were right. This was no earthquake."

Natalie's view of what was left of her car blurred. A tear slid down her cheek and dropped onto Macon's hand.

"You all right?" Macon's grip had loosened, but she was still wrapped in his arms.

Oh, how she wanted to lie about how she wasn't panicked that Leon had found where she worked. Lie about how Jeremiah's last look at her never haunted her dreams. But most of all, she wanted to lie and say she didn't need Macon or anyone else.

But...

She licked her dry lips.

Nothing came out.

"I've got you," he whispered.

And as much as she wanted to believe that, no, he didn't.

No one did.

6

The flames destroying Natalie's car had arson written all over it. Macon sprayed what was left of the front of the vehicle with a fire extinguisher, yet the white foam only weakened the blaze.

He glanced over his shoulder. Natalie had followed him out into the parking lot. She was far too close. "Let's get you back to the sidewalk."

She'd wiped the tears from her cheeks. All professional again. Except instead of answering him, she chewed on the edge of her bottom lip.

What if she'd been inside her car?

Macon swallowed. He backed up four paces and Natalie followed. The flames were as high as his chest, but without his trucks here, he'd done all he could.

At the last minute, he'd decided to go to the center to try and make a better impression. He'd wanted to admit that his crew was struggling with Mickey's death. But that was a given and shouldn't hinder them from doing their jobs. If he had just emailed the evaluation like they'd agreed upon, he wouldn't have been here to protect her.

The color of the flames was no longer white, which meant the fire's temperature hadn't risen anymore. Black smoke whipped upward as the setting sun reflected a piece of metal amongst the shards of glass on the asphalt. Could it be a clue as to what trigged the explosion?

Natalie silently matched each of Macon's steps. She bent at the waist too, except her big blue eyes had a glazy haze to them as she blinked over and over at the flames. Just like when he had carried her away from the house fire.

After a checkup call from Allen this afternoon, Macon had learned Natalie hadn't been the one to file the complaint, which would have been a conflict of interest. Yet Macon wasn't sure Allen had read the entire report that detailed how Natalie had been extracted from the house fire. Even if that wasn't some level of conflict, Macon couldn't seem to get Natalie out of his head.

When he'd overheard that she had a restraining order out against someone, it had been the faint tremor in her voice that had made him interrupt their conversation to check on her. It'd gone downhill from there.

Or uphill, depending on perspective, because he'd found her in his arms—albeit innocently—again. And somehow, in that brief moment, he'd wanted to help.

That's all. Just help. Because she'd looked alone. Even afraid. Now that he knew about a restraining order with a client, he could guess why Natalie's car had exploded.

Macon pointed to the metal on the ground. "Do you recognize that?"

Natalie didn't take her gaze off the persistent fire.

The receptionist was back on the sidewalk where Natalie needed to be. Dean was now beside her with his ear pressed to his phone. Kelsey must still be inside with all the clients.

When Natalie didn't answer, he touched her elbow, and she jumped.

Macon held out his hands. "Sorry, I—"

"No—yes—I mean, I'm sorry." She took a deep breath. "What are you...what have you been looking at?" She reached for the button but then pulled her hand back as if it might be hot. "Do you have any guess as to what happened? I don't believe my car suddenly burst into flames."

Her attempt at humor failed as her lips quivered on the edge of her half smile. She cleared her throat and brushed her fingers through her bangs. A few sections of hair from her bun had slipped out sometime between when he'd caught her in the hallway and when she'd kept pace with him around her car outside.

Maybe it was crazy, but part of Macon wanted to tuck the loose hair behind her ears and tell her everything would be all right. But as a fire chief, he knew when something looked deliberate. And the arsonist was still out there.

Sirens stopped him from answering, and they both stepped back from one another. His crew had arrived before the police. The counselor was about to get exactly what she'd requested—more time to observe his crew. Unfortunately, it was at her expense.

Ridge blasted the horn and drove the fire truck into the parking lot, coming right up beside the destroyed vehicle. Amelia hopped out and raced to the back of the truck. They reached for the hose at the same time.

Macon wanted to reprimand them both. Now was not the moment for stubbornness or a power struggle or whatever flowed between them. Never on call, but especially not when the person responsible for evaluating their mental health had a front-row seat to what resembled an arm-wrestling match.

Another siren pierced the air. If Macon had still believed God was on his side, he would have offered a glance skyward. Instead, he kept his attention on his crew. He put his fingers in his mouth and whistled. When he gained Amelia's attention, he yelled, "One hose should do it."

The police car pulled in front of the building, and Police Chief Conroy Barnes stepped out. He nodded at Dean first, then at Macon.

Ridge knelt, Zack right behind him to keep him steady, and he aimed the hose at the fire.

As the sizzle and pops competed against one another, Amelia did a perimeter check.

But where was Dave?

"Chief James." Conroy stepped up on Natalie's other side. "I'll need to take any witness statements."

Macon turned to Natalie. "You want to go first, or would you rather I go?"

Natalie arched her shoulders. "It's my car." She walked over to the police car, her posture straight, but wrapped her arms around her waist.

When Macon twisted back around, Amelia was now with Ridge on the hose.

Zack stepped up beside Macon. "I didn't know extra crispy was on the menu today."

"Stephens!" Amelia yelled over the gush of the hose. She waved Zack over.

Zack sighed. "First, I apparently wasn't doing it right, and now she wants me back over there." Zack shook his head. "I wish she'd make up her mind."

Macon scanned the dwindling flames. "Did Greene make it on the truck this time?"

"By the skin of his teeth," Zack said. "And if you want Patterson on your good side, I wouldn't ask her about it."

When had Amelia ever been on his good side?

The hose shut off, and Amelia jogged toward him and Stephens instead of having her attention on the car. The fire was out, but they needed to watch for any leftover fuel that could reignite.

"Stephens." This time Amelia's voice came over Zack's walkie. "Leave him alone. He's off duty. Come help Ridge while I do another perimeter sweep. And where is your TIC?"

Instead of answering over the radio, Zack picked up his thermal imaging camera and shook it in front of him. "I forgot it one time. Once."

A rumble groaned in the distance as a cloud of smoke that had nothing to do with fire drifted above the trees. A silver car rounded the curve into the parking lot and jerked to a stop, the tires half on the curb in front of the entry. A woman spilled out along with a few items of trash. She never glanced toward the fire truck or police car as she ran for the center.

Dean stepped in her way. The woman flailed her hands, her keys jingling with her movements, her glare directed at Natalie.

"Where have you taken my Joey?" Tears tracked down her red face. "Please tell me he's okay. No one at the hospital will tell me anything." Her hands shook as she tried and failed to remove a section of her frizzed hair stuck to her wet cheeks.

Macon positioned himself in front of the woman, but Natalie shifted to stand beside him. "I left word for you at Creekside Therapy, Angie. Joey is unharmed. Safe."

Angie scowled at Natalie. "You should have called me. I'm still his mother. If he's been in a fire—"

"If you had returned to Creekside yesterday, you would have gotten all the information. This is all I can offer you at this time."

"I need to see him now. To make sure he's safe." She laced her fingers together. "Please, I'm begging—"

"If you want to write Joey a letter, I can see that he gets it," Natalie said.

"Can you give him his suitcase too?" She opened the passenger side of her car.

Conroy had his palm on the butt of his gun as the woman pulled out a hard red suitcase.

She held up the square suitcase by its single handle. "I packed the things he had at my place."

Conroy's shoulders relaxed, but Macon kept on the toes of his feet.

Joey's mom sniffed. "I don't want him to feel alone. I went by Peter's house and..." Tears appeared again. "Is Peter okay? Will you give him a note from me also? It's really, really important."

Natalie took the suitcase. "Why don't we go on inside? I have paper you can use."

Dean followed the women into the building.

With Natalie occupied, it was Macon's turn to provide his account of the explosion to the police chief. Not that he had much information.

And he left out a few things too. Like the fact that right after the explosion, Natalie had looked at him just like she had the day of the fire. Like he'd saved her world.

Like he mattered.

Macon shook his head. He had to wipe that from his mind. The woman held the future of his fire department her hands. Allen had forwarded him the oversight committee's evaluation form. No one seemed interested in Macon's view of his crew. Only what Natalie thought.

If he didn't measure up, he could kiss the chief position goodbye.

Conroy circled something on his notepad. "Any strange people or vehicles when you arrived at the center?"

All Macon could think of was Natalie landing safe in his arms. "Nothing appeared out of the ordinary."

The building was flanked on all sides by sturdy, grandfather-like trees. Ones that had been around and weathered life's storms.

Macon rubbed the back of his neck. "With this much coverage and how the vehicle was parked at the edge of the lot, someone could have detonated a planted bomb easily. The problem was, who would want to hurt Ms. Atkinson?"

Had Natalie mentioned the restraining order to Conroy yet?

Conroy paused note-taking on his phone. "That's my job to worry about."

Macon crossed his arms at the same moment the fire truck's door slammed shut. He turned to see Ridge with a roll of caution tape, which Amelia snatched from him. Who was making sure the fire stayed out? Zack stood in view of the smoking ashes. Another thumping sound came from the direction of the truck.

"Can you give me a moment?" Macon didn't want to draw any more attention to his crew.

Conroy returned to his notes. "Don't you wish you could send them into timeout corners sometimes?"

Of course the police chief had noticed his crew's clash. If only getting his crew to cooperate was that simple.

Macon clenched his jaw. "The fire report will have our best guess for the explosion. We'll also get our arson specialist on this as well. But the restraining order might provide more leads than my department can supply."

Conroy's brows raised. "Restraining order?"

Macon matched the police chief's expression. "She didn't tell you?"

Conroy slid his notepad into his pocket and took out his phone. "Appreciate the heads-up."

"If I think of anything else, I'll call you." Macon hustled over toward his crew. He rounded the truck where he'd seen both Amelia and Ridge storm off. When he found Dave sitting in the backseat, Macon redirected. Finally. There was the missing firefighter. Except the newest hire had his head leaned back and eyes closed. The others may have nicknamed him Ghost, but that didn't make him completely invisible.

"Greene! This is the opposite of naptime."

Dave blinked and leaned out the open truck window. "Yeah, Chief?"

At least he'd called him by his title. "Why are you sitting on the job?"

He rested his head back again. "Because the boss ordered me to. And unlike Foster, I listen to her."

Macon reached the front of the truck to find Ridge holding the end of the hose and Amelia standing at the front, their eyes locked in a scowling match.

At this point, he was more of a babysitter than a chief. Macon folded his arms over his chest and forced air out through his nose. "Do you know that everyone at this crime scene is staring at us? And it's not to recommend us for any awards."

Macon pushed out a breath and called back, "Lieutenant Patterson, why on earth did you order Greene to sit in the truck?"

Before she could answer, Macon spun toward Ridge. "Is there a reason why this area isn't roped off already?"

Amelia changed her scowl from Ridge and deepened it Macon's way. "Greene said he hit his head. He might have a concussion. Since Trace and Izan haven't arrived yet, and I haven't had time to check him, I ordered him to rest. The police are here, so I assumed it's their jurisdiction to rope off the area, not Ridge's duty when there's other stuff he's *supposed* to be doing."

Ridge released his death grip on the hose and, for the first time, stepped toward Amelia instead of away. Great, all he needed was for Ridge to jump ship against him.

"Hey, Chief James, one more quick question." Conroy's

voice made Macon look over his shoulder, but it wasn't the police chief that gained Macon's attention.

Natalie was no longer inside with Angie. She stood on the sidewalk, watching, her arms crossed over her chest. Her eyes zeroed in on Macon, and she frowned.

So much for making a better impression.

7

Natalie pivoted between the mop bucket and the box of toilet paper in the janitor's closet that doubled as the center's security room.

She often told her clients not to wish they could turn back time. Usually it caused more anxiety than it helped. But there was so much she wanted to change about the past twenty-four hours. Her session with Macon. Her car. Those tears he had witnessed.

Right now, she wished she had already told Chief Barnes about Leon. She would have. Probably. Except Angie had shown up.

Natalie's gaze flicked to Macon, who leaned against the door. Her boss, Dean Cartwright, sat in the lone computer chair while Officer Olivia Tazwell and Chief Barnes squinted over his shoulder at the computer screen. They were all boxed in by shelves of cleaning products. None of which could help her clean up this situation.

Because now she was going to have to tell the officers about Leon. *With* Macon listening.

Conroy pointed at the computer screen. "Stop it right

there."

Natalie paused her pacing. Dean clicked on the keyboard and froze the frame.

Olivia leaned closer to the recorded time-lapse view. "Do you think that's a navy or black truck?"

Did Leon own a truck? Natalie pivoted back toward the mop in the corner. The recording had only caught two cars which were unaccounted for. The center was off the beaten path. Typically only people who were lost or who had an appointment traveled out this far. Along with the cars, there had also been a motorcycle and a single truck visible in the feed. Everything was black and white and blurry at best.

Natalie tried to figure out why Leon would want to blow her up. He'd imagined things between them that had never happened—things that had created an unhealthy attachment. He'd even tried giving her a thousand-dollar necklace.

Of course, that had been before the restraining order.

"It never parked." Dean swung back and forth in his chair, and his gaze snagged on Natalie. "It's my fault that we don't have an image of the person who did this. I should've put up more security cameras."

Natalie inhaled for four counts and exhaled. She laced her fingers together in front of her. "I have a restraining order out against someone."

The two cops twisted in her direction.

Dean tilted his head to the side. "You haven't told them about the restraining order yet?"

She stood up straighter. "Angie interrupted things."

Macon's jaw clenched. Maybe he believed she wasn't capable of evaluating his crew now. Would it be professional to ask him to leave?

Once again she could recount her litany of failures. Enough for Dean to remove her from the firehouse evaluation and assign it to someone else if he wanted to. Despite her reaction to the car explosion, getting close to Macon wasn't one of her sins—she was not going to fall into his arms again. If Dean allowed it, she would continue to do her job.

Conroy clicked the pen in his hand and shared a glance with Olivia.

Natalie pressed her lips together. "At my last job, I had a patient overstep boundaries. When things worsened, my boss recommended I take out a restraining order. Allen got me a job here, far away from Leon Polmes. But he apparently called the center today looking for me."

Conroy widened his stance. "We've already been looking into the restraining order, but we'll need to see if we can get his number from the incoming call list."

Natalie nodded. The police chief worked fast if he already knew about Leon. "Wren took his calls. I'd just found that out moments before the explosion."

Dean shook his head. "I still should have had more cameras up."

Olivia sat on the edge of the desk. No one was giving Natalie a shameful glare for not coughing up the info on Leon sooner.

Conroy tucked his pen into his pocket. "More cameras may not have helped. Polmes could be a suspect. But there's also another option."

He pointed back to the computer screen. "Anyone could have parked along the road and hiked through the woods. Get in, get out. Set up the explosion and, with a zoom lens, they could've filmed the latest of the 'Smash the Bug' videos."

"It's a horrific social media craze," Olivia added.

Macon uncrossed his arms. "Is her car already trending?"

"Not yet. But the MO does match all the others," Olivia said.

Natalie opened her mouth. Then closed it. "So you believe the explosion is linked to the car bombing challenge and not Leon?" If today could have a silver lining, having Leon far from here would be it.

Olivia nodded. "Correct. This craze has been happening all over the country. Here." She motioned toward the computer. "Let me show you."

Dean scooted out of the way, and Olivia brought up an online posting of another VW Beetle being exploded. One that wasn't Natalie's.

"Since the original video aired six months ago, the state police have been receiving calls identical to the one we got today." Conroy sent a compassionate shoulder lift toward Natalie. "There was one only fifty miles from Last Chance County a week ago."

Natalie glanced over at Macon, who still didn't look convinced as he watched the next video. "How many times has the perpetrator not been found?"

Conroy rested his hand on his gun belt. "Only a few."

Olivia clicked back to the parking lot video. "Predominately teen suspects."

Conroy tilted his chin at the computer screen and then looked to Dean. "We'll need a copy of this video. If Natalie's car explosion is posted online, it'll immediately be flagged. The explosive report should provide leads as well."

"I'll get right on that copy, and we'll tighten security here." Dean rolled his chair back in front of the computer.

Macon stepped forward. "Are you sure it's safe for her to return to work? And what about at her house?"

Natalie inspected Macon's wrinkled brow. Was he upset for her or because she was still the one evaluating his crew?

"There's a chance it's related to Polmes. I'll send out patrols by your house," Conroy said.

Olivia moved closer to Natalie. "Or if you'd feel safer, you could make other arrangement to stay—"

Natalie shook her head. "I can take care of myself. If Leon wanted to hurt me, he would have exploded my car when I was in there, right? It looks like any vehicle that fits the online challenge description is in more danger than me."

"Sounds like we're on the same page." Conroy extended his hand to Natalie. "Wish I had better news. We'll keep you posted as the investigation progresses."

Natalie willed her grip to be steady. "Thank you. Would it be all right if I see if anything is salvageable in my glove box?"

Conroy shared a glance with Macon, and then said, "As long as Chief James approves."

"I'll go with you," Macon said, his voice not quite a whisper. "I'll wait out front."

Natalie tightened her arms around her chest. The memory of Macon steadying her in the hall had been the calm before the day's storm. She didn't know what she would have done if he hadn't been there during the explosion.

Once the officers and Macon left, Dean sighed. "Natalie, I'm sorry. We'll figure this out. But I want you to know you handled Joey's mom like a seasoned counselor, even with everything you were dealing with."

At least one thing had gone well. Angie's note and suitcase could be given to Joey. But it would have to remain in Natalie's office until she called Tosha for his location.

"If you don't need me, I'm going to go check on my..." Natalie's eyes watered and she swallowed back the word *car*.

Dean frowned. "You want me to come with you?"

"I'm good. Thanks." She sped out before Dean observed her falling apart.

The outside air hit her flushed cheeks as the fire truck's flashing lights circled overhead. She rolled her shoulders back as if marching in formation. Earlier she had told Macon she wanted more time observing his crew. She'd gotten what she'd asked for.

When she'd volunteered to go to Angie's car and get her purse for her while she finished her notes, Natalie had caught the power struggle between Ridge and Amelia. Then Amelia and Macon. She believed the underlying problem wasn't about the need for control but about hiding their feelings from each other. They were taking the pain of losing Mickey out on their teammates.

However, this trip outside, none of the fire crew were arguing. The amount of smoke in the air no longer burned her nose.

She searched for Macon, but when she didn't find him or Amelia or Ridge, her gaze drifted to the bright red lights flashing on top of the fire truck. Her mind jumped back to the night Jeremiah died. She'd been wheeled away on a gurney. All she'd seen was the flashing rescue lights, pain not only surging along her forehead but also in her heart.

Her legs wobbled beneath her and she blinked. *Stay in the present.* She locked her focus on the trees across the road and refused to allow the bright red lights to lead her to the last explosion she'd endured.

Tonight, she'd only lost her car, not a friend.

As if in tune with her emotions, the fire truck turned off its lights and pulled out of the parking lot. So much for Macon waiting outside for her. Yet with a closer view of her car, she realized there would be no approval needed to explore the vehicle. Nothing was left except the metal frame and shards of glass on the ground. Anything that had been fabric or leather or a precious memory was long gone. The dried flower from her mother's funeral she'd kept in her cupholder was gone. Just like the last photo taken of her and her mother. The Bible in the glovebox also gone. So much of Natalie's life...turned to ash.

Her vision blurred as the wind tugged at the loose hair around her bun. She glanced skyward and blinked. Was God even up there seeing this?

She closed her eyes. Of all the types of cars for some

demented challenge, it had to be the one her mother had pledged to buy her when she turned sixteen. Natalie had hated bugs when she was little. Apparently, she'd even screamed at ladybugs until one night a monster bug had haunted her dreams. Her mother had shown her a picture of a Volkswagen Beetle in a magazine.

"*See, little captain, not all bugs are scary.*" Her mother had nestled Natalie's head against her shoulder. "*Anytime you have a bad bug dream, imagine you and me riding in this Beetle car. One day, we'll drive in one together for real.*"

Natalie wished she could ride with her mother. But now she didn't even have the right car.

Macon cleared his throat behind her.

With two swipes to her cheeks, she hopefully removed all of her tears. She forced a smile so he didn't witness her at her lowest moments yet again and turned toward Macon. "I was going to ask if I could check my car for my belongings, but..." She gestured to the blackened carcass.

"Here." He held out a handkerchief. "I got stopped by my crew before I could get this for you."

Natalie squeezed it in her hand. So much for hiding her weaknesses. But the man could be sweet. She wiped her cheeks with the cloth. A stitching thread on the smooth fabric rubbed against her skin. Inspecting the handkerchief, she expected to find initials, but it was three crosses stitched into the corner. Natalie ran her finger over the blue threads.

He tilted his head toward a truck across the parking lot. "Do you want a ride home?" His gentle tone almost made her tear up again.

She sniffed and scanned the center. She should wait for Dean, but he might be a while, especially if he was going to order more cameras online. She should call Allen, but it would take time for him to drive out here. And she was ready to be home now, taking a bath to wash off the stress of this day—and maybe the residue of explosions past.

"It's not really appropriate, considering I'm assigned to evaluate your crew."

He tipped his head to the side. "I'm pretty sure that applies to normal situations where your car didn't just explode."

All she could think about was the photo of her and her mother—the last picture of them she'd had. Not trusting the strength of her voice, she nodded. It wasn't like anything unprofessional would happen while he was her client. He might seem to want to be her hero, but she didn't need one.

By the time she came back out with her things from her office, Macon had pulled up beside the door. She hopped in. She inhaled the smell of mint and cedar, bringing her right back to the moment they'd had in the hallway. She buckled her seatbelt and locked away any unprofessional feelings she had toward the chief.

He'd just been here to help. Again.

Macon tapped his fingers on the steering wheel. "Do you think maybe you need to go to Frees's house instead of home?"

"Just home."

His brows pulled in. "Sure you wouldn't be safer at Hope Mansion?"

She arched her back, sure she wanted a soaking bath tonight. "You heard the police chief. Apparently, only my car wasn't safe."

With a noncommittal grunt, he followed her directions to her house. But when he parked in her drive, he didn't offer her a wave or a simple "goodnight." He got out with her and walked around the front of his truck. His headlights formed a spotlight on his toned body.

She averted her gaze. "Thanks for the ride."

His eyes narrowed on something over her shoulder. He

swayed around her and took off toward her front door. "Stay here."

She hoisted her purse higher on her shoulder and marched after him on the sidewalk. The man was the fire chief, but he wasn't *her* boss.

Natalie stepped onto her porch. Macon's truck lights caused her potted plants to cast angry shadows on her door. Wait. Not only was Macon not on her porch, but her door was ajar.

Again.

She quickened her last steps and pushed the front door wide. "Chief James?"

Inside the narrow entryway, the house was quiet. Not even the hum of the refrigerator echoed from her nearby kitchen. A flash of light let her know Macon was down the hall, more than likely checking each of her rooms for an intruder. Just like she had last night.

She flipped on the entryway light. Then turned to the left and switched on a lamp. Her television still hung over the short bookstand across from the couch where her three throw pillows sat untouched. Her DVD player was still lit up. Nothing was out of place. No one had broken in.

She walked back to the entryway and set her purse down on the console table by the ceramic bowl Allen's girlfriend's adopted niece, Victory, had painted for her. "Stand down, Chief. It's okay."

Macon finished checking the left side of her house and finally came back to where she stood in the entryway. "Smash the Bug Challenge or not, it's not safe for you to stay here. An explosion *and* your house open." He headed for her kitchen. "Unless you usually leave your house unlocked, which isn't safe."

She jiggled her front doorknob and tried to turn her lock, but it wouldn't move. "I didn't leave anything unlocked. It's broken. This is probably why it was unlocked last night too."

The dishes in her cabinet rattled. He was at her side in four long strides. "Two days of unlocked doors? Did you tell this to Conroy?" His hand brushed hers and a tingle spread through her body. "Two unlocked doors and a possible bomb with a restraining order feels like more than coincidences, Natalie. I'm definitely taking you someplace safe."

Her first name on his lips made her blink up at him. "They said I was fine."

If she said fine a few more times, would the stubborn man listen? Her breathy voice wasn't helping her case. She was an ex-soldier. She could take care of herself.

She squared her shoulders. "There's no proof Leon was even in town. Why would he call the therapy center if he only wanted to blow up my car? Chief Barnes is right. It makes more sense that it would be the Smash the Bug Challenge. I'm staying here." She wanted the comfort of quiet in her own home where she could process what all she had lost and plan how to go forward.

He held her gaze for a moment, then frowned. "Hold on." He slipped past her and walked out the door.

Hold on to what? She stepped out onto her porch as her mind slipped to when he'd last held on to her, which was two too many times now. As a counselor, she had to be strong enough to hold on to herself and others.

He jogged back and held up a screwdriver. The sudden grin on his face had her reeling to put professional space between them.

She moved back into her house. "Wait." Her arm landed on his. "I can fix—"

"I'm sure you can." He bent over and inspected the lock. "But this"—he inserted the screwdriver and twisted—"will only..."

A clink made her lean over his shoulder.

"There. All done." He turned the handle, and the lock and knob performed as they should.

When he stood, she realized she'd made multiple mistakes. Her hand still on his shoulder. And even worse, her face now close to his.

All she could manage was a hushed, "Thanks."

If she were a half a step closer, she'd be practically in his arms again. She could not end up there anymore, or she may not have a job tomorrow.

"You're welcome." His muscles rolled underneath her fingers, and her gaze dropped to his lips. "Natalie, I think you're—"

She jumped back to reality and grabbed the doorknob for support. Whatever drew her to this man had to end right now.

Yes, he'd been kind enough to bring her home and give her his handkerchief. He'd fixed her doorknob, and she didn't even need to think about the other reasons she might find Macon attractive. The point was, he was the fire chief—and even more, her client. Which meant off-limits.

She had a job she wanted to keep.

Macon ran his palm over his face as if he, too, was putting space between them. He scooped up the screwdriver that had fallen on the floor, slid it in his pocket, and pulled out something else. By the time he'd unrolled a piece of paper, all the tingles Macon had caused earlier had left her body.

The fire department evaluation form.

"I had an extra copy in the truck. I thought—"

Natalie crossed her arms. Compassion wasn't the reason he'd fixed her door. There was a chance it wasn't the reason why he'd offered her a ride home either. He was a chief on a mission.

At least now she was thinking like a professional.

She held up her palm. "I understand a lot has happened since I told you earlier that I wasn't done evaluating Eastside, but it remains true. I need more time observing your crew. And what I saw tonight doesn't change that stipulation."

Macon had the decency to wince. He opened his mouth only to shut it. After shifting on his feet, he finally said, "With our evaluations finished, it might help you process what you endured today." He rolled the paper back up and slid it into his back pocket. "I wasn't trying to be selfish. I was only"—his gaze didn't leave hers, as if he was wanting her to see what he wasn't saying—"thinking of you."

"That's not your job."

He puffed out his chest. "I would do my job, but because no one else besides *therapists* can supposedly help, I'm stuck watching my crew, the people *I've* been working with for weeks now, be evaluated by someone who has no clue what it actually takes to be a firefighter."

Natalie slanted her head. His anger didn't appear to be centered around pride but genuine respect for his crew. She leaned her hip against the console table. "Thank you for fixing my lock and driving me home. As far as your crew and my signature, I'll see you tomorrow morning at seven."

He fixed his stare over her head and pressed his lips together. "For more of your one-on-one therapy sessions?"

She wasn't sure how much her emotions could take of that. She needed something hands-on. Active. Something where the crews weren't giving monotone, one-word answers like teenagers. Something that would prove to the chief that she was there to help not hurt. "No. You have a point."

He met her eyes.

She lifted her chin. "Tomorrow your crew is going to teach me how to be a firefighter."

8

Macon rang Natalie's doorbell and slid his hands into his uniform pockets. As the tone echoed behind the door, he eyed the lock that had spurred his protectiveness into overdrive last night. Or rather, it had been the woman behind the lock. He'd only added to his list of mistakes by asking her to sign off on his crew last night. However, he wasn't sure her plan for this morning was any better.

Despite the drizzle of rain, the sunrise crested over her neighbor's roof. A car drove by on the road, but not another noise beside the birds. He pressed the bell again.

He checked his watch. It was four minutes after seven. Maybe she was making him wait to teach him a lesson. Even if he had been trying to do right by her and his crew last night.

He ran his hand along his buzzed hair, and his gaze landed on her scuffed-up doorknob. At least his motives for fixing her door had been pure. Yet, based on her return scowl, she had believed otherwise. The golden handle caught the sunrise, revealing a loose screw. Hadn't he tightened them all? When he had finished securing the lock, she'd been right next to him, her eyes wide with shock and maybe a little gratitude. But it had been her touch on his arm that had glued him to the moment.

What if the police had gotten it wrong about her car, and it wasn't an internet prank?

He jiggled the handle. It was secure. But what if her lock wasn't only broken last night and the day before from old age, like she'd said? Someone could have tried to get into her house yesterday and when they'd found it empty, gone after her car at work.

"Ms. Atkinson!" He knocked against the wood until his knuckles throbbed.

He stepped to the side to glance in her windows and tripped over a concrete planter. His shin stung as he limped over and shielded his eyes against her front window. But the blinds were drawn. What if the reason she hadn't answered the door was because the intruder was inside her house? Leon could be in there right now.

He beat on the door. "Natalie!"

He scanned all her windows. No lights were on that he could tell in the daylight. He jogged around the side of the house and found the back door. He turned the handle. Still locked.

He could break the window on the back door and get inside. Yet what if she had simply overslept? He wouldn't exactly coax her into signing off on his crew by becoming an intruder himself.

He banged on the back door. "Natalie, are you okay?"

There was being paranoid, and then there was saving someone's life. He just didn't know which side he needed to lean toward. Except he should have insisted she go to her cousin's or the shelter last night. A piece of paper wouldn't stop Leon. What if the explosion had gone off too early by mistake? Leon could be angry that it didn't cause any harm. Or perhaps it was only meant to terrify her. Cause her to run home unprotected.

Macon scooped up a palm-sized rock from the landscaping at the same time his phone rang.

The firehouse number flashed on his screen, and he swiped to answer. Amelia's voice answered his rushed greeting. "Did you go for a cookie run?"

Her irritation at him was only good for one thing: building his character. "Patterson, if this isn't an emergency, I'll stop by your office as soon as I arrive. However, I may have a situation here."

"We have one ourselves. The therapist is back. Didn't you think we needed to be told?"

Macon released his hold on the rock and cradled his forehand with his palm. There was no intruder. No stalker. Natalie wasn't even home—she was already at the firehouse. He took a deep breath and kicked the rock back into place.

Hadn't Natalie said she'd see him at seven? He'd assumed that meant he'd pick her up because she no longer had a car.

Macon gripped his phone. "I only found out late last night she was returning. I'm on my way."

He hung up before a snide comment about getting her own cookies from now on erupted from his mouth. No matter how his lieutenant treated him, he had to be the example. If no one else would step up to their duties, he'd have to figure out how to make up for it until he got everyone working as a team.

Teamwork had been so easy with his other jobs. Why not this crew?

Macon jogged back to his truck. His gut had failed him, but this time, it was a good thing. Hopefully, her neighbors wouldn't call the cops on his odd behavior. That's all the committee needed to hear to send him packing.

He connected his phone to his truck's Bluetooth speaker and punched in his old hotshot crewmember Logan Crawford's number. The so-called friend who, along with his twin—rescue squad lieutenant Bryce Crawford—had gotten it into his head that Macon could be the chief.

It took three rings, but his buddy finally answered. "Yup," Logan said groggily.

Macon backed out of Natalie's driveway. "I'm not sure if I should feel offended that I haven't seen you in almost three months and that's the only thing you have to say or—"

"Let's go with option two." Logan's yawn crackled over the phone.

Macon glanced at his dashboard clock. "Sorry, man. Forgot about the time difference." The eastern part of Australia was sixteen hours ahead of mountain time. It had been a struggle adjusting to the differences when he'd returned stateside.

"No worries. It's just been some days."

Macon grunted. "I feel that. Do you need me to come back down there and help you guys out?"

A pause carried over the line until Logan finally said, "What's going on there, Chief?"

He sighed. "Didn't your brother tell you about the therapist evaluating the crew?"

"Haven't talked in a few." Logan let out a whistle. "I bet it's been a struggle for you." Logan knew about his horrible experience with counselors years back.

"She's got to sign off on everyone, including me, before the board meets again or—"

"Hold on, let's circle back to the whole *she* thing in a moment—"

"There's nothing to come back to." The stoplight before him turned red, and Macon slammed on his brakes. But even as he did, the memory of Natalie leaning against him last night zipped through his mind.

"Right." Logan's tone flattened. "That's why you're totally

ignoring my comment. But seriously, Macon. I know you don't want to hear this; however, you're a great firefighter."

"You're right. That's awful to hear."

"Hilarious. Just jump through the hoops the committee wants, and then you'll be good to go as chief."

Unless Natalie blamed him for the lack of teamwork.

Macon glared at the stoplight in front of him as rain sprinkled on the hood of his truck. If he did get fired, he'd find another job. That wasn't the problem. But he didn't want to fail in front of his hometown. In front of his brother. He wanted to prove himself.

So far, all he'd done was the opposite.

"You're being your own worst enemy again," Logan said. "You're a natural leader. Shoot, you were doing the work of three guys down here. I have no doubt you're a great chief. That's why you're there. That's why Allen hired you."

Much to the committee's disapproval.

Macon pressed the gas pedal too hard on the wet pavement, making his tires squeal. "What if Allen hired the wrong guy?"

He hadn't meant to overhear the woman from the committee in the hall outside Allen's office. Always the wrong time. Wrong place. Ignorance was bliss for a reason.

"Did you know raccoons like to dunk their food in water before they eat it? Doesn't mean they won't eat without it. Doesn't mean you're in the wrong spot at the wrong time. God doesn't make mistakes."

No, but His creation sure did. Especially Macon.

Rain pooled on his windshield, and he turned on his truck's wipers. "Racoons. Really?"

"Shut up, I'm tired. Racoons were the first random fact that popped into my head. But my point is still the same. None of this second-guessing taking the position. Oh-woe-is-me isn't a good color on you. You like that fact better?" He laughed.

It was Macon's turn to roll his eyes, but this was why he'd

called his buddy. The comradery missing at Last Chance County. "Don't make me come over there and embarrass you in a game of ping-pong."

Macon chuckled. It was the one thing Logan could beat him at. "After that, we'll play some basketball and darts. Best two out of three."

Logan's laugh tapered off into a cough. One that hinted at being around too much smoke.

"Thanks, man." For listening. For reminding Macon to keep going. For being his friend. Because this guy didn't discuss his feelings with a stranger. At least, not in a sit-down-face-to-face therapy session.

Get him on the basketball court and he expressed all kinds of feelings.

"Hang in there, Chief," Logan said. "And keep me posted. I'll be studying up on my random raccoon facts for you. Maybe some dolphin stuff too. Until then, I've got to go back to bed. Early shift's coming whether I sleep or not."

Macon ended the call, and a smile broke as the windshield wipers swiped away the rain. By the time he made it to the station, he figured he might not have any more answers than before he'd spoken to Logan, but his attitude was at least ready to start new. If only he could talk Logan into coming home to Eastside Firehouse, he'd at least have one ally. Bryce did all Macon asked of him, but they just didn't share that history.

The rain had slowed to a mist. His boots had no trouble walking through the pooled puddles, but his steps faltered when he spotted Natalie. Not in his or even Amelia's office reading through their handbooks. No, Natalie was outside running drills. In full turnout gear.

She weaved around a set of orange cones lined up across the pavement, a hose draped over her shoulders. Faster than Dave, she reached Ridge and Zack lined up at the truck and dropped the hose onto the ground.

Amelia pointed to the ladder secured against the building. "Climb to the top and bring the dummy back down."

Hesitation spread across Natalie's face.

Natalie had said she wanted to see what it was like to be a firefighter, but this was too much for her first time.

Macon was about to call off the drill when movement beyond them caught his attention. A truck parked across the street. He heard boots slipping and twisted back toward the ladder. Had she fallen?

But Natalie was already halfway up.

He looked back at the driver in the truck. The guy had a pair of binoculars pressed to his eyes.

It wasn't uncommon for people to stop and watch them train. Usually, it was older folks or families with children. This was a single man who wore a beanie on his head. The truck wasn't running, and he'd been there long enough for the bottom corner of his front windshield to start to fog up.

Macon stalked out in the man's direction.

Just as Macon got to the curb, the truck started up.

Macon broke into a jog, but the truck peeled away, just barely missing him.

License plate. Macon turned and just grabbed the beginning. 342A. Conveniently, his batting average his junior year of high school.

But more importantly, that, along with the make of the truck—a red F-150—should net some answers to who might be after his surprising rookie firefighter.

He spotted Natalie now climbing back down from the roof, the dummy over her shoulder. If she didn't fall to her death first.

9

Ridge held up a high five toward Natalie. "That was awesome. You'll make a better rookie than Stephens."

Zack shoved Ridge. "Take that back."

Natalie bit back a groan as she pushed herself up to stand. Her legs shook, screaming for her to sit back down on one of the giant tires placed for training along the fire station's drive. She hadn't been this tired since basic training. "I think I'll stick to counseling."

She unsnapped her helmet, her muscles protesting even that small movement. Her arms ached from holding on to the firehose today—or more like trying to hang on while Ridge and Zack did most of the work. It was amazing how powerful a stream of water could be. And right now, her sides weren't thrilled about all the laughing, either. She'd quickly learned that being around Zack and Ridge, there would be no hiding from laughter. Professional or not, she hadn't ruled out the effectiveness of using comedy to cover up their stress.

Eddie jogged over from the freshly washed rescue truck parked outside the fire station. Rescue hadn't joined in Truck's training, but Eddie had been out there cheering Natalie on for most of the afternoon. He offered her a fist bump. "If you ever want a spot on the crew, I wouldn't stop you. I'll even train you for Rescue instead of Truck. It's where the best belong." His eyes twinkled even in the gloomy light.

The morning's rain had dried up by the time she'd finished climbing the ladder. However, the sun had refused to come out to watch her beat Dave at all of the exercises.

Dave sat on the back bumper of the truck. He was a stout and short man with a baby face. It hadn't been too difficult for Natalie to beat him in the sprints, but there was no reason why she'd gotten her ax swings against the giant tire in before he'd finished his.

Zack took off his helmet. "After we get off, we're all heading out to the Backdraft Bar and Grill. Want to go? Celebrate an easy—"

Ridge shushed him. "Don't you dare finish that, or we'll be called out one minute before shift change."

There had only been one run the last few hours, for Ambulance 21. Macon had prompted her to ride along. She didn't know if it was for her to watch Trace and Izan in action, or to get out of Macon's hair. He'd been nearby today, but never as close as they had been last night.

Natalie took in the firefighters. Everyone seemed to be in agreement with Zack's invitation. It would give her an opportunity to observe the crew outside their work habitat. Get a read on their everyday emotions. Body language. Interaction outside work. Macon's too. Her eyes searched for the chief. He stood in his starched uniform beside the cones with Amelia, arms crossed over his chest. She shook her head at her clipboard as Macon said something in a hushed tone.

Natalie adjusted the SCBA strap on her shoulders. "Sounds good, actually. I haven't worked this hard since my last PT test."

All three sets of eyes widened. Eddie opened his mouth

first. "Which branch? One of my foster brothers is in the Marines."

It wasn't unusual for people to be surprised she had been in the service. "Army."

"Cool." Zack grinned. "Hey, Chief." He yelled over his shoulder. "We have the best therapist. She was in the Army. I bet she can do more—"

"Settle down, Stephens," Amelia answered before Macon could. "You and Foster get ready to do another round of tire flips."

Ridge growled. "I think it's past time for her to put her clipboard down and—"

Macon stepped away from Amelia. "Hit the showers. Let's call it a day."

Amelia glared at Macon but turned toward Eddie. "Rice, the least you can do is put the tires away since Rescue didn't bother to join us today."

"Except we did do training. Thankfully, not under her watch," Eddie mumbled to Zack.

Macon avoided Natalie's gaze. Would it hurt him to give her an ounce of recognition for her hard work today?

Ridge showed her where all their gear went. Natalie cleaned up and told the guys she'd meet them at the nearby restaurant. She found her bike still chained to a young tree at the edge of the parking lot. She untied the plastic store bag she had used to protect her seat from getting wet and stuffed it in her backpack.

When she told Macon last night that she'd meet him at the firehouse at seven, the fact she didn't have a car had somehow slipped her mind. Taking the bike had been a brilliant idea at the beginning of the day. Now, with her body aching, not so much. But the car rental place would be closed by the time she got there. So she fought through her exhaustion and pedaled to the restaurant. Unexpectedly, it provided her a quiet moment to process after being inundated with the training and the crew all day.

Rescue and Truck didn't mesh well. But it was probably because Amelia and Bryce had two different methods of leadership. Eddie liked to be where the action was, which might be why he'd put up with Amelia's snide comment. Dave did the minimum on everything. Ridge and Zack hid behind humor. All of them had a hollowness in their gazes when they glanced at the tires, and she had a feeling it had something to do with Mickey.

Backdraft Bar and Grill was only a few blocks from the fire station. By the time she entered, most of the crew had arrived. The place wasn't overly bright but had a "come hang out together" vibe. Dart boards hung on the far wall near the pool tables. The guys were seated at the long tables in the center. Rescue at one end and Truck on the other. Amelia sat at a smaller booth by herself. Her shoulders were hunched as she scrolled on her phone.

Natalie glanced around the rest of the seating area. No Dave or Macon yet.

"He's not here." Amelia clicked on something on her phone. "The chief's always the last to arrive. You'd think it'd be the opposite."

Natalie held a neutral expression. She wouldn't have thought Macon arriving later would be a negative thing, since he'd have the most to do to finish up for the day. Plus, in the Army, officers didn't fraternize outside of work with the enlisted personnel.

She slipped into the seat across from Amelia. "Mind if I sit with you?"

Amelia set her phone down. "You surprised me today."

Natalie took off her backpack. "Haven't had that hard of a workout in a while. I'm definitely going to reward myself by vegging out in front of the television tonight. Probably the rest of the week too, if I'm honest."

She spied the menus at the far end of the booth and grabbed one. "What's good here?"

"I ordered boneless wings and an extra veggie salad. But I suggest you order on the app." Amelia flicked her gaze to the booth where most of the crew sat, longing in her eyes. "Or I guess you can waste your time and flag down the waitress. But you might want to change seats. Maeve always heads to the guys first."

A waitress swept past. Natalie read *Maeve* off her nametag. Sure enough, the waitress went straight to the long booth. "Does that bother you?"

Amelia picked up her phone again. "Why? I'm the best firefighter. It doesn't matter if I'm the only female or not."

Amelia was almost as good at deflecting as Macon. So she hadn't jumped in with her own hobbies earlier, and she didn't hang out with the crew. Natalie sized Amelia up. Did she not have anyone else? "Do you have family nearby?"

She barely shook her head before swiping on her phone to make the time display. "Not many of us at Eastside have family nearby. That's why my crew is so important."

Her crew. Not Macon's.

Amelia's eyes narrowed at something over Natalie's head. "Macon has his brother."

Natalie turned to find Macon entering the seating area. Alone.

"But from what I understand, he doesn't even see him." Amelia leaned back against the leather booth. "Eastside needs a leader who knows what they've been given and doesn't waste it."

Natalie only offered her a closed-mouth smile. Not all families were healthy to be around. There was a sadness in

Macon's eyes. Maybe it had to do with his family and not just a firefighter's death.

Maeve walked by and Natalie waved at her, but she headed on past. Amelia raised her brow and went back to her phone.

Whether Natalie ever received her food or not, the outing had been a success. She'd homed in on Amelia's unrepressed opinions about Macon, which clouded her view of his leadership. The brother thing she would look into, but she should also examine the craving for family Amelia had.

Macon pulled up a chair at the end of the table, beside Bryce.

After Natalie finally broke down and ordered on the app, she rested her elbows on the table. "If the guys usually exclude you, why do you come?"

Amelia held her attention on one of the televisions on the wall before finally saying in a hushed voice, "It wasn't always like this." She wrapped a folded napkin around her finger. Then unwrapped and repeated the movement. "Mickey was good at bonding the crews together. He was like the older brother you always wanted." She blinked over and over at the ceiling. "When Macon was hired, Mickey said change was a good thing." She shook her head, and anger replaced her tearful gaze. "I should have fought harder against Macon's pairing change-ups on his first day."

Natalie waited a beat before answering. "You believe Mickey's death wasn't an accident." That's what the report said. A wall had collapsed on Mickey. "That Macon should have been disciplined?"

Maeve suddenly appeared at their table with two to-go containers, two cups, two plastic forks, and a frown. She set their food down and spun away from them before Natalie could say thanks.

Amelia opened her container and slid her fork into a cucumber. "Allen failed to see Macon's fault in Mickey's death."

Her cousin had said the mayor had requested that Allen evaluate the crew before Macon could take over leadership officially, but he'd mentioned a complaint filed in-house. It wouldn't be surprising if it were Amelia. Natalie glanced over at Macon. Did he know?

As if he heard her mental question, he pushed his chair away from the table and headed toward their booth. He nodded at Amelia, who only lifted a brow before grabbing her drink.

Macon looked at Natalie. "I'm not sure who gave you a lift over, but I'm heading out if you need a ride."

Her entire body screamed at her to agree. The ache in her legs from the day's exertion had seeped in since she'd taken a seat. As much as she wanted to go home, she had to focus on her job. She needed to dig a little deeper with Amelia. The lieutenant had things locked up inside that produced a compulsion to be in control. "I'm going to hang out here a bit more. But thanks."

A frown pulled on his face, and she was about to change her mind until he knocked his knuckles on the tabletop. "Let me know when our paperwork is ready."

Natalie fisted her napkin in her palm. She assumed he was speaking to her, but Amelia mumbled a reply. So, he wasn't talking about the evaluation again.

In fact, as she spread out her napkin, she caught Macon glancing back at her, a sadness buried in his gaze. He gave her a half smile, and an unwanted flutter in her stomach floated toward her chest.

"See. The right chief for us would stick around," Amelia said. "Be there for his crew."

Natalie's gaze followed Macon out the door. Through the window, she watched him climb into his truck parked under a streetlight.

"He didn't stay around when his brother survived that fire either." Amelia glared out the window. "Macon James doesn't belong back in Last Chance County. He's let too many people down. But the oversight committee will soon fix that mistake. The sooner the better."

Natalie moved her food around with her fork, but the hurt she'd just seen in Macon's eyes made her stab a tomato harder than necessary.

To get the firehouse on track, she needed to start with the chief.

Whether he liked it or not.

10

If only Macon could have been in two places at once tonight. He flipped on his turn signal and pulled out of the fire station parking lot. Being a responsible chief had meant skipping out on a round of darts with the crew and completing paperwork back at the office instead, even when he didn't feel like it. Except, in the time he'd sat at his desk, he hadn't even gotten much done. Not with the memory of Amelia's glare and Natalie's probing inspection of him at the Backdraft Bar and Grill.

He rested his elbow on the center console. Maybe tomorrow would go better, but it was hard to guess with the station's sponsored Easter egg hunt on the docket. He'd never been responsible for such a community outreach before being chief in Last Chance County.

He didn't have many memories of the event. His father had only ever taken his brother—at least, from when he was old enough to remember. Houston got to do all the fun town events while Macon had to stay in his room. His parents blamed it on his cancer, but really, it was easier to have him locked in a bubble.

He eased up to a stop sign and noticed a shadow move on the dark road ahead.

As he drove closer, his headlights lit on a bicyclist. Not a wise one at ten o'clock at night. Near the edge of the road without any reflectors, the rider was an accident waiting to happen.

Macon eased beside the cyclist and rolled down his window, expecting to educate the cyclist. Then he saw who it was. "Natalie? You said you had a ride."

Her steering wobbled, and they both sucked in a breath. She managed to make it through the pothole on the side of the road and kept peddling. "I'm fine."

Macon inched his truck alongside her. Avoiding the counselor had been the opposite of helpful. "Why don't you hop in?"

She pulled her bike to the shoulder and waved him on. Of course she was going to be stubborn about it.

He drew up to her again and leaned over to the passenger window, one hand on the seat. He called out, "I'll just drive behind you, then, until you're at home."

She adjusted her helmet and combed her bangs with her fingers. "Go home, Chief. I'll sign the evaluation when I think it's time. Not before."

"This isn't about that." This was about her safety.

But based on the way she lifted her chin right then, he wasn't building a sturdy foundation with this woman.

"It's hard to see you. There are no reflectors on the back of your bike or your backpack, and you're wearing..." Her jacket was a blue that wasn't as bright as her eyes. He did not need to tell her that. "I'll drive behind you, or you can load the bike in the back and I can take you home. We'd both arrive home faster that way."

She rested on her handlebars, and a tired expression

surfaced. She tilted her head in that professional way of hers. "Has anyone ever told you that you're stubborn?"

And you're not? "I believe that's what helps me be a good leader."

She stared at him. "I'll put the bike in the back."

Macon hopped out. Once they finished the tug-of-war of who would put the bike in the back—he let her win, he wasn't always stubborn—they headed to her house. He turned up the radio only for her to turn it back down and fold her arms.

Well, two could play that game. "Why didn't you tell me you needed a ride?"

"I didn't need a ride. I have my bike."

"But it's five miles from your house to the station." He squeezed the steering wheel and tried to tamp down the urge to wring her neck. "And even farther to your job. What if it rains again? Can't you get a rental?"

She sighed. Looked at him. "Why do you care?"

Oh. He swallowed and glanced back to the road. "Because I'm a chief and I...well...you were sort of my rookie for a day."

Her laugh held an edge. "I hope you encourage your real rookies more than you did me."

Macon bit back a growl. "Fine. I don't want you to get hurt. Basic human caring 101."

Silence stretched between them. "Turn up here on Maple. It's a shortcut between Orchid and Carpenter—"

"I know." He took the turn.

"Oh, that's right. This is your hometown."

He glanced at her again. "Was that in my file?" Or had Amelia talked about his past that she didn't know the half of?

Natalie didn't look back at him. "Is your family still here?"

If he had known they'd be playing twenty questions, he would have doubled down on his suggestion of following her home. "My brother's here." He hoped he didn't sound as bitter as he felt.

"And do you see him often?" At his hesitation, she added, "You said you wanted me to sign off on Eastside as quickly as possible. These questions may not seem necessary to you, but it's part of my process."

Sure it was. "You're telling me you asked everyone if they have a brother?"

More than likely, Amelia had sent Natalie unlocking his better-left-closed doors. The past needed to stay there in order for him to build a better future. Except that was proving near impossible.

"I'm not sure how my family information is necessary for you to determine whether or not I can do my job today. What about you? Where's your family from? You know, to make sure you're the right therapist for my crew." He should be the one evaluating his station, not a near stranger. Not someone who had panicked in a fire.

Only the hum of the truck engine and the bumps of the road filled the moment.

She reached her hand to her mouth before laying it back on the armrest. "My family moved around a lot growing up. But we're talking about you, and apparently your family had a house fire growing up?"

"Yeah." He didn't want to get angry when that was common knowledge. But the fact she'd been poking into his past when there were more important issues concerning his crew...

"Is that why you became a firefighter?"

It seemed like when she wore her therapist badge she could avoid questions, but there was no such escape clause for him.

He could maybe offer her this much. "Yes, it's why I decided to be a firefighter. Without their quick actions, so much more would have been lost." Like his brother's life. All because of his own dumb decisions, thinking for once he could be the first choice.

Macon pulled up at the house. Before he put it in Park, she

opened the passenger door. "Thank you for the ride. I'll get my bike myself."

He wasn't the only stubborn one. "Please don't ride your bike without reflectors. We don't want to have either of the crews coming to your rescue." He bit back the word *again*.

"I'll take that into consideration, but I'm still going to need some more time with the crew."

Of course she did. Nothing in Last Chance County had ever been easy for him. "You could come to the egg hunt tomorrow."

Even in the truck's dome light, he caught how she wrinkled her nose.

"Or not. Whatever. The station sponsors an egg hunt for the community. Has for years. In case you didn't know, traditions run long in this town." Especially old judgment and nicknames.

The wrinkle turned to a frown.

He rested his arm on top of the steering wheel. "You can see the crew interact without the stress of answering a call. It starts at nine."

She considered him, those blue eyes on him—so blue, the color of the ocean, with mystery and a current that tugged on his heart.

He swallowed and looked away. He didn't need to be turning into Eddie and thinking of compliments.

"That sounds good, actually, thank you."

"Sounds good as in you're going to meet me there at nine?" He hazarded another glance at her, but she was typing something into her phone. "Or will you let me assume I'm supposed to pick up a vehicleless person at her house again?"

She looked up, held his gaze. "You came to pick me up at my house this morning?"

"Silly me, I assumed—"

"Macon, I'm so sorry." She actually *looked* sorry, frowning, worry in her eyes.

He shrugged. "Thought you might be trying to teach me a lesson."

"Seriously, we only got our signals crossed. I hadn't meant to—"

"Don't worry. It isn't the first time I've misunderstood what a woman meant."

Her mouth hung open.

He pinched his lips together. He should have kept his mouth shut. Because he knew, just knew, she was filing that in her head.

Next car ride, he'd be confessing a story from twenty years ago and how it had led to failure of the worst kind.

"You want to meet here or there?" He bit the words out.

"Let's do here." Her features softened. "If you don't mind. I forgot to call the rental place back."

"Can we exchange numbers?" When she wrinkled her nose again, he hurried on. "In case one of us is running late." It still sounded like he was asking for her number for a date. His throat tightened. Shoot. He should leave before he said something else stupid.

Her smirk made her eyes shine. "Or changes their mind about being there or here."

He managed a nod. After they exchanged numbers, he waited until she unlocked her front door and wheeled her bike inside. But as he backed out, his lights highlighted a familiar truck.

Too familiar.

A red F-150. No driver this time.

Macon pulled in behind the truck parked on the street. Got out and shined his flashlight app on the license plate. He tightened his hold around his phone. The numbers matched his old batting average.

Parked by the fire department was one thing, but again, this time near her house? Not just that, but at night. The day after her car exploded.

He jogged to the driver's side of the other truck. A beanie had been tossed on the dash, along with a motorcycle parts magazine. A pile of coffee cups on the floorboard. No binoculars.

Was it good news or bad the man wasn't in the vehicle?

It could be one of her neighbors, who followed her on her bike today to the station to make sure she got where she was going safely. That would be strange. But he had just offered to do the same thing. If it wasn't one of her neighbors, was it Leon? And most importantly, where was the man now?

Macon switched off his flashlight app and dialed Natalie's number.

After the fourth ring, he got voicemail. He dialed once more and, on the third ring, sprinted for Natalie's house. If she didn't answer her door on the first knock—

The door swung open. "No, Chief, I haven't changed my mind about—"

Her words broke off.

"Natalie, you all right?"

"Sorry." She wiped chocolate from her lip. "I was too busy slicing myself a piece of cake. I don't know why I only ordered a salad tonight."

He stared at her mouth. Then blinked at the plate in her hands. She was eating chocolate cake. Not in danger.

He took a step back and ended the phone call. "No one is in your house?" At any other time, he would have shuddered at the way his words sounded. It didn't matter if she thought his question was odd. She *had* a restraining order against someone who could have blown up her car.

She set her plate on the console table by the door and placed her hands on her hips. "Macon, are *you* okay?"

There wasn't time for that. "Have you heard anything back from the police about your car?"

She squinted as if trying to calculate where he was going with this.

"You've heard something?" Her hand touched his arm long enough for his pulse to spike.

Most of her hair was now piled on top of her head. Her bangs and a few strands framed her face. She brushed back a longer piece behind her ear, revealing a bit of scar on her forehead.

Had someone done that to her? Was that why there was a restraining order? Conroy had to have looked more into a possible connection between that and the explosion.

He turned and eyed the red truck again. He was going to have to jump all in. She might never sign off on his evaluation, but that didn't stop the need for her safety. He inhaled deeply. "What kind of vehicle does Polmes have?"

His heart beat three times as hurt flashed across her face.

"Chief James..." Her tone lowered to her professional one.

The jump had been as icy as he predicted.

"That has nothing to do with our current client-therapist relationship, something that is already crossing lines considering the circumstances. You shouldn't have heard about it in the first place."

Maybe not, but sometimes the past had a way of sneaking up and messing with the future. His usually did.

She crossed her arms. "I have confidence that the police department is doing all they can about the explosion. They have double-checked the video's time stamps and clues. They still said I was safe, and I believe them. I'm an ex-soldier who knows how to use the weapons I keep at my house. I'm afraid you're obsessing over Leon to hide from your own issues. It's past time for you to go home, Chief."

"I think you'd better check in with Chief Barnes." He matched her tone so she'd think this was over.

She started to close the door. "I'll take care of it." She paused. "And there's been a change. I'll be meeting you at the egg hunt instead."

Macon clenched his jaw and bit back another argument. What was the point when they were both exhausted? "Fine." And she called *him* stubborn.

Her eyes flared with surprise. "Thanks for the ride. I'm fine. Go home. Get some sleep." She gave him a brief nod, then shut her door.

He marched for the stranger's truck, where he snapped a picture of the license plate. It was expired. He pounded out a text and sent the picture off to Conroy.

Seconds later, the police chief replied that he would have a patrol car swing by her neighborhood a couple extra times tonight, just to be safe.

Go home. Right. Until she signed off on his crew, she was a part of his life. If something didn't feel right, he protected those in need. Because if a fire chief didn't rescue people, what good was he?

He got in his truck. He'd just stick around until the first patrol came by.

Who was he kidding? He leaned back on the seat, stretching out his legs. At least he wouldn't miss her leaving her house in the morning.

11

Morning sunlight glittered across the plastic eggs spread against the park's grass. All the slides and swings in the background had been deserted as families continued to flock from the lot where the fire trucks had been parked. Natalie sandwiched herself between Zack and Eddie in front of probably a hundred children, all wide-eyed and smiling.

She'd had a long text conversation with her boss, Dean, last night and this morning. She felt better since she'd filled him in on everything happening. Hopefully after today she could sign off on their evaluation. Or at least be two steps closer. There was no doubt the crew needed ongoing counseling—but it wouldn't be Natalie doing it.

Zack handed Natalie a small flag with Truck's emblem on it. "Here. It only makes sense for you to cheer on the winning crew." He sent a smirk Eddie's way.

Natalie waved the flag. "Go Truck."

Eddie crossed his arms. "If I hadn't passed all Rescue's flags out already, you wouldn't be stuck with the loser's flag."

A girl with a purple headband ran up and tapped Zack on

the arm. "Mr. Firefighter, do you have another one of those flags that I can give to my sister?"

Eddie broke into a grin as he eyed Natalie's flag. "Yeah, Stephens, do you?"

Natalie handed over Truck's flag. "You can have mine."

"Make sure you cheer really loudly for the Truck team." Zack pointed to his chest. "That's the crew I'm on."

Eddie walked over and put his arm around Zack's shoulder. "Or yell for Rescue if you want to pick the winning side." Before Zack could respond with a comeback, the girl smiled, revealing two missing front teeth, and ran back toward her family.

The rest of the crew circled around, and Macon moved to the center of the group. He handed out clipboards to Amelia and Bryce and kept one for himself. Dark circles under his eyes matched the ones Natalie had covered with makeup this morning, and she wondered if he'd wrestled with sleep last night because of their last conversation too.

He was the reason a cop car had been parked at her house when she rolled her bike outside this morning. But she could have sworn Macon's truck was still parked on her road when she got up to get a drink at one a.m.

She shouldn't have answered him so sharply last night. He'd caught her off guard when he brought up Leon. Having a restraining order didn't exactly scream *capable counselor*.

"This may be a team building exercise, but first and foremost it's for our community. Let's go out and be herolike examples." Macon's phone buzzed, and he frowned before taking the call.

Zack struck a pose worthy of a movie poster. "Who needs a cape when we have hoses?"

Ridge snickered while Dave stared at someone out in the crowd.

When Amelia's glare landed on Zack, he hunkered behind Ridge.

Macon turned around and tapped his wrist, still on his call.

Amelia brushed past Bryce and flipped over the first page on her clipboard. She stomped over to Macon and waited until he ended the call, then punched her fists onto her hips. "Why is our egg race last?"

Macon tucked his phone into his pocket and readjusted the megaphone he held under his arm. "Because I wanted the community to get to do their fun first."

"It's tradition to—"

"I discovered at my classroom visit that the younger siblings get tired before their egg race, so I switched up the schedule."

Amelia opened her mouth twice before shaking her head. She whirled around and barked out orders to Ridge.

Macon sighed.

Natalie painted on a smile and stepped forward. "Can I help with anything?"

There was a brief hint of gloom in his gaze, and then it was gone. "I'm sure you'll be busy enough observing." He looked past her. "I'm guessing you didn't have any other problems last night?"

Maybe it had never been sadness she'd observed in his eyes, but rather, fatigue. He had a leadership role in the community, and it seemed he'd added the burden of watching out for her when she was around his crew. Like he did everyone else in his department.

Perhaps the questions she'd had about him didn't have to do with the grief she thought he was hiding. Maybe it was his response to taking on too many problems. Stress affected the body in different ways.

"Greene!" Amelia yelled as she jogged toward a red-faced Dave, who stood near the roped off section by the crowd.

Natalie and Macon turn around, reminding her that Macon's leadership included those who didn't appreciate him.

Not exactly the best environment, but it was what he did with the pressure that mattered.

After Amelia steered Dave back into his position, the first three egg races went off without any problems or complaints. Until the firefighters lined up for the next race.

Macon ran across the field. "It's not your race time."

Amelia scribbled an arrow on her clipboard. "We need to move up our race."

Macon hooked his thumb behind him at the crowd on the sideline. "This isn't about us. It's about them."

Amelia pushed Dave back behind Zack in her crew's lineup. "Greene says he's not feeling the best. And no, this is also about you and how you've changed a tradition. The youngest kids did their race. Surely the older kids can wait until the race right after ours. Then Greene can go rest."

Natalie didn't have time to dissect all the motivations and feelings waging war right in front of her at this very moment, but she had one suggestion for a quick ceasefire. "I could take Dave's spot if he's not feeling well. If that would help."

In front of his squad, Bryce shrugged. "What do you want us to do, Chief?"

"I'm good with Natalie joining in," Eddie said from Rescue's formation.

Macon eyed Dave. Then Natalie.

Natalie inspected Macon's clenched jaw.

"I-I can do this." Dave rubbed his palm down his face.

Amelia handed Natalie her team's clipboard. "We're all ready. And the people are ready to watch. It's not like they have the schedule."

Macon raised his chin at Amelia. He held the bullhorn to his mouth and faced the crowd. "Who's ready to cheer on their favorite squad? Everyone rooting for Rescue, let me hear you."

The crowd hollered and waved the different colored crew flags.

A group of kids chanted the crews' names as Macon counted down the start of the race. "Go!"

Amelia and Bryce went head-to-head carrying a spoon balancing an egg in their mouths. They filtered through their lineup, and Truck had the lead until Dave wobbled and dropped his egg. Instead of picking it up, he scowled at the west section of the crowd, where a man in a hat unwound his arms from around a woman.

The guy cupped his hands around his mouth. He yelled something that was muffled by a couple of kids fighting over a single team flag beside Natalie. Dave threw his spoon down and sprinted right for the chuckling man.

Apparently he'd heard what the guy had said. And had been all healed from whatever ailment he supposedly had.

Macon yelled, "Greene!"

Dave never stopped. He went right over the crowd's boundary lines and punched the man wearing the hat. The man covered his face and fell back on the ground. Dave jumped on top of him.

The crowd erupted in gasps and a smattering of cheers. Despite being at the opposite end, Macon reached Dave first. He pulled him off the guy. Natalie wasn't far behind the rest of the crew.

"Greene! Get off him. What's the deal?"

Dave bounced back, breathing hard, a look in his eyes that Natalie had never seen on him before. "He can't say that about my sister and get away with it."

Macon pushed the man back by the shoulders, kept his voice low. "Breathe. Walk it out."

Dave shoved away from Macon.

The man with the bloody nose stood on his feet. "You bet I'll be pressing charges!"

Dave spun back around. His focus set on the now laughing man.

Macon wrapped his arms around Dave. Bryce joined in and helped secure their rogue firefighter. Macon glanced over at Zack. "Find Trace." He turned his head and locked his gaze onto Natalie's. He didn't need to speak for her to see what he wasn't saying. Whether he'd wanted her help earlier or not, he needed her now.

"I'll settle the crowd." She jogged to where he had dropped his clipboard. Before she could grab the bullhorn on the ground, someone else picked it up—a man with burn scars up his arm to the sleeve of his tee, and then above the collar stretching to his bald head. He held up the bullhorn without any hesitation of anyone noticing his exposed wounds.

She gaped at his skin that matched the angry scars on her forehead. The wounds she had cut her hair to cover.

The man smiled, and the movement pulled on the healed scars on his face. "What race do I need to announce next?"

His voice had a soothing quality, like he should be a podcast host. Maybe he was, and that's why he sounded familiar.

Natalie blinked. Her empty hand flitted to her bangs, but everything was in order. Her wounds remained covered. If that fiery board from the explosion on the day Jeremiah lost his life had stayed on top of her a second longer, her face could have completely matched this man's skin.

He didn't even wear long sleeves. How had he gotten to the point where his scars didn't bother him?

She ran her trembling finger down the schedule. "I think..." She forced her gaze to remain on the page and not on the scarred man. The crew had gone out of order, but if she went back to the last race and... "It's either the eight— or ten-year-old race?"

"Hey, Gunner," the man asked a nearby boy. "Has your sister raced yet?"

The boy shook his head.

The man said, "Let's go for the eight-year-olds."

After the man addressed the crowd and got a few parents to take over the finish line duties, he stuck out his hand to Natalie. "I'm Houston, by the way. Youth pastor at Last Chance County Church."

His skin was both smooth and rough. Just like her burn scars. "I'm Natalie Atkinson. The newest counselor at the Ridgeman Center."

His grin dimmed. "No wonder you came to Macon's rescue. But a word of advice? When my brother comes over to thank you for helping, don't mention your job."

She barely held onto the clipboard. "He already knows." But right now she wanted to know about Houston. "Macon's your brother?" Her words sounded like a question, but they both knew the answer.

"Best brother I've got." He tipped his head toward Macon and Dave, walking to a police car that pulled up by the fire trucks. Houston was the one Macon had clammed up about last night.

Interesting. And ninety-nine percent of the time, there was a reason—or usually reasons—why. Looking at Houston and his scars, a thousand questions rose in her mind. His brother had to be the real reason Macon was a firefighter.

When she searched past the scars, Houston had the same color eyes as Macon. Similar in build, though Macon was taller. More muscular.

As if reading her mind, Houston said, "We looked more similar before..." He motioned to his wounds.

Had Macon seen her scars on the day of the fire or the explosion? He seemed overly protective of her, maybe because she reminded him of his brother. Which could have been why he'd been so protective last night.

The egg hunt had ended up being even more educational than dinner.

Another boy younger than Gunner came up to him. "Pastor

H, got a problem. Can you come talk to my momma about the lock-in? She don't think I'm old enough."

Houston's chuckle nearly matched the one time she'd made Macon laugh. He extended the bullhorn to Natalie. "I'm not in the business of bribing parents. But I can provide the details."

The boy's face fell.

"Perhaps she could still let you go if you get picked up early?"

The little boy pulled on Houston's scarred arm without a thought, and they disappeared into the crowd.

"Thank you." Macon's voice made her spin around. He stood behind her. "Dave calmed down a bit. He's nursing a migraine amongst other things. Thanks for reorganizing everyone."

With robotlike movements, she handed over the bullhorn. Then the clipboard. "Your, uh, brother helped too."

Macon's jaw tightened. "I'm sure he did."

Without another word, he lifted the bullhorn to his mouth and called for the next race.

Natalie kept pace with him. He couldn't ignore all her questions if he wanted her signature. And perhaps this wasn't the right time, but then again, with Macon, maybe there never would be a right time. "Were your brother's injuries why you wanted to become a firefighter?"

She wanted the real reason. Not the apparent half story he'd given.

This time, he scrutinized the list on his clipboard. "It's complicated."

She flung her hands out between them. "Macon, I'm good with complicated." Or she used to be. He was deflecting. Hiding. Again.

Would he ever trust her enough to open up? When he had finished fixing her lock, she could have sworn there was something flowing between them, and maybe it couldn't be anything more than friendship, but she thought they were building some level of rapport. But maybe she was reading him wrong. He was better at closing her out than most.

As if he read her thought, Macon gestured with his head for her to follow him. "Officer Ramble is taking Greene's statement now. I'll need to head over there and give mine as well." He rubbed his temple. "My brother...our relationship is..." He swallowed. "He got caught in our house fire. One I should have been home for."

He could have shouted *And I blame myself* for the expression on his face.

Or maybe there was something else. "Do you think he holds a grudge against you?" Because it certainly hadn't seemed that way, the way he'd jumped in to help. Unless he wanted something more to hold over Macon. But she hadn't gotten that vibe.

"Chief!" A boy wearing a baseball hat called his name from the crowd of kids.

He waved at him instead of answering Natalie. Until he whispered, "Yes, he's the real reason I'm a firefighter."

She ran his words against the things she had learned about him. He was bossy. Yet... protective. The memory of how gently he'd held her as they escaped the fire warmed her. He was a natural leader. Helper. But...did he feel the need to save everyone? "Being chief is a heavy burden."

"I'm willing to carry it." He stepped away from her, but she still made out his mumbled "I *have* to carry it."

Fine. She'd wanted him to open up, and technically, he had. He'd turned on the spigot and allowed a few drops of information to trickle out.

The problem was, it only made her thirst for more.

12

Macon would not hit this man.

He squeezed his fingers around the arms of his chair as red-faced George Greene shook his finger inches from Macon's nose. "Janice was right. You are too young. Too inexperienced. How dare you fire Davey!"

How dare a city hall oversight committee member barge into *his* office. Macon rose to his feet. "Allen Frees agreed with my recommendation to terminate—"

George swung his head back and forth. The fluorescent office lights bounced off his balding head. "Termination is right. I'll see the mayor terminates your contract at our next meeting. Pack your bags!"

George slammed Macon's door on his way out.

Macon fisted his fingers. Allen had warned him this job wouldn't be easy. Macon had said nothing worthwhile was.

He lowered into his chair. Had he made a mistake leaving Australia?

A glance at the clock revealed it was past time to finish Truck's training booklet. He stomped down the halls toward the conference room to set it up. Except, when he entered, his needed firefighters were already there. And so was Natalie.

She wore a striped skirt that hit at her knees and a pair of pointed heels that matched her black shirt. She smiled when she noticed him. “Perfect timing, Chief. We’re having an informal group session. Please join us.”

No way. He took one step back. Group sessions were *not* something he wanted to relive. He’d rather endure a round two with George.

“I promise it won’t be long.”

Like that was the only problem here. He should have known her smile hadn’t meant anything good. But he couldn’t give George any fodder to make his case to get rid of Macon at the next meeting.

Macon held back a growl as he grabbed a seat at the front.

Thank you.” She smiled again at Macon. “I’ve told everyone that it’s okay to have opinions. Even...feelings about one of your team members having to be let go. Sometimes we don’t realize those around us are dealing with similar things. This is a safe space.”

Safe for who?

Macon bristled under Natalie’s side-glance.

Letting Dave go was supposed to have been what Macon had wanted all along. What was best for Eastside. Especially when Natalie had outperformed him in her firefighter training, proving to Macon that Dave had only been truly hired because he was George’s grandson. But seeing Dave, distraught over his regrettable choices, felt too close to Macon’s own past. If Macon could go back and make different choices, he would.

It hadn’t helped that Natalie had watched Dave’s outburst, or that Houston had cozied up to Natalie. Her probing questions when he had already been down could only have been his brother’s doing. Now she was interfering more.

Macon massaged his temples. This group therapy session wouldn't work. Hadn't for his family. He couldn't afford to lose anyone else from his Truck crew.

Amelia raised her hand.

Macon held his breath.

"Go ahead, Amelia," Natalie encouraged.

Amelia glanced at Macon and then at Natalie. "I think... never mind. Someone else go."

Natalie shook her head. "Please continue. We want to hear your thoughts. Right, Chief?"

No. He knew how group counseling worked. And he could almost guarantee by Amelia's expression he was not going to like the words from her mouth. He leaned his back against his chair. But he also wanted Natalie to sign off on his crew.

Macon clenched his jaw and said, "Your opinion matters, Patterson."

"I think it was a mistake." Amelia's tone was calm. Level. But her words struck his heart.

Of course she did.

Ridge lifted his coffee mug up toward Macon as if to say *Good luck.*

"And why is that, Amelia?" Natalie's chair squeaked. Her therapist's gaze always seemed to observe his failures. He never should have invited her to the egg hunt. She would have missed Dave's disaster. Avoided Houston.

Amelia placed her hands under the table. "I think people should never be penalized for what they've inherited."

If some stomach problems were the "heredity" portion Amelia referenced about Dave, they had nothing to do with his actions at the egg hunt.

Ridge shook his head. "We're still talking about Ghost, right?" He paused, as if to allow Dave's nickname to sink in. "He can't go around punching people. And he missed out on at least two fire runs. That puts the rest of us in danger. I have to be able to depend on our people."

"Exactly!" Amelia's hand went up, framing her face.

"This is good, you guys." Natalie turned toward Zack. "Any thoughts?"

How was this good? Amelia and Ridge were back to glaring at one another, and Zack looked half asleep as he simply shrugged.

Then Zack said, "I'd like to trust the guys who have my back."

"The *people* who have your back." Amelia tapped her pen against the table. "By the way, that was an old bully from school and Greene's sister's ex who hurled insults at Greene. He shouldn't be penalized for what a family member did. You'd know their situation if—"

Natalie held up her hand. "Easy, Amelia. Don't allow your feelings to twist—"

Macon moved to the edge of his chair. "Greene had a blood alcohol level worth firing over alone. And if you suspected and didn't report it, that hurts the entire team too. The community will remember how a firefighter lashed out at one of them. We will be carrying that millstone around for weeks. Months. Second chances..." He swallowed. "Some choices don't get one."

He still hoped he was worth the second chance.

Natalie flipped her notebook closed. "Why don't we take a break and circle back to this after we've had a chance to clear our heads."

"Actually"—Macon stood—"we need to go over some training booklets. That is, if you're done"—he held back the word *interrogating*—"interviewing all of us for the moment."

Ridge grunted. "Therapy or booklets. Not sure which is worse."

He knew which he'd pick. Macon cleared his throat. "Turn to page fifteen."

Zack grabbed a booklet off the table and flipped to the page. "Beat you."

Natalie pointed to her open booklet. "Not hardly, slowpoke." She sent the youngest in the room a wink.

Macon's shoulders tensed. Was there something growing between them? Several years separated the two. However, it wouldn't be out of the realm of possibility.

Except, Natalie had made it ultra, crystal clear that her relationship with him—and he'd thought, all of them—was strictly professional. So, probably it meant nothing.

Still, it bugged him.

"You don't have to take this course, Ms. Atkinson."

"You can't get rid of me that easily." She tilted her head at Macon again. "I want to see what they have to deal with and think through."

Macon pulled up his slides on the laptop connected to the projector. He picked up a booklet and used it to block Natalie's scrutiny. "Can anyone tell Natalie a different way, other than a 911 call, that we can be alerted to a fire?"

"Certain sprinkler systems give us direct alerts when their units detect smoke. Especially warehouses and factories that deal with expensive merchandise or that use flammable equipment," Amelia said.

"Teacher's pet," Ridge muttered under his breath.

Zack flashed a huge grin Natalie's way. However, her attention remained on the booklet.

Macon clicked on the PowerPoint. "This is why customers spend extra on those sprinkler systems." A picture of a warehouse filled with smoke popped up on the projector. "It only took three minutes for this security camera to be blocked by a smoking conveyer belt. Being directly connected to our stations saved valuable time."

Natalie was no longer staring at her booklet but at the screen. Her lips pinched together, and Macon wondered if she was reliving the fire she'd endured with Joey. Or something else.

He clicked off the slide, which brought up the smoke house. Based on her blanched expression, he wasn't sure it was the best plan for her to join in their training today.

"In our training house"—he went through the slides as quickly as possible—"we practice how—"

"Natalie, I apologize." Amelia pointed at the screen. "I should have thought about having you do the smoke house instead of the ladder exercise."

Would their minds ever be on the same page? Amelia had been there the day Natalie had to be carried out of the fire. Surely she'd seen how their counselor had reacted.

He shook his head. "That won't be necessary."

"Wouldn't that be a perfect opportunity to let her experience what we do? More so than this." Amelia held up her booklet. "Sir, I'm not trying to override you here. If it's about time and you're busy elsewhere, I'll take the lead on this. I think Natalie learns best like I do. Hands-on."

"Or I'll do it." Zack raised his hand.

"I had the fastest time cleaning my gear this week," Ridge countered.

"Doing your job correctly should be the objective, Foster," Amelia snarled.

Macon needed to shut them all down.

Until Natalie's voice squeaked. "She's right." She cleared her throat. "I need to experience the smoke house. I'll be better able to evaluate..."

Macon walked to her table and dropped his voice. "You've already experienced a real-life fire."

She snapped her chin up. "Not as a firefighter. This will prove that I'm capable of making the call for your crew."

He raised his brow. "Has someone mentioned otherwise?"

She met his gaze. "The sooner I observe and experience all I need, the sooner I can get out of your hair."

Perfect. *Exactly* what he wanted. Evaluations finished before the committee's next meeting.

"You're the therapist... Get your gear on. Be ready in twenty minutes." Macon motioned for Zack to put his hand down. "I'll be the one taking her. Stephens and Foster, you both get the training set up."

Their groans wouldn't change his mind. He wasn't going to allow one of his crew who hadn't witnessed Natalie's reaction in a fire to lead her through smoke. He'd had a buddy at his last stateside position experience PTSD from a collapsed roof. And it could be triggered by anything.

If she wanted to do this, he was going to protect her.

Macon looked over a report and then readied his gear. Natalie was outside waiting for him wearing turnout gear. "Sure you're ready?"

She tightened her helmet strap. "I can handle a little smoke."

He double-checked her air tank and mask. Everything was typical protocol. All except the rate of his pulse. It was years since he'd been a probie. The first few times he'd been nervous about going into a smoke house. But now, he shouldn't be.

At the training site, he lowered his gloves enough to touch the back of his hand, the most sensitive portion, to the doorhandle. When it wasn't hot, he still went ahead and ducked lower as if they were entering a burning room.

He opened the training door, and smoke splashed out into the fresh air.

Macon didn't have to beckon Natalie. She was close enough to bump into his SCBA. "Fire Department! Anyone in here?"

He held out his thermal imaging device, and Natalie copied his actions. In the hall, his TIC registered the heating blanket they'd put over the dummy. He helped her reposition her TIC so it mirrored his results. Except, normally, the easiest level was the bedroom with multiple exits, where they usually put the dummy. Not the far corner room.

The smoke grew thicker, but there would be enough visibility if they hunched lower. He motioned for her to take the lead. To be the one to experience how it felt to rescue someone. She blinked at him through her face shield. The determined gaze from his in-class training session had vanished. Doubt and fear had slipped in.

"I'll be with you each step. But it's your call. You don't have to prove anything to me." Someone might have doubted her abilities as a therapist, but it wasn't Macon. He'd seen her listening and observing. Offering compassion. Nothing like the therapist his parents had visited after the fire. Who'd seemed to egg on the tension. Then again, maybe no one could put a family back together after that kind of tragedy.

She adjusted her helmet again and then stepped in front of him, holding her TIC out in front of her like a trained firefighter. It made him proud of his crew for teaching her the correct ways. Even with their downfalls, they had been a good example when it mattered. They reached the dummy, and she did everything by the book, minus announcing who she was.

Yet when she lifted the doll, the only door to the room slid shut.

Macon looked around. This wasn't the right simulation.

With the door blocked, the smoke pumped back through vents in the ceiling. It had nowhere else to go but to swaddle them into darkness.

Natalie dropped the dummy and pressed to his side. "What's happening?"

Macon grabbed his radio. "Stephens, has the simulation malfunctioned?"

"Everything looks fine on the computer...wait."

Natalie backed away.

Even stooping over further, he could barely make out her form. "Don't move out of reach."

His radio crackled. "Chief." It was Ridge. "Looks like the program has been overridden."

Only a few people had the codes to change a scenario. "By who?"

"I'm not..."

Natalie banged against the locked door.

He twisted around and headed for the door. The banging continued as he wrapped his gloved hand over hers. "Ridge, override the system. Open the door. Right now."

Natalie kept banging with her free hand.

Ridge came on. "It says it's already overridden."

Natalie shook beneath his touch. She edged away from him, deeper into the smoke. Deeper into fear. He had no doubt she was imagining herself trapped with Joey.

"Natalie, you're okay. It's only smoke. It's only..." He could no longer see her. She had disappeared into the darkness.

He pulled out his TIC and located where she had curled up in the corner. He dropped to all fours and put his mask right up against hers. "Hey. I'm right here." Her eyes opened and he again saw the fear coursing through her. "I'm going to get you out. Just like I did before."

She reached for him then, her beautiful eyes fully opened. She wrapped her arms around his neck.

Except he needed her to let go. "Natalie, do you trust me?"

Her grip on him lightened and she nodded.

"Stay here while I go open the door. I'll be right back for you."

His words seemed to sink in, because she released him.

He grabbed his axe from his belt. First, he'd get Natalie to safety. Then he'd figure out why the system had already been overridden. Or malfunctioned.

As his axe splintered the wood, two options shot through his mind. Either someone really wanted to set him up to fail in front of Natalie...

Or worse, someone really was after her.

13

She couldn't breathe. Someone had filled her lungs with sand while something stabbed her back.

Breathe, Natalie! She heard a voice—maybe her own—and forced herself away from the cloying fog of panic.

But she had to get this board off her chest. She had to get to Jeremiah. Please, Lord. Help! Let him be alive—

She forced her eyes open to find sunshine and trees.

Wait. She wasn't being burned, or her head would be on fire.

And her friend Jeremiah wasn't caught in the flames of an explosion.

In fact, no one was screaming. Except her.

"Breathe, Natalie!"

Someone removed her helmet. They rested their hands around her hair. Near her scars.

Macon. He leaned in front of her, and the activity of the smoke house crashed into her mind. Training. She'd panicked during the training. That was all.

She sat up. The movement released the pain in her back but not her chest.

"Easy." Macon's hands moved off her face, and she was able to take in a short breath until he moved them to her shoulders. Warm. Solid.

They sent a tremble right through to her bones.

No, she was just relieved, her panic cascading over her common sense.

"You're all right," he said, his voice soft. "Just keep breathing."

Oh, heaven help her, she just let his voice caress her and leaned into his support. How was she going to keep her counseling job? Not only could she not fall for a client, it probably wasn't a great idea to let him see her weakness.

"Anything hurt? I can get Bently or Collins out here if you don't want me." Worry lines had engraved themselves along his forehead, but it was the concern in his coffee-colored eyes that made Natalie rest her face back in her palms.

Her pride, that's what was hurt. But she couldn't depend on this man to save her. She had a job to do.

She scooted over and brushed away the rock she had been sitting on. Probably what had poked her back. What had made her think she was reliving Jeremiah's explosion? The smoke, or being confined?

She shook off those thoughts. "I'm fine."

There was no other option.

"Did your air tank malfunction?"

She couldn't let him believe he was at fault for her reaction. "The fire equipment was fine." She removed the only glove she had and put both hands on top of her head. "I needed to know what you all do."

His expression darkened. "This was a bad idea. Not with your recent fire experience."

She held his gaze, hearing what he *wasn't* saying. That she shouldn't be counseling his crew—and he was right. She needed her phone so she could call Dean and tell him she was done.

"Chief, everything all right?" Macon's radio crackled with Zack's panicked tone.

Macon eyed her as he radioed back. "We'll be in to inspect the controls in a bit." He sat beside her.

She had nothing for him.

Because, for a moment, she considered he might be right. If she was going to panic every time she tried to get into their point of view, understand the crew, she could hardly help them, right?

She pressed her chapped lips together. "Sorry."

He worked off his jacket, revealing the sweaty shirt underneath. "We all have struggles, Natalie."

"I'm supposed to be the one *fixing* the problems. Not creating them." She sighed. Oh, she was tired of fighting it. "I have PTSD. It was after an explosion, and I have it handled—"

"Until you're in a locked room. It's understandable."

"Not for a therapist to firefighters. I...I'll call Allen and get Dean or Kelsey over here instead of me—"

He put his hand on top of hers and she froze. "Or I'm here if you want to talk about it."

His husky tone was probably due to the smoke, but she leaned into it anyway.

No, oh no—

She yanked her hand away. "No, really, Chief."

"Macon's fine, Natalie. You call everyone else by their first names."

She cleared her throat. "Knowing isn't going to make you like me being here any better."

He didn't reach for her again, but he met her eyes. "Try me."

Maybe. What if...she studied his expression. Took a breath. Closing her eyes, she could still picture Jeremiah's face. "I failed to see the signs of a fellow soldier's depression...and he'd apparently taken C4 from the armory, molded it around his office chair, and..."

Macon didn't even blink, just held her gaze.

"He died."

Macon nodded.

Her eyes filled. "As a counselor, I always prided myself on being the person to support others. I was supposed to be the strong one. Dependable. The one with the next step, the answers. Help them sort through and even carry their burdens."

He had taken her hand again. She hadn't even noticed.

"I was preoccupied that day. I had...something else on my mind..." She wasn't sure she wanted to tell him about her father's suicide attempt. "I didn't know he'd gotten orders to go back to Afghanistan. I didn't even see Jeremiah's desperation not to return there. Not until it was too late."

He reached up and touched her forehead. "Did you try and stop him?"

She froze and he removed his hand, but let his question hang there.

"I failed. The MPs had already barricaded Jeremiah's building by the time I found out." Her hand went to her scar on her leg from when she'd jumped over the barricades. "I was positive if I could just make it to him, I could talk him down." She shook her head. "I got close enough to view his expression from a long hallway from inside his office. His pain was obvious. Then he was gone." She shuddered. "And I was trapped."

Macon almost looked like he wanted to pull her into a hug, but she lifted her chin. How long had it been since she'd trusted someone else with her burdens? If only she'd met him under different circumstances. "I was hospitalized for trauma and burns. Then medically discharged."

"No wonder being in a smoky room—"

"I'll be fine."

His lips made a grim line, but he nodded.

"Are you going to tell Allen or Dean about the smoke house?" She stood. "I'm fine now. I promise. My PTSD isn't magically going to go away, but it shouldn't affect my ability to wrap up my evaluation of your crew."

He drew in a long breath, and uncertainty clouded his eyes. She needed this job. After out-processing from the army, then the disaster situation that had happened at her next job with Leon, Dean had been the only one who offered her an interview.

She bustled under Macon's gaze. "In case you ever have one of your guys deal with an episode, get them to water. Give them a drink, or just washing their hands will work. Get them moving. It sometimes helps. Okay, Chief?"

His title seemed to shore him up and he nodded. "Good idea, *Counselor*."

She dredged up a smile, trying to restore space between them. Despite their moment, nothing had changed.

She grabbed her mask and jacket off the ground.

"Here, let me..." He reached for the gear in her grip, and his fingers brushed hers. He dropped his arm and took a step back. Maybe he felt it too—the heat that simmered between them.

So not good. He didn't reoffer to take her gear, which was fine. She followed him toward the training shed.

Zack looked up from where he sat at a desk, and his gaze darted back and forth between Natalie and Macon. "What happened?"

Macon rested his helmet beside the desk. "I had to cut the door, and we headed out the back."

Ridge sat beside him at a computer and clicked on the keyboard. There were buttons for the airflow and each of the training house windows and locks. "It looks like the training sequence was overridden so the doors locked when they shouldn't have."

Macon squinted at the screen.

Ridge frowned. "What we thought we selected isn't what happened."

Zack rubbed his chin. "Uh, we stepped into the kitchen to grab a drink before heading here." He shifted his feet. "Patterson was already at the controls. She had everything turned on."

Macon turned toward the guys. "Could you give us a moment?"

"No problem, Chief."

After they'd stepped out, Macon lowered his voice. "At first I thought this might be connected to your car explosion..." He ran his hand down his face. "But on duty right now, only Bryce, Amelia, and myself have the admin password to change a simulation. So unless someone outside of us is skilled at hacking and predictions..."

He assumed Amelia had done this.

Natalie held up her palm. "Let's slow this down. We don't know for sure who or what happened."

He blew out a hard breath. "Patterson's the one who suggested we take you in there even after witnessing the effect that residential fire had on you. She could have done this to try to get me kicked out as chief."

Natalie took a step back. "Amelia doesn't seem the type to take revenge on an innocent. Even if she wanted to prove you incompetent, I have a hard time believing she would put me in danger."

Macon folded his arms and leaned against the wall of the shed. "But it was only smoke. Not fire. She has hated me as her superior since the accident where we lost Mickey. Who's to say she didn't sabotage this?"

"She may blame you for Mickey's death. But she also

blames herself." Her posture at Backdraft Bar and Grill hadn't been only anger but also guilt. As if she had failed to do something too.

Natalie rested her palm on his forearm. "Don't allow your emotions to rule you. Emotions aren't always wrong; however, they can't be the truth we rely on. I think it's time we talk about what happened with Mickey and..."

His nostrils flared, but he didn't say anything else.

Okay, so she'd cut right to the point.

"Listen, all your people are still hurting over Mickey. Or something else in their life as well. Let's take Ridge. His humor and sarcasm is a crutch. Zack will jump on that too; however, he also pretends he's young and dumb, especially to avoid conflict. Eddie is loud and everywhere because he doesn't want to be left out. Charlie pretends he's happy-go-lucky, but the guy's wife left him and now he's estranged from his family. He misses them."

Macon just blinked at her. Twice.

"And Amelia. She challenges your every move because she feels like if she lets her guard down, she'll lose someone else. Did you know she felt the closest to Mickey of all the crew?"

Macon frowned. "I didn't know that."

"While observing everything, I've witnessed that you and Amelia are both talented firefighters. And I believe you know that. She wouldn't jeopardize anyone's life, training or not. Nor her own job. She loves it too much." Natalie paused. "*That's* why she's so hard on you."

Macon didn't move. Neither did he speak. Was he still listening, or had he simply built his wall up higher?

"Facts may prove me wrong, but I believe Amelia's attitude is a shield. Protection. Beneath that, she wants to fit in with your crew. That's why she's so standoffish. So desperate to do it her way. But even if I'm wrong, jumping to a judgmental conclusion won't make you a good leader for your crew."

Macon opened and closed his mouth before finally nodding.

"I know you have your reasons for not trusting therapists. But you can trust me."

And once she turned in the final paperwork, she wouldn't be his counselor anymore.

14

Macon had never liked dancing. And he was past the point of being tired of dodging everyone's opinions—the committee, the crew, the town. He led Natalie to the door so they could head inside.

His phone rang. Houston's name lit the screen, but Macon sent it to voicemail.

Now he was even dodging his own brother. If the counselor wanted to know him, she was going to get the full storm.

Come what may.

He held open the back door to the fire station for Natalie and marched into the bay. Amelia stood from the lobby chair, facing the doors, as if she'd been waiting on him. Or at least news on their training session.

She set down her boots and shine kit and kept her gaze on Macon until they met at the end of the fire truck. Wasn't that guilt in her eyes?

Macon crossed his arms and lowered his voice. "Did you set up the smoke house controls?" He caught a glimpse of Natalie standing behind them against the wall. A few of his guys were now peeking in from the hall. Perhaps here wasn't the best place for this conversation.

Even if Amelia was guilty, Natalie had been right. He couldn't let his emotions take over.

Natalie hadn't been hurt. Just scared. And there was no real proof Amelia had done anything. At least not yet.

Amelia widened her stance. "I didn't have anything to do with the simulation malfunction." Her cheeks seemed more puffy than normal, and her eyes had a touch of red around them.

"I tasked Foster and Stephens with setting up the simulator, but you got there first."

She licked her lips. "I could get it done quicker than—"

"I asked them to do it because Stephens needs to feel more confident in setting up the program."

Amelia opened her mouth only to close it. "I wasn't aware. I'm...sorry."

"Why did you set it up and then leave?"

"I had a phone call that I had to take." She sniffed, and her gaze darted to her extra pair of boots on the bay floor.

Had she been crying? He ran a hand behind his neck and squeezed, glancing at Natalie. Maybe she'd been right and he'd jumped to conclusions about Amelia. Natalie had been correct about all of his crew's personalities, and she hadn't been around them as much as he had.

"Excuse me, Chief?" Bryce brushed past the eavesdropping crew and jogged toward him from the engine bay.

"As soon as I finish with Patterson, I'll be right with you. You can have a seat in my office."

Bryce shifted on his feet. "Actually, this affects Patterson. I'm to blame for the smoke house incident. Not her."

Amelia folded her arms across her chest. The momentary look of gloom was gone. Instead, she cocked her head.

One of his crew members shushed another from the other

side of the kitchen. Macon ignored them. He also refused to glance at Natalie. An I-told-you-so was sure to be waiting for him. He hadn't been wise in confronting Amelia in front of everyone. No wonder Natalie hadn't signed off on his release—he wasn't sure he'd have signed off on himself either.

He motioned down the left hall, toward his office. "Let's head to my office. Patterson, I'll need to speak to you immediately following Crawford."

He noticed that Natalie headed for the locker room, probably to shed her gear, maybe shower.

But her story still hung in his head. She was brave—he'd give her that.

Inside his office, Bryce stared at Macon's desk. "I changed the specifications for a drill to include a barricaded door. Apparently, I failed to change it back." He lifted his gaze only to drop it again. "Feel free to take out of my pay what is needed to fix whatever had to be broken. Even if there should be a higher penalty."

Macon rested his elbows on his desk. The wall clock ticked with the pulse thumping in his temples. He could not lose any more of his crew, especially firefighters like Bryce who were great at the ins and outs and didn't give him lip. "Did you perform this new drill alone?"

"No, it was for Rescue. We needed to practice more scenarios that are out of the ordinary. I thought we should have more experience with an escape situation."

Macon clicked his pen and grabbed a sticky note. "How did the new simulation go?" This might need to be added to his "must improve" list.

Bryce leaned forward in his chair. "Better than I pictured. Rice crawled through the air duct—the smoke-producing one—and dropped into the next room."

"Quick thinking. Also, good practice for low visibility."

Bryce cupped his hands together. "So, am I still the lieutenant of Rescue?"

The surprise in his tone made something Amelia said earlier ring in Macon's mind. "You're worried about your position?"

"Never mind, sir. Thank you." Bryce shot right to his feet.

Macon waved him back down. "Bryce, you helped your brother talk me into applying for this position. Of course I'd like to hear your thoughts on where your concern stems from. It sounds like it wasn't only because of the training house ordeal. Is this about Greene?"

Bryce sat down on the edge of the chair. "Ghost deserved to be fired. It's just that the atmosphere hasn't felt all that welcoming toward ideas outside of the box, I guess."

When had any one of them tried to come to him with different training? Macon had a whole page of different ideas to implement. Was he somehow unapproachable now that he had moved from his twin's friend into being Bryce's boss? But he was spot on about the firehouse's atmosphere. It wasn't up to the standard Macon wanted either. He needed time to get them there.

Macon sighed. "It's easier to know you'd like some changes if you'd talk to me. Especially as Rescue's lieutenant. Please don't make me fill another position. You're a great firefighter, as good as your brother. I'm not promising to agree with everything you say, but I want this place to be a team."

"I'll keep that in mind, Chief. Thank you."

At least one of his lieutenants used his title. "Could you send Patterson in here when you leave?"

Soon Amelia shut the door to his office and stood by his desk.

Macon rose to his feet. He inspected Amelia's eyes. Not as red or puffy, but still showing signs of stress. "I apologize, Lieutenant. I jumped to conclusions. It wasn't fair to you." He cleared his throat. "And if you ever need any help with your crew's training or attitudes, feel free to come to me."

Her gaze flicked to his before seeking the window as she nodded once.

After she left, Macon sank into his chair. The clock showed it was well past time for his normal shift to be completed, yet the reports on his desk wouldn't be approved by themselves.

He'd go grab a coffee and come back to finish up the other stack of reports.

When he walked by the conference room, Natalie was hunched over her computer. Guilt caused him to stop. He needed to tell Natalie she'd been right about Amelia.

Needed to tell her about his past.

He unclenched his fists and walked around the front of her. She wasn't looking at her screen. Just a far-off gaze and her thumb tapping her chin. He understood a little how she felt. How the present and the past could both work against you. Hearing her take the blame for her friend killing himself had almost gutted him. Mostly because he got it—sometimes, just looking at Houston. Suddenly he was right there in the ER, listening to his brother scream.

So yeah, he got panicking, and PTSD, and the feeling that you'd never escape the choking smoke of guilt.

Macon waved his hand in front of her eyes.

She blinked, a good sign until she said, "I'm fine."

It was the lie he'd told their family's old counselor. The one he'd believed. The one Macon still gave when remembering his family's fire.

He sighed. "You were right. I jumped to conclusions about Patterson. Crawford had run a different simulation for Rescue and forgot to change it back."

"Oh." She nodded. "That makes sense."

He wanted to end it there. To walk away and hope whatever she knew about him would be enough. But he needed that signature if he wanted to stay in Last Chance County. "I like to go on a hike when I have a rough day. Fresh air helps me gain a fresh perspective."

She tilted her head. He always had the sense that when she did, she could see the things hidden inside. "You have rough days?"

There was the Natalie he'd grown used to. Intuitive. "Is that one of your regular therapisty questions?"

She laughed, and it was light and sweet. It erased some of the tension in his shoulders. "I'm not sure that's a word."

"If you promise not to ask too many questions, I'll answer them while we hike."

"No hiking today." She lifted up her black heeled shoes. They certainly weren't hiking boots. "We could meet in your office."

Nope. He didn't need his crew accidently overhearing anything. Besides, he was technically off shift.

The last place he wanted to be was around memories of fire when he was talking about, well, memories of fire. "I don't think so."

She studied him. "You're right, it's past time I get some fresh air. I could be talked into a horse ride. I've been wanting to ride all week."

Macon grimaced. "Horse air isn't exactly fresh."

"Better than smoky."

Better than his office. "I've never been horseback riding."

"Then it's time we change that." A spark returned to her eyes that hadn't been there since before the fire simulation, and when she smiled, his heart gave a small jolt.

He needed to chill. It wasn't going to be fun.

Just a part of his job.

15

"Macon, watch out." Natalie tightened her legs around the spotted mare, Breezy. She leaned her body to the left as if she could move Macon out of the way of the tree branch.

But Macon was not leaning. Not steering. His borrowed horse, Candy, kept trotting forward. Right for Macon's head to gain a pump knot in about five seconds.

Natalie reached for Candy's leads. But she was too far away. "Macon, duck!"

He pulled harder on the reins. "Whoa!"

Finally, Candy stopped. Macon's face was a mere inch from the tree bark. He maneuvered around the branch and turned to Natalie, sending her a glare. "Thought you gave me the smart horse."

"You wanted one that went in a straight line."

Nothing about Last Chance County's Fire and Rescue teams was straightforward, but she'd typed up her evaluation. She was done. Almost. All she had to do now was proof and send it off.

"Yeah, well, I also wanted one that wouldn't let me get my

brain smacked either." His arms were stiff, holding the reins on each side of the horse's head as if he were the tin man in need of some oil.

"Feel free to relax your body. She can feel how nervous you are."

If anything, Macon's shoulders became more rigid. "How's this better than hiking?"

Natalie stroked Breezy's black mane. "Because it reminds me of the good times." She pinched her lips together. She shouldn't have said that. She was supposed to be a professional. "Gently press your heels against Candy."

"This may be my first rodeo, but even I know that prodding a horse will make them go faster." He finally rested his hold on the reins on his thighs. "What good times did you have with horses?"

Asking questions was supposed to be her job, not answering them. Perhaps if she offered him something, he'd feel more comfortable to share the worry in his eyes. "I'll tell you, if you can keep up."

She nudged Breezy into a trot. When Macon pulled up beside her, Natalie smiled. "Are you ready to admit riding is better than hiking?"

"I'm ready for you to keep your end of the bargain."

She fixed her gaze on the horizon. The mountains in the distance reached the clouds. The same sky her mother used to tell her they were both sharing, no matter if she was overseas.

"My mom used to tell me stories about her pony growing up. Write about them, actually. She was in the army. So she was gone with training a lot. She used to send letters with a short horse adventure in them. One letter told me how I'd get to have horse lessons too one day. Our last PCS move had a stable nearby. But then she was deployed and didn't make it back to teach me."

She closed her eyes and felt the breeze tug at her hair. "She died a hero. Rescuing the rest of her unit. But that didn't make much of a difference for my father and me." She peeked at Macon out of the corner of her eyes. "Though I suppose I didn't really share any of the good part of riding."

He shrugged. "Horses remind you of your mom."

True, in a roundabout way, even though what brought her to riding horses every day wasn't good either. The burdens of her job and of the past.

As she slowed Breezy to a walk, the trusted mare twisted her ears back for a second, letting Natalie understand she'd have preferred the higher speed. As if any of them got to choose what life threw at them.

"I'm sure she'd be proud. You're almost as good a rider as you are a therapist."

"You think I'm a good therapist?" She snapped her head around.

Macon shrugged. "You're completely different from the last one I had."

"I'm sorry, Macon. I understand that feeling. And I think my wanting to be a counselor has similar reasoning behind it as you becoming a firefighter."

Horse hooves thudded along the worn path, filling the silence. Until Macon said, "Doubt that."

She glanced at him. Could she trust him with her full past to help him share his?

He met her gaze. Pain. Regret. Not fear. The look in Macon's eyes did not match Jeremiah's. Or her father's.

"My father didn't take my mother's death well," she whispered. "He...tried to commit suicide."

She squeezed the reins, but it did little to steady her on the inside. This was why Macon hid from those around him. The same emotions she carried with her. They both carried the regret of not seeing another's pain.

The sound of running water joined the slow hoof beats. A

bird sang from the branches shading them above. Anything but silence, yet it was the stillness she craved. Riding was exactly the fresh air and perspective she needed. It was out here that she most wondered if she could trust God the way her cousin did.

At the fork in the trail, she had Breezy take the path on the right. "After he made it home from the hospital, a counselor helped my father process everything. While he was receiving mental care, I came to live with Allen and his family. But with only two boys to hang around with, the horses quickly became my haven."

She had been so lonely. So confused. Hurt.

Natalie clicked her tongue and steered Breezy to the right of the path. "So I knew that when I grew up, I wanted to be just like that great counselor." She wanted to prevent others from feeling like they weren't enough to live for. "I joined the army because being on base was where I felt closest to the memory of my mom. Her last words to me were, 'Bug, while I'm gone for long work, be a brave little captain for the other soldiers here. For your father too.'" She blinked away her blurry vision. "I wanted to help people work through their pain."

He rode quietly beside her, and for some reason, in the telling, the sunshine found her bones, stress evaporating from her body.

Natalie continued. "After studying, I learned that each person adjusted and responded to events differently. But I could be right there with them. Not as a crutch they'd always need, more like someone who would be on standby for life's unsteady paths. Yet I couldn't do my job well if I was too occupied by my own pain."

"Or stuck in the past." His jaw flexed.

"Exactly." She didn't want to force something he wasn't ready to offer. She only needed to be patient.

The water trickling ahead grew louder, and Natalie pulled Breezy to a stop. "Let's give the horses a drink."

He followed her down to the creek, then got off Candy and led her to the water.

"Pretty day," she said.

He shot her a look. "I would say I've somehow been tricked into a counseling session, but I was the one who invited you out for fresh air."

She smiled and watched Breezy drink, running her hand along the mare's neck.

"I didn't want any of this." Macon racked his fingers through his hair.

Her foot crunched on a stick. "The horse ride or something else?"

His heavy sigh made her look up. "When I was ten, the town knew me as the boy with leukemia. If I wasn't in the hospital, I was stuck at home. My father always took my brother Houston on trips, just the two of them. Even took him to get a baseball signed by *my* favorite player."

"I didn't know you had leukemia." Natalie gave herself a second to absorb the implications. "That's tough at ten. And how do those memories make you feel about yourself?"

Macon tensed. "That question makes me think back to those awful group counseling sessions with my family."

No wonder he had been tense in the conference room today. "Let me rephrase, then. Could that be why you and Houston don't get along, because you believe your parents favored him?"

"Everyone favored him. And before you talk about how that's my opinion, facts back me up. Everyone had reasons to favor him. He's more of a hero than I'll ever be."

Natalie schooled her expression. Macon must have seen some kind of shock, because he turned away.

"At twelve, he donated bone marrow to me. The doctors had

promised no risk for him, but there was a complication. He ended up dealing with pelvic pain all through high school."

"It's not your fault your brother was hurt."

"Except it was," he whispered.

Coldness had seeped from the edge of the water into her borrowed barn boots. But it was Macon's guilt that made her suck in a breath. No wonder he wore pain in his eyes. "The fire at your family home?"

Silence stretched between them, so long she thought he'd never speak. Finally he said, "I should have been home that night. His life was even more ruined because I was only thinking of myself."

"What happened, Macon?" She pointed to a tree that must have fallen not long ago, because the downed log wasn't covered with moss or ivy.

Anger. Guilt. Sadness. He kept pushing it down in hopes it would disappear.

After they were both seated on the log, she turned toward him. "Is that when you saw a therapist, after the fire?"

He shook his head. "My parents went to one when I was sick. And then went to another one after I got out of the hospital. The therapist insisted we do family group sessions. He kept on with the feelings questions, and my dad kept getting angrier. Until one day the therapist called the police in the middle of a session because the yelling got so out of hand."

He rested his face in his palm. "They divorced before I was officially in remission. It was terrible. I wish their therapist had been able to help them stay together." He picked up a rock and plopped it into the stream.

Natalie realized he believed it was the therapist's fault. As much as she wanted to argue with that assessment, she understood.

"After the fire, I tried to apologize." He picked up a different rock and tossed it into the water. "I'd snuck out of the house to meet a girl. Only, the girl I thought I was meeting had actually left the note in my locker because she believed it was Houston's, not mine. So I went to the batting cages to...deal with that disappointment. If I'd never snuck out or had gone straight home, I could have saved Houston. So that's the whole reason why I became a firefighter—to make sure no one else has to go through what Houston had to."

She laced her fingers together to keep from reaching out to comfort him. "Thank you for trusting me with your story. I'm thinking you became a firefighter for the same reasons I'm a counselor. To help others avoid their pain, and to keep them from experiencing more."

His mouth tightened around the edges, but he nodded.

A lizard slithered away from its hiding spot on a rock, but Breezy caught a glimpse and pulled back. Natalie hiked up to grab the reins and managed to step in mud between two rocks. A suction noise encased her foot.

She tugged on her leg. "That's a heavy burden to carry, trying to save the world."

"Isn't it only fair when I caused others to hurt?"

His words plunged into her chest. The memory of Jeremiah's funeral flashed through her mind. She'd watched his tearful family, knowing she could have stopped his death if she hadn't been distracted.

When she tugged on her foot again, Macon stepped closer. "Here let me—"

"No, I can—"

He pulled up on her lower leg.

The mud released her foot, and she wobbled backward. Macon grabbed her. The momentum brought her against his chest...and sent them both spiraling for the creek.

Macon turned as they fell, and tucked her against him. Natalie gasped. He hit the ground, but only their sides landed in the ankle-deep water.

The water splashed against her hip. "That's cold!"

Macon scooped her to her feet.

As he rose to his full height, she failed to hold in her laugh. "Please tell me you're not going to have a giant bruise on your hip tomorrow." She covered her smile with her fingers.

One entire jean pantleg was completely soaked, as was half his chest. Water dripped from his sleeve. Mud had splattered on his face and neck, but it was her muddy handprint on the dry portion of his shirt that had her biting back her grin.

He wiped his mud-caked fingers on his pants. "You think this is funny, do you?"

She schooled her face. "Of course not. You just have a little"—she crinkled her nose—"mud right here." She reached over and wiped a chunk off his cheek. Then wiped it off her finger onto his other cheek.

His eyes widened.

She tilted her head. "There. Now it looks even."

"Oh, you want even, do you?" He smiled and stepped toward her.

She squealed and took off sprinting down the creek. "Don't you dare, Macon!"

Except she didn't hear him splashing behind her. She turned around only to be caught around the waist. "Did you really think you could get away from me?"

She swatted at his chest. "You dirty dog! You went along the bank."

His heart raced as fast as hers. He smelled like cedar and mint and somehow like comfort. That dark gaze slipped from her eyes and fell to her lips. Her breathing hitched.

When she'd first arrived at Eastside Firehouse, she'd thought his gruff management style hid something that would prohibit him from being a good leader. Now she knew his past had been an uphill battle. Like hers.

And all of it made him a better leader, not worse.

"You don't have to save the world alone." Her words faded into a murmur, and she didn't know if she was talking to him or herself.

Macon swallowed, his gaze searching hers. His hands had left her waist, and now his fingers moved along her arms. The touch sent a shiver through her.

She wasn't sure who leaned against who, but she lifted her chin. His cheek brushed hers and her eyes drifted close. She lifted on her toes and lightly pressed her lips against his.

The kiss was soft and sweet. And completely wrong.

She pushed against his chest. They both took a step back. But no space between them now could erase what she had just done.

He blinked down at her, his mouth a little red from her cherry lip balm.

Oh no. "I'm so sorry, Macon." She covered her still tingling lips. "I mean, Chief James." She squeezed her eyes shut. What had she been thinking? She hadn't thought. That had been the problem. She had done what she told her clients not to do—allowed her emotions to take over.

Breezy nickered and Natalie turned in a full circle.

She shouldn't kiss her client. But she had.

She touched the spot where his cheek had rested on hers. Her skin still prickled from his five-o'clock shadow. But in the perfect kind of way.

Natalie stomped toward Breezy. "Time to turn back. We're losing sunlight."

"Natalie..."

Counselors did not kiss their patients or clients, or whatever Macon was. She could not afford to lose her job. Couldn't lose her last chance at helping people again.

She whirled back around. "For both of our sakes, *nothing* happened. Okay?" She couldn't meet his gaze. But she felt it.

The rest of the way back to the barn, Macon kept Candy

beside Breezy, his jaw as tight as his grip on the reins. His gaze focused on the path ahead. How she wished they hadn't ridden together in his truck on the way here. Now it would be so awkward.

No. She couldn't let it. This was her fault. She'd just wear her counselor hat more securely.

He didn't say anything until they dismounted at Allen's barn and his phone chimed twice. "I guess I didn't have a signal earlier."

As he listened to his messages, his frown made her erase the distance she'd put between them. "What's wrong?"

"Houston wants me to coach a youth baseball team."

Natalie nodded. "That could be good—"

"Except I don't play baseball anymore." Before she could dig into that statement, his frown deepened. "Do you know an Angelina Ross?"

"What?" She wouldn't let him deflect this time. Time with his brother would be a great start at healing their relationship.

Macon slipped his hand into his pocket. "Apparently, she owns the truck that was outside your house the other night."

Natalie hung the horse's reins on its hook and spun around. "Conroy should have updated me with that information. Not *you*."

With a huff, she pulled out her phone. She had one new voice mail. It was more than likely Conroy.

Macon moved in front of her. "The same truck was also parked at the fire station earlier that day. When you ignored my concerns, I got the plate number and Barnes ran the plates."

She crossed her arms. She hadn't ignored him. She'd had her gun within her reach all night. She just didn't want Macon so focused on her instead of himself. "And was it *your* truck that I saw parked outside my house that same night?"

He sent his fingers through his hair. "I stayed until a patrol car came twice and inspected the truck."

"You had no business doing that."

He frowned at her. "To worry about someone's life? That's my entire job, Natalie. I'm not trying to overstep here. But like it or not, I know about the restraining order."

She shook her head. "And again, you're a client. That is—"

"None of my concern. I know, you've said." He took a deep breath. "But..."

His hesitation gave her a moment to process what he'd said, what she didn't want to think about.

"What if the police are wrong and your car exploding isn't only a copy of the Bug Challenge or whatever the stupid thing's called?" His next words lost their edge. All that was left was compassion in his eyes. The way they had looked at the creek. Like she was worth the risk. "What if this Angelina is connected to the explosion, or to the restraining order, or *both*?"

She wanted to ignore what Macon suggested. But if Leon had a new girlfriend, and she believed the warped lies Leon had concocted as truth, it could send a mentally unstable person after her.

Natalie leaned against the wooden workbench.

"You're in danger, Natalie." Macon's touch on her arm was as tender as his voice. "And yes, maybe...this"—he gestured between them—"can't happen..." He ducked to look in her eyes. "But I promise, I'm going to make sure you're safe."

16

He could really go for some batting cages right about now. Macon adjusted his grip on the wheel. Except he'd given up baseball years ago. And coaching with his brother spelled disaster. But at the moment, there were bigger issues.

He snuck a peek at Natalie in his passenger seat. And apparently, he'd also have to give up the memory of kissing the woman beside him, who was wrapped up in one of the two old towels he kept in his truck.

"Are you still cold?" he asked.

"I'm fine."

"I can turn up the heater if you want."

"I'm fine, Macon." She sighed. "Chief James."

He swallowed. "Natalie, you call the other firefighters by their first names and you didn't kiss them. So I think it's safe to still call me Macon."

She played with the frayed edge of the towel. "I don't kiss clients, Macon."

Right.

For both of our sakes, nothing happened.

He clenched his jaw. She'd smelled like vanilla and fit in his arms perfectly.

The cool creek water seeping into his clothes had been forgotten when she had closed the last distance between them. He should have been surprised, but more than anything, he'd liked the kiss. Seconds before she'd realized what she'd done, she had looked at him with desire. But more than that. Like she cared. About him. Not just his problems or his past.

He waited for the regret of sharing his story to kick in, but it didn't. Was it because he'd finally shared the whole of it, or because he'd shared it with *her*? He peeked at her again.

He was glad that, despite having a rental car now, she'd talked him into riding out to Allen's barn together. She probably hoped to focus on getting him to open up, but instead, he was trying to show her things didn't have to be awkward.

Her body angled toward the passenger window. Was she regretting all she had shared with him about her past, or was that what she told all of her clients? He frowned at the windy road before them.

"Do you tell a lot of your clients about your past? Is that your way of getting them to open up? Or just the stubborn ones?"

The truck's engine hummed, and the radio murmured in the background. But Natalie didn't speak. A yes, then. Which meant he wasn't special to her. Not in the way she was becoming to him.

The truth was, he shouldn't be interested in the person standing between him and the job he wanted. For all the precautions he'd taken concerning his crew, he was the one that'd fallen prey to temptation.

"No," she finally whispered. "I've never told anyone all of it. Allen knows most of it, but..."

He couldn't keep himself from another glance her way—at the same glossy gaze she'd worn after the training house mess.

She'd helped him with the burden he carried. However, he hadn't helped her at all.

Yes, he'd opened up. But she was still technically in a professional position with him, despite the personal side to their relationship. Maybe things could be different after the forms were signed. After the committee meeting and swearing him in as chief. Until then, she needed him not to share his feelings.

He would show her how professional this could be.

He cleared his throat. "Do you want to pick the music?"

She opened her mouth, but flashing lights ahead caught both of their attention.

Macon slowed. The rescue squad truck was parked at the site up ahead, their hose stretched down into the ravine. The air was more foggy than smoky, but the smell of oil and fumes couldn't be ignored.

Macon pulled off the road and unclicked his seatbelt. "I'm going to check in with the crew."

She unbuckled, and there was no point in asking her to stay in the truck.

Down in the ditch, a silver car had not only wrapped around a tree but the front end had at one point been on fire. No skid marks in the ground. It was as if the car had flown off the road. Which meant it had to have been traveling fast.

Bryce had the cutters out. Yet not running. Jayson aimed the hose at the burnt car engine. Charlie and Eddie were unfolding a tarp on the ground. Had someone been thrown from the car and was already gone?

Macon looked for Ambo 21, but they hadn't arrived yet. No cops or Truck 14 either.

He jogged toward the scene. He stepped on a wobbly stone and paused. But Natalie went past him. "Natalie, you need to stay back."

Macon once again sprinted after Natalie. The wet valley grass squished underneath his boots. "Natalie. Stop!"

"I recognize that car. We have to help her."

There was an honor student bumper sticker on the rear bumper. Not even a scratch on the backside of the silver car, but the hood was smashed. The entire front bumper had become one with the tree. Glass and bark sprinkled the ground that wasn't burnt. The smell of gas clogged his lungs. The tarp off to the right hinted at something or *someone* Natalie didn't need to witness.

Macon wrapped his arms around her waist. It was too close to the memory of the day her car exploded.

"Please, Macon."

The hydraulic pistons rumbled to life as his crew forced their way into the car.

"We've got to stay back and let them work."

Charlie jogged over to the rear of the car and waited for Bryce to cut through the driver's side door. After the door was removed, both men just stared inside.

"Why aren't they getting her out?"

Bryce must have heard Natalie, because he lifted his gaze and barely shook his head at Macon. Natalie sagged against Macon's chest.

"I'm sorry."

"She was supposed to be at rehab." She covered her mouth.

"Chief!" Eddie ran up behind him, and Macon let go of Natalie. "We thought you were still at the station. That's why we called you."

Macon pulled out his phone. "I don't have a missed call."

Natalie's throat sounded raspy. "No signal past the barn. It wouldn't show a missed call if Eddie didn't leave a message."

Eddie frowned, and he looked at her, back at his boss, this time his brows raised. Then he said, "Police department's delayed. But we didn't touch the suicide note. Just put a tarp over it. The paper had floated out of the window, saving it from the flames."

"Suicide note?" Natalie brushed past them both, her gaze darting around the ground. She ran over, ripped the tarp back, and grabbed the paper.

"Rice, you aren't a rookie. You can't share that stuff with bystanders."

"I forgot." He held up his hand. "It's like she's one of us."

The piece of paper shook in her hands. "This doesn't make sense. But it relates to one of my clients, so I'll need to talk to the police about this." She let her hand drop.

And then it hit him. Her past. Her father had tried to commit suicide—oh, Natalie.

Macon slipped the note away from her.

"Oh, poor Joey." Her voice cracked.

Police sirens blared in the distance. He'd have to hand deliver the evidence since they'd both touched it. He took in the position of the car against the grouping of trees and the road above. It appeared Angie hadn't even hit the brakes on the curve.

Natalie turned toward the officers coming toward them. "I don't want a stranger telling Joey his mother's dead. It made it worse for me, the unfamiliar people. I should be the one to tell him."

He squeezed her arm. "I'll take you as soon as I square things up here and we get confirmation from the coroner. But only if you repeat after me."

She sniffled and blinked back tears that were about to spill down her cheeks. "What?"

"This wasn't your fault."

Natalie opened her mouth only to bite down on her quivering lip. She tucked her thumb inside her fist. She was trying to be strong, but for who?

He opened his arms. She hesitated for a second and then

leaned against him. Her tears damped through his extra T-shirt he'd had in his truck. They were hot against his chest and a coolness followed. He rested his chin on the top of her head and brought her up against him. Why had he ever thought this woman was the worst thing about his job?

She was compassionate and funny, and she only wanted to make him the best chief he could be. Natalie needed someone to help her.

And he wanted to be that someone.

17

No one was ever ready for the worst day of their life.

And she'd never be ready to tell Joey about his mother either. But both Dean and Tosha had agreed that Natalie should be the one. Their confidence in her didn't make things any easier.

Natalie double-checked the address Tosha had texted. "It's that gray bungalow with green shutters."

Macon nodded from the driver's seat. She still wasn't sure if she'd made the right decision, having him drive her straight here versus to the fire station.

Sturdy trees lined the sidewalks and dotted the neighboring front yards, shielding the houses from the sunshine. A playhouse and swing set stood in the side yard of the bungalow. Both things Joey had requested from his dad.

Natalie let her head hit the headrest.

She should have visited Joey before now. After the egg hunt, Natalie had called Tosha for an update. The social worker had been near the Ridgeman Center, so Tosha had swung by to pick up the suitcase and the letter from Angie. But now Natalie had to tell him his mother was gone.

She exhaled and pushed her shoulders back. “Thanks for dropping me off.”

Macon put the truck in park and faced her. “I’m not just going to leave you.”

“That was the plan.”

“No, that was your plan.”

She shook her head. The man was still so stubborn. “Then I should have had you drop me off at my rental car.” He’d already swung her by her house to grab a change of clothes.

“You would have had to backtrack and lost a good thirty minutes or more.”

“But I don’t think you realize how long I may be needed here.” She closed her eyes. “Macon, I still remember the faces of the solider and chaplain that arrived at our on-post housing to tell us the news about my mom. I knew before they even came inside that life was about to go from bad to worse.”

But when would it get better?

Macon unbuckled. “If I’m in the way, I’ll slip out. But there’s no rush. Whatever time you and Joey need.”

She stared back at the house. Would it help Joey to see the man who’d saved them from the fire? Maybe.

Macon remained on the top step while Natalie knocked on the wooden front door.

A boy younger than Joey opened the door and smiled at them. “Heya.” He held up the three cookies in his hands. “Do you like cookies?”

Through her teary vision, Natalie smiled back.

Macon was the one who answered. “You better not offer us cookies yet; you don’t know how many this one eats.” Macon hooked his thumb at Natalie and bumped his shoulder into hers.

Always skilled at redirecting emotions. It was the perfect thing for her to get herself under control, especially since Joey poked his head into their line of sight.

"Ms. Natalie," he mumbled, his mouth full of cookies. "You here to take me home? Did you bring pretzels?"

"Oh, Joey, I forgot." Why hadn't she grabbed a bag when she'd changed?

A woman with a pair of puppy slippers came into view. Her eyes widened behind her glasses. "Benjamin, you can't be opening the door for strangers."

Joey pointed. "That's Ms. Natalie. She knows my dad."

Natalie pulled out her replacement Ridgeman Center ID. "I'm his counselor, and this is Chief James."

Joey tilted his head. "Like the firefighter chief?" At Natalie's nod, Joey set the other cookie on the side table by the couch. "You're the one who got us out of the fire?"

Macon dipped his head, and Joey ran over and wrapped his arms around him. "Thanks for getting us out of the closet and for carrying Ms. Natalie. She would have been too heavy for me."

Macon's cheeks turned red as he patted the boy's back.

No, Macon didn't have a hero complex.

"Mom." Benjamin tugged on the woman's arm. "Can they have some of your cookies?"

Ready or not, this was it. Natalie said, "That's a really sweet offer, but if we could have a moment alone with you first, Mrs. Cunningham?"

Mrs. Cunningham rubbed her hands, and a bit of flour drifted onto the carpet. "Boys, stay in the living room."

She motioned for Macon and Natalie to follow her to a sunroom off to the side. "Is this a surprise inspection? I assumed Tosha would be performing all of our meetings, but this is our first placement." She held up a finger. "Before I forget, the school sent home a note about some friend of the family of Joey's trying to visit him at school. I was pretty sure all visits had to be run through you, correct?"

Through the glass doors that separated the kids from the

adults, Natalie watched Joey grin at Benjamin. How long would it be until he smiled again?

Macon elbowed her.

"I'm sorry." Natalie laced her fingers together and squeezed. "Tosha would be the one to bring that visitation question to. I'm unaware if they had located any other family. But...I'm not actually with CPS. I've been counseling his father. Did Tosha not tell you we were coming? She's stuck in a meeting across town."

"Oh, well, I left my phone in the bedroom. My husband's on swing shift this week. I didn't want to wake him." She patted her chest. "I'm a little nervous. Joey has been such a wonderful treat to care for. He really is the perfect playmate for Benjamin. Not that that's why we're doing this."

Natalie licked her lips. "It looks like Joey is doing well here."

Macon moved his hand behind her on the back of the wicker loveseat.

"I-I wish this was some kind of surprise inspection. Unfortunately, we have bad news to share with Joey. I thought it would be best for you to hear it first." Natalie picked a string on her pants. "I asked Tosha if it would be all right if I was the one to share."

"Good heavens, what's happened? Please don't tell me his father passed away."

"His mother, actually."

Tears filled Mrs. Cunningham's eyes. "The poor boy. How?" She looked at Macon. "Or can you not share that information?"

If only Natalie didn't utter the words, then the sadness wouldn't be true. But that wasn't how life worked. "A vehicle accident appears that it may have been a suicide."

"No!" Joey shoved open the glass door. "Mom would never leave me on purpose."

Natalie's eyes widened. Why hadn't she double-checked to see if Joey was listening? She wished he was too young to understand what that word meant, let alone have to endure the aftershocks.

"Joey." She went to stand, to hold him, but her legs went limp. "I'm so sorry."

He shook his head. "She promised to get better."

Natalie reached out, and he fell into her.

"She promised to take me to Jump Club for my birthday."

She combed her fingers through the top of his hair. "I know, Joey."

He jerked back. "No, you don't. You're wrong. She always kept her promises. Even when she was on drugs. I know that's why her and dad weren't married anymore. That's why she had to go get help. But she always took care of me. Even when she wasn't allowed to."

Benjamin came in, bringing the suitcase Angie had pleaded with Natalie to get to Joey. Now Natalie was so glad she'd said yes to the note and suitcase. That would be the last thing Joey would remember about his mother.

Benjamin opened the suitcase and pulled out a teddy bear.

As Joey took it, tears trailed down his freckles. He turned and sprinted through the house.

Natalie wiped her eyes and then wrapped her arms around herself. She'd failed another family. Two families would still have their loved ones if only she'd helped them sooner.

"Natalie?"

Macon's voice sounded urgent, but what would be more pressing than making sure Joey was all right? She took a step to follow Joey, but Macon's hand on her arm stopped her.

He spun the open suitcase around and pointed inside.

Crayon scribbles in a suitcase couldn't—

"It says Angie here." He drilled her with a look, then indicated a section of smaller printed letters. "And also, Angelina Ross."

18

Seeing Natalie curled up on the top bunk comforting Joey had proven what a dedicated counselor she was. And whether Macon should admit it or not, her concern did something to his heart too. Except Natalie wasn't ready to know that.

Would she ever be?

Tonight wasn't about Macon, which was why he'd stayed on Mrs. Cunningham's porch and called Conroy three times before the police chief finally picked up.

Macon needed answers. The problem was, no one had any. Conroy had told him nothing had been posted showing her car explosion, despite other recent postings. Then he'd told Conroy about Angelina Ross's name on Joey's suitcase.

When he'd explained it was the woman who'd shown up the day of Natalie's car explosion and the same person as the suicide driver this afternoon, Conroy had told him he'd get to work trying to figure out if there was a connection.

Now, back in his truck, Natalie's head rested against the door.

"You okay?" Macon asked.

"I'm not worried about me."

"Obviously, for Joey...but Natalie, I'm also worried about you. And before you tell me how wrong that is, Angelina is the registered owner of that red truck outside your house and outside the fire station. So she is connected to the man who has been watching you. She was there the day of your car explosion."

"*Was,* Macon. Now she's dead." She shook her head. "I failed someone else."

"Her death isn't your fault. Was she even your client?"

"I still should have noticed—"

"You're a great therapist. Period." She had just spent an hour holding a boy when she could have allowed someone else to do the hard stuff.

Before either one of them could say anything else, her phone rang.

Hopefully, it was Conroy with actual news.

"Hey, Amelia."

Macon gripped the steering wheel.

"Oh..." Natalie's shoulders drooped. "No, I'll take care of it. Thank you. Yeah, no kidding... You too. Bye."

When she lowered the phone, Macon asked, "Everything okay?"

Natalie scrolled on her phone and sighed. "Looks like my rental has a flat. I have to call the rental company."

"I can just change it—"

She waved him off. "I bought the full coverage." Then said into her phone, "Yes, hi. I have one of your rentals and it has a flat. Can I just... Yes, I did. It's under Natalie Atkinson." She closed her eyes. "Yes, of course. It's at the Eastside Fire Station. Okay. Thanks."

After the call ended, Macon waited a moment, then said, "I could have easily fixed your tire."

Natalie rubbed her forehead. "I was just following the

instructions I was given. Plus, the rental doesn't have a spare. And it's also *not* your job to worry about my car, remember?"

Right.

"If you could just drop me off at my house, I'd appreciate it."

Her phone rang again.

Finally, Conroy.

She blinked at the screen before swiping and saying, "Hello?"

A second later she sat up straight. "H-how did you get this number?"

His muscles tensed. Not Conroy.

"No, listen, Leon."

Macon hit the brakes and whipped around to look at her.

"You can't. We don't—" She leaned forward and placed her palm on her forehead, displacing her bangs. "Leon, that is none of your concern. Why don't you call your current therapist? I'm no longer that person, remember?"

Macon squinted at the red stoplight ahead. The guy she had a restraining order against had her cell number. Macon shouldn't be taking Natalie home. Leon probably knew where she lived. Should they go straight to the police station?

"That doesn't matter. It isn't... Leon. No. I have to go." She pulled the phone away from her ear and stared at it.

"What did he want?" The truck suddenly was too quiet.

"I don't know what to do anymore."

He struggled to hear her. She had both hands on her face.

"He thinks I'm cheating on him. Not sure how he got my number. I've already switched it once."

"We need to go to the police. Then I can take you to the phone store."

She blew out a breath. "Could this day get worse? No. I just want to go home. I'll call Conroy from there. Today's been..."

First the smoke house incident, and then seeing Angie's

wreck. Plus having to tell Joey about the death of his mother. Then a flat tire and now Leon. He got it—she was spent.

But was she safe?

Natalie tucked a piece of hair behind her ear. "It's getting late. The phone store would be closing soon."

"But you need to file a police report. Leon can't contact you like that."

"We're only two blocks away, and I don't want you to drive back across town. I've already made you wait with me all afternoon."

She hadn't made him do anything. "Do you have Chief Barnes's cell number?"

"I'm a regular person, not a fellow chief. Why would I have his direct number?" As soon as he pulled into her drive, she unbuckled and opened the truck door. "Thanks for taking me home. And everything. You were…a great partner today."

He opened his mouth to call her out on sidestepping his question…until the dome light reflected in her eyes. There weren't tears in her gaze, but the sorrow couldn't be missed. *Oh, Natalie, you don't have to carry this alone.* Macon hopped out and jogged around his truck.

"Macon, you don't have to check my front door each time you bring me home. It's been perfect since you fixed it. I'll call Conroy, I promise. But I also want to be rational when I do."

The words sounded like hers, but there was a slight tremor at the end of her sentence. "How about you grab some things and I take you back to Frees's?" Her cousin used to be a cop, so he'd know what to do, and he could probably convince her to listen. "That way, you don't have to call anyone tonight. Talk it out with your cousin. Get some sleep, and then you'll be ready to face this with help tomorrow."

"I'm a professional counselor. If I can't handle my own problems, what does that say?"

"This isn't a problem you try to face alone. Leon has your

number. What if he knows your house location? What if he's been behind the car bomb this entire time?"

"It was an internet prank."

"Chief Barnes told me nothing had been posted showing your car explosion, but there have been other recent postings." Before she could argue that proved her point, he said, "If it was simply a copycat to get to you, there wouldn't necessarily be any online postings. And do you honestly think the Angelina thing is just a coincident?"

She said nothing.

"People come to you to ask for help. Owning up to a problem and wanting help doesn't make you less of a counselor, just a smart woman."

Natalie shook her head. "Allen has enough to worry about. I don't want to interrupt his time with Pepper and Victory."

"Then what about Hope Mansion?"

"That's for women who need rescuing."

He placed his hands on her shoulders. "And what if you do?"

She pulled away. "My doors will be locked. I was a soldier, so I can take care of myself. Tonight, I just need some sleep."

"At least one of us will sleep."

She frowned. "Thought you weren't on call tonight."

Did she memorize all his crew's schedules? "I won't sleep while you're here and Leon's wherever he is."

She blinked at him, and then yanked out her keys. "For the last time, Macon, I'm not on your crew. You don't need to worry about me."

Was she serious, or seriously trying to hide from this problem? "It's good you're not on my crew, because I'd probably have to look for a new job."

She whipped her head around. Confusion and something else lined her brows as she stood in the doorway. Just because I haven't physically signed the evaluation yet, doesn't mean things will go south."

She thought this was about his evaluation?

Mason swallowed. "I might have told you all my deep, dark secrets just to keep my job. But it...it felt like more than that. Like we agreed earlier. We're friends. And now I want to share the past because I want to know more of yours."

The soldier who he'd bet was a great leader. The girl who'd lost her mother and nearly her father. The counselor who'd held a crying boy. All those pieces made up the woman standing before him—the woman he was falling for.

The way she challenged him. Smiled because she cared. If she'd only allow herself to let him help carry her load, like she did for him. Not because she had to but because she wanted to.

"If I were your chief, and you were on my crew, I'd need to get a different job for everyone's safety. Because my mind tugs your way when you're near. Even when I don't want it to."

He stepped closer and brushed a piece of hair behind her ear.

She didn't move away, but her voice trembled. "I may not be on your crew, but our relationship should be professional."

"For how much longer?" He kept his whisper tender as his hand moved to caress her cheek. He knew he was heading back into dangerous territory, but she still didn't move away.

He'd done what she wanted as the fire department's counselor. He'd opened up. Nothing else would keep her from releasing them. Which meant if they wanted to spend time together outside of the evaluation, they could.

Only the tiniest of gaps remained between them. Enough to allow her the decision to either back away or explore the reason his heart hadn't stopped galloping since their horse ride. Or if he was honest, the day he'd carried her out of the fire.

She put her hands on top of his arms. "Macon—"

Their lips touched, and just like last time, a flame erupted in his chest. The desire to deepen the kiss coursed through his body, but he stayed gentle. She'd been through too much today. He was about to move away when her fingers slid up his shoulders and traced the hairs on the back of his neck. The smell of vanilla made him hold her tighter...

He needed to slow down. Think. He pulled back. "How about the firehouse?"

"What?"

He pressed a kiss to her forehead to keep from kissing her mouth again. "You could stay overnight in the women's bunk room. That way we'll both maybe sleep. Tomorrow we can dig into everything."

She shivered, and he pulled her close, rubbed his hands up and down her back. He was already used to having her in his arms.

"Please, Natalie. Only for tonight. And we'll call Chief Barnes together."

Her fingers skimmed along his neck, and it did nothing to stop the heat flooding him.

"Okay," she whispered.

He hoped her answer wasn't simply for him taking her to safety tonight but also to figuring out what was burning between them.

Because for once, he wasn't ready to put out the flames.

19

Natalie hugged her bag to her chest. The dim hallway in the fire station felt a bit too much like the first night she'd had to stay at her aunt's house when she was younger, after her father was rushed to the hospital.

The day she'd found him unconscious in the car from his suicide attempt. If their garage door hadn't had a dog-bite-sized hole in it from a previous pet, and she hadn't changed her mind about staying overnight at a friend's house, carbon monoxide would have killed her father.

"All the bunks have clean sheets." Amelia flipped on the light to the bunk room. Four sets of bunks stood like military headstones, straight and uniform. The blankets were all folded with a crease at the corners and tucked under the mattresses. "Pick whichever. You're the only one in here tonight."

"Thanks for staying over to help get me set up. And for noticing the tire on my rental." Natalie chose the first bunk. She dropped her bag onto the bed and tried not to grimace at the texture of the blanket and the condition of the pillow. She should have at least grabbed her pillowcase; it wasn't like she was at basic training anymore.

Amelia took a step inside. "I can stay if—"

Natalie held up her palm. "Promise. I'm fine. I'm only here out of precaution."

Natalie pressed her lips together and unfortunately remembered Macon's kiss and the way he'd looked at her. Why had she let him kiss her? She had rules for a reason, and yet she couldn't seem to stay away from him.

"Thanks again, Amelia." Natalie covered a yawn. She kicked out of her shoes and sank onto the bed. If only she could just go to sleep and restart the day.

Instead of leaving, Amelia marched over and sat on the bed right across from Natalie. She wiped at the wrinkles her weight made on the blanket. "I, ah, I'm sorry about the accident. And your friend?"

Her client's ex-wife. But Amelia didn't need to know all that.

"It's just... I thought...when we first pulled up to the scene, I misread the way the chief was...holding you." She cleared her throat. "But I can see what it actually was now. Losing people... it's hard. I understand."

Natalie crossed her ankles and sat up straighter. Time to put her own needs aside and use this opening. "How are you dealing with losing Mickey?"

Amelia stood. "Things are better. I think. Just...slow."

"Slow is not bad. Or wrong. Dealing with loss is not a one and done type of situation. And I'm always available to talk, even after my work here is done. As a professional or as a friend. Or both." She offered Amelia a smile.

Amelia tugged on the sleeves of her uniform as if erasing away her emotions. "Noted. And I'm glad James wasn't inappropriate with you today. Or any day." She locked eyes with Natalie. "It would look bad on more than just him as chief. His crew. All of us. No one needs another scandal. This fire station has had enough of those already."

Natalie fisted the blanket beneath her. The itchy texture

didn't bring any comfort. How did this turn so quickly into what felt like an interrogation?

A knock on the door saved Natalie from Amelia's inspection. Macon had another blanket in his hands.

"Patterson, did you lock the back up tonight like I asked?"

"Yeah, but I'll double-check it on my way out."

After she left, Macon extended the blanket to Natalie.

"Thank you." She ran her hand along the edge. The heat of the fabric surprised her more than the desired softness. "It's warm."

Macon's cheeks flushed. "I popped it into the dryer. When I was sick, my favorite nurse brought me quilts from the warmer. She also made me that handkerchief."

For days, he had been silent about his past. Now he shared it with her freely. She hugged the blanket. She was finally seeing the real Macon.

"I'm sorry. I keep forgetting to give it back."

"Why don't you just keep it."

He was sweet, funny, and put others first. And she would probably dream of their kiss tonight. However, Amelia had a point.

Natalie clung to the blanket tighter. "Macon, we can't do this."

He glanced around the room. "Of course you can. It's not the first time we've housed people in trouble. Especially during storms." He leaned his shoulder against the bunk. "This is a life storm. I didn't tell the crew anything except to be on the lookout. There's been some suspicious activity around. Plus, you are counseling us. No one thinks it's strange."

That was the real reason right there. "We can't do this as in *us*." She pointed to him and then herself, as if he couldn't figure out who she was talking about. "You and me. It's unethical."

His eyes didn't shift from hers. "Let's get some sleep. We'll talk out the easy solution when we're rested."

Among the great qualities blossoming from him, he was still very stubborn. "It's not a simple solution, Macon. We can't ignore the fact I was hired to assess all of you. I can't allow that boundary to be crossed once again. I know that I kissed you. Twice. But I think maybe we need to take a step back."

Macon frowned.

"Leon..." She could barely say it aloud.

He jerked his chin up. Hurt settled in his expression. "You're comparing him to me?"

She shook her head. "I *have* to do this the right way." She needed a win. "Macon, I enjoy my job here. I like being in Last Chance County near family. Allen stuck his neck out for me to get Dean to hire me after my failures with Jeremiah and with Leon."

Macon narrowed his gaze. "Those weren't failures on your part."

She was the qualified therapist. She should have seen the signs. Dealt with the information better. "You and me...it's just too complicated."

He straightened. "You think I can't handle complicated?" His gaze, laced with swirls of anger and hurt, remained on hers. As if daring her to see his emotions—the ones he showed and the ones mirrored by her own.

No matter what conclusion she had already formed about the firefighters, there would be a conflict of interest.

His cell buzzed, and he frowned as he checked the screen. "Do you need me to get anything else for you tonight? Or stay with you when you call Chief Barnes?"

"I can take care of everything myself." She squeezed the blanket to her chest. It had grown cold, much like Macon's expression.

She needed time to wrap her head around Angie and what clues they had. If someone was after Natalie, the last thing she wanted was to drag Macon into her mess.

20

The promise of coffee kept Macon upright. He wasn't in his twenties anymore. Four hours of sleep was not enough. All the what-ifs kept spinning in his head last night. Most of all, the way Natalie had pushed him away. Yes, she could talk to Conroy by herself. She had proved over and over how strong she was. Didn't mean she had to do it alone.

It hadn't helped that his bed at the firehouse had felt like a brick last night. But there was no way he was going to head home with Natalie here.

He closed the door to his office and walked by the women's bunk room again. The door was still closed. At least one of them was getting sleep.

Somehow, he made it into the station's kitchen and only ran into one wall.

"Morning." Eddie leaned over his plate on the kitchen island as he mumbled through a mouthful of food.

The kitchen smelled like sausage and eggs. But Macon veered straight toward the coffee pot. An eclectic variety of mugs hung from pegs above two different coffeemakers and one electric teakettle.

Macon took a sip and then inspected Eddie's plate, piled high with what looked like a breakfast casserole. "Who was in charge of breakfast? I think they might be gunning for a raise."

Eddie shoveled in another heaping spoonful. "She needs a raise all right, and I'm thinking we just need to keep Natalie on full time."

Macon stared at Eddie. "Natalie fixed breakfast?"

Eddie squinted at him like he'd gone crazy. Or hadn't had enough coffee. "She was up at, like, five and then started rummaging in the fridge."

Macon blinked. "Huh."

"I told her anything was up for grabs unless it was labeled." Eddie shrugged. "And the next thing I know she was making this gloriousness." He scraped up the last of his food and dug out another helping. "Hey, Chief, did you give any more thought to coaching that rec baseball team? Your brother said he'd talk to you about it."

Macon grimaced. So much for ignoring Houston's voicemail. His brother went behind his back for reinforcements. "I think it sounds like a great opportunity for you to give back to the community."

"Except I never played baseball," Eddie said. "So I need to be one of the assistant coaches who knows all the kids' names. Who cheers them up when they miss a ball. We need *you* to be the coach with all the knowledge. You know, do your chief thing, but on the field. Houston said you were good."

"My brother was good too. He's the only head coach you need."

Macon pictured Natalie tilting her head and asking why he built walls around baseball. He shook his head. "I think it's great you volunteer with the area foster care kids and are forming a team, but I can't give you the answer you want. And I need to go tell Natalie thanks for breakfast."

Eddie's shoulders drooped. "She already left."

Macon spun back around. "Left?"

"She called a ride share. Apparently, the rental company said her car wouldn't be ready until the afternoon."

Of course she had. Macon tightened his grip on his coffee mug. Was she hiding from her problems like she'd wanted to do last night? Had she even called Conroy about Leon?

"Thanks, Rice." Macon pulled out his phone and headed to his office. Pulling up Conroy's number, he hit Send.

Conroy answered on the fourth ring. "You wouldn't have any free time today, would you? I've got some questions about this arson report." He asked the question as if he'd been the one to call Macon.

Macon glanced at his schedule. "Nothing that can't be postponed." Or at least, nothing that Amelia and Bryce couldn't handle. "I've got some time now."

"Perfect. If you can get here before ten, that would be great."

Once they hung up, Macon sent out texts to his lieutenants informing them of the day's change. It only took seventeen minutes to get across town. Somehow Macon had hit every green light. He hoped it was a sign that his day would go much better than yesterday.

The police department lobby was empty. Ruby, the part-time receptionist, stood behind the front desk, watering a row of tiny plants. "Morning, Chief." She glanced toward the chief's office and tucked her short white hair behind her ears, revealing huge red earrings that matched her bright lipstick. "Looks like he's on the phone for the moment. Want a coffee while you wait?"

"I don't want to trouble—"

"No trouble whatsoever, hun." She set the watering pitcher

down and popped a hand on her hip. "But if you don't tell me how you want it, you'll get it black."

"How about just a splash of creamer?"

She returned with two steaming mugs. "One's for Conroy, if you don't mind delivering." She glanced over at her phone. "And it looks like you better hurry before someone else calls."

Sergeant Donaldson nodded as Macon headed down the hall.

Conroy opened his door before Macon could worry about having to knock with his hands full. "Ruby read my mind. Thanks." He took the black coffee mug and held his door open wider.

Macon sat in one of the two chairs for guests. A variety of awards hung on the back wall, and a group of picture frames faced Conroy on his desktop. Probably his wife and kids.

Macon stared down at his coffee. "What's wrong with the arson report?"

Conroy sighed. "Nothing. Except it matches most of the Smash the Bug Challenge's typical MO ingredients."

"So you don't think it was Leon?"

"I never said that."

"What kind of car does Leon have?" Macon asked.

"Doesn't." Conroy leaned back in his chair. "License has been stripped."

"Last known address?" Macon asked.

"An army base in Texas. I've put feelers out, but unless he's picked up, I don't know where he's at to even ask where he's been."

"Since Leon called, Natalie stayed at the fire station last night. Should she keep doing that, or can you put a car at her house overnight until Leon is spotted? And did you find any connection on Angie?"

Conroy frowned. He lifted his hand. "Wait. Back up. Leon contacted her? When?"

It was Macon's turn to frown. "Last night. Natalie didn't call you?"

If she didn't want Macon to help, fine. But she couldn't keep putting herself in jeopardy. Of course, maybe that was on her to-do list for today.

"Hold on." Conroy clicked a few things on his keyboard. "No. It doesn't look like she filed a report last night or this morning. I'll call her this afternoon if I don't hear anything from her before."

"Shouldn't you send a patrol car to watch her? What about the Angelina connection?"

Conroy finished his coffee. "I cross-checked with Angelina Ross, also known as Angie Johnson, in the recent suicide accident on Hangman's Curve. She's caught at a streetlight camera for the time leading up to her pulling into the Ridgeman Center parking lot after the explosion. The truck outside Natalie's house and the fire station had last been registered to Angelina five years ago. She only had one up-to-date registered vehicle—the one in the wreck."

"So what are you thinking?"

Conroy gave him a look that he felt often as chief. "The therapy center camera footage is grainy at best. No one went near Natalie's car that we can tell, just patients and workers coming in and out. They're all verified. The only other unaccounted vehicles were a car, motorcycle, and a truck. But none of them parked. Most people going there just make a U-turn in the entry of the parking lot. So no, nothing new. And except Angie's drug charges, nothing else points to her."

"Except Natalie helped get her ex full custody of her son." Macon rubbed his temples. They really had no facts to trust, and the recent connection had committed suicide. Was it out of guilt?

Conroy's radio, tucked on the shelf on the wall, crackled to life. He had the volume low, but Macon still caught the words *Ridgeman Center.*

Macon was on his feet before Conroy spoke.

"Easy, Macon. Don't go jumping on your white horse yet. We've had calls of distress from their resident Mr. King before. Couple times a month actually. He's got schizophrenia. Every time he's called, it's because he's quit taking his meds."

The radio buzzed again. "Officers responding."

Conroy picked up his pen. "I'll call if it ends up being related."

"Sure." Macon wouldn't jump to any conclusions. He'd just drive on out there to check for himself.

Whether he and Natalie had a future together or not, he didn't like the twist in his gut.

The one that, as a firefighter, meant he should hurry.

21

She did not need one more thing.

Natalie couldn't hit Send on the finalized firefighter report until she talked to Dean. But he had not answered her text about a meeting time. She and Tosha were playing phone tag about Joey. Since she'd not made it over to her office yesterday, her inbox was overflowing. And she still needed to call Conroy. She should have allowed Macon to help her call last night, but she'd done what she always advised against. Ignored the problem. But she would call right after she located that new file she'd made on Peter.

Natalie closed her filing cabinet and rounded her desk, hands on her hips.

She'd made a new folder for Peter just three days ago. The hospital had emailed an update this morning, and she needed to place the physical copy in his folder.

Except it'd disappeared.

She'd already checked her bags. Had she left it at home? With last night's sleep on a strange mattress and overanalyzing all she'd told Macon, she wasn't exactly working on one hundred percent brain power.

A glance at her empty trash said the cleaning company had been in last night. But certainly, she wouldn't have knocked the file into the trash.

Natalie picked up the phone on her desk. No dial tone, again. The message light wasn't flashing either. So much for the phone getting fixed. She unplugged it from her desk and tucked it under her arm.

Outside in the hallway, Kelsey was leaving her office. Her hand pressed against her chest and her brows pulled in worry.

"Kelsey, what's wrong?"

Her fingers went to her hand. "I can't find my ring. I'm heading to go check the security camera just in case someone entered my office. Maybe one of the residents..." She bit her lip. "I don't know. I just have to find it."

Natalie matched her steps. "I'll help." Maybe the change in scenery would help her remember where she'd put Peter's file.

Kelsey pointed up to the corner of the hallway. "Since the explosion, Dean's added a few more security features; however, some of them aren't up and running fully yet. He said it's harder than stopping a coup in a tiny African country. Probably more time than he has, too. I hope this newer family program isn't a waste of my time. If I can get us through all the hoops, it can bring extra funds."

Natalie took in the makeup around Kelsey's eyes. It was thicker than her typical, more natural look. It more than likely covered deep circles under her eyes like the ones Natalie also wore today. Everyone's workload was heavy.

Which was why Dean had authorized Natalie taking on the fire station assignment. And also why Natalie couldn't put her professionalism and the center's reputation in jeopardy over her growing feelings for Macon. She'd hated the look of hurt in his eyes, but it was the only thing to do.

Kelsey was the first to reach the extra closet turned security center.

Natalie flipped on the lights as Kelsey woke the computer. Natalie placed her broken phone on the desk. After the password and a few clicks, they watched last night's footage.

The cleaning van pulled in around nine. A motorcycle pulled in about a minute behind them, parking beside the van. In the grainy feed, it sort of looked like the motorcyclist spoke to the driver of the van before he left.

"Wasn't there also a motorcycle in the parking lot on the day of the explosion?" Kelsey glanced over, a frown on her brow.

Natalie willed her heart rate to slow. "Yes." She didn't need to get worked up yet. Not before there were facts to prove a problem. "I'm not sure of the model though. I don't know anything about motorcycles, but one of the EMTs at the firehouse drives one."

The next thing on camera was the two cleaning ladies. One rolled a vacuum down the hall, and the other carried a couple of buckets and a broom. The footage went black before either of the cleaning members made it to a door in the hallway. And none of the residents left their side of the wing.

"I don't know what I expected." Kelsey sniffed. "My best friend gave me that ring before..."

"I'm so sorry." Peter's misplaced files didn't compare to a ring.

Kelsey's sigh felt as heavy as the weight on Natalie's shoulders from the past few days. "I think I'm going to need an extra coffee today."

After locking up the security room and grabbing some caffeine from the break room, they headed back down the hall.

Kelsey nudged Natalie. "Other than this morning, how is the job going?"

"Honestly, not much has worked right in the last week. The fire, explosion. That woman's death." Not to mention Natalie's unwanted feelings toward a client. "But the hospital gave a promising update on Peter."

"If you ever need to talk...whether as a therapist or as a friend, my door is literally just up the hall."

Natalie smiled. It was almost what she'd told Amelia last night. "Thanks, I appreciate it." She took a sip from her mug. "Same goes for you."

As they reached the welcome desk, Wren stood with a haggard expression. Her smile was only at half-mast.

"What's wrong, Wren?" Natalie asked.

The receptionist ran her thumb over the edges of her polished nails. "Mr. King has been at it again."

Kelsey deeply inhaled. "Another false alarm to the police? Does Dean know? Have officers already responded to Mr. King's call?"

Wren nodded quickly. "I've already updated Dean. Officers Tazwell and Ramble are here doing their normal check as we speak."

Mr. King and his schizophrenia kept everyone on their toes. Too bad Conroy hadn't come. Natalie would have to call him after lunch.

"Sounds like it's all being taken care of. Oh." Kelsey turned to Natalie. "Speaking of a call...your phone."

Natalie stared down at her cup of coffee. No wonder she was misplacing files. Natalie pressed one of her palms to her forehead. "Wren, I'm so sorry. My phone's broken again. I meant to bring it here—"

"My fault. I sidetracked you." Kelsey bit her lip.

"I left it in the security room." Natalie hooked her thumb over her shoulder. "Let me—"

"Leave it. I'll just order you a new one." Wren glanced down at her desktop. "I don't have any new messages for either of you, but Kelsey, your eleven-thirty arrived early." Wren checked the sign-in clipboard. "Matt Smith. He's a new patient. I offered for him to sit out on the patio, but he was quite antsy. I thought he might really need to talk." She laced her hands together. "I escorted him to the chair outside your office."

Kelsey grimaced. "Well, from now on, we'd better just keep people out here in the main lobby. I've had something go missing from my office recently."

The brightness dimmed in Wren's eyes. "I'm so sorry. I will do better from now on."

Natalie offered Wren an encouraging smile. "You're doing a good job, Wren."

"Yes. Thank you for being thoughtful, Wren. I appreciate you taking special care of our clients. But we need to be more cautious with all that's going on." Kelsey glanced at Natalie.

"Right. Of course." The main phone rang, and Wren waved to them as she answered.

Kelsey took a sip of her tea as they headed down their hallway. Natalie pointed to the empty chair by Kelsey's office. "Perhaps your Mr. Smith decided to wait on the patio after all? Or made himself at home in your office."

"I don't know if that would be a good thing or bad. But if it helps a new patient become more comfortable about sharing his struggles, then a little confusion over where to wait won't be the end of the world." Kelsey offered a forced smile. "Let's hope our day gets better."

Natalie opened her office door, set her cup on her desk, and headed straight for her chair. She relaxed against the leather, closed her eyes, and took in a deep breath. She wished she'd gotten more rest. But the coffee would help. Eventually. Soon the little problems of the morning wouldn't feel like nails on a chalkboard.

If only Macon hadn't kept coming to mind.

Half the time he looked sad that she'd rejected him, and the other half he held out a paper, asking her to sign. If only she hadn't been tasked to evaluate him. But if not, would she have gotten to see the real Macon?

A noise clicked in front of her. She popped her eyes open and jerked her gaze toward the door.

A man she hadn't noticed stood in the corner, where he'd been hidden from view when she came in.

Natalie sucked in a breath.

He stepped out from the space behind her open door. A pair of ripped jeans paired with a bleached, stained hooded sweatshirt. A gun in his hand. It shook in his grip.

"Did you break it off with him?" He spat the words, and it was a voice she recognized. The long hair and straggly beard she did not.

The bloodshot eyes glued in her direction belonged to Leon. She'd been trained in hand-to-hand combat and self-defense, and she'd had weapons aimed at her during her time in the army. She was a therapist. She could handle Leon. She just needed to remain calm.

He pointed the gun at her. "Tell me."

Natalie inched her hand toward her phone, except it was gone. She swallowed. Kept her face void of emotion. Why hadn't she dug out her cell phone before heading to drop off her landline?

A quick knock sounded as Kelsey opened the door. "I found my ring! But, bad news, now I can't find—" Her eyes widened. "Oh—"

Leon hit her across the temple with the butt of his gun. No time to react.

Kelsey's yelp was cut off, and her legs buckled beneath her.

"Kelsey!" Natalie dove around her desk for her friend. Half cupping her head and half shielding her from smacking her head against the filing cabinet, she eased her friend to the floor.

Natalie grunted as she was sandwiched between the floor

and an unconscious Kelsey. She shifted Kelsey's weight off her legs. Blood covered Natalie's hand.

Leon shut the door and locked it.

Natalie's chest burned with each rapid breath. "Leon." She pressed the side of her shirt to Kelsey's bleeding face. "Let me get her help. Then we'll talk. Okay? Just put—"

"No!" He aimed the gun right at her chest. "Where's the locket I gave you?"

Natalie gasped.

The gun rattled in his hand.

She swallowed. Her mouth was so dry. She locked eyes with Leon. "Leon, why don't you—"

"You know I like it when you call me Leo." He reached out and touched her cheek.

Natalie jerked away and hit her back on the filing cabinet.

Kelsey moaned.

Natalie pulled her coworker closer, covering her the best she could. Kelsey whimpered and shifted. Something hard brushed against Natalie's knee.

It vibrated against her leg.

God was looking after her. Kelsey's phone must have been in her pocket when she collapsed.

Unless the patrolling officers heard the commotion, the cell phone was the only hope they both had to signal for help.

Leon narrowed his gaze. He reached down.

Natalie shielded Kelsey more. "Leave her alone!"

But instead of Kelsey, Leon grabbed Natalie's collar. "Where. Is. My. Necklace?" His breath reeked of garlic and sour milk.

Natalie shoved against Leon, and he released her. She pulled her arms back to protect Kelsey again. "I didn't wear it today."

Her main goal during a session was to listen. Help make goals. To encourage. *Counselors don't lie.* But never did they give false hope. However, this was not the time to remind Leon that his thousand-dollar necklace wasn't something she could ever have accepted. Nor was he supposed to leave her anything after the restraining order.

"The police were supposed to give you that necklace back. Did you not receive it?"

Leon shook his head. But not as if to answer—as if trying to clear his head. He shuffled closer, his arms now down at his sides. The weapon pointed at the floor.

With a kick of her right leg, she could swipe his legs out from under him. But if he didn't release the gun, he might take out his anger on Kelsey instead of Natalie.

That couldn't happen.

Leon's head snapped up. He narrowed his eyes. "That's because you're wearing *his* necklace instead. Aren't you?" Leon spat. "Tell me the truth! I saw you with him."

He raised the gun, hands no longer trembling.

Natalie stared down the barrel, wondering if her next heartbeat would be her last.

"If I can't have you, no one will."

22

The Last Chance County police car in front of the Ridgeman Center failed to settle the knot in Macon's stomach. He parked his truck and pulled out his cell phone. Still no return text from Natalie. The simple reason was she was busy, and he was making something out of nothing. Again.

Or she was hiding from him.

But with Leon's call last night, not to mention the 911 call—despite Conroy's words—he wanted to check with his own eyes. Otherwise, he wouldn't get any work done today.

He shut his truck door gently and took in each car in the parking lot. Nothing out of the ordinary or in the surrounding trees. No vehicles that matched the grainy surveillance video.

Inside, the lobby was quiet. Only the melody of the receptionist's nails clacking away on the computer keyboard. No officers. They could be finished with their patrol and have gone to get Natalie's statement about Leon's call last night.

"Hey, Chief James." Wren smiled at him before he reached her desk. Her eyes suddenly widened. She sprang up from her chair and glanced around him. "Please don't tell me the fire department had to respond to Mr. King's call too."

Officially, no. "It's just me." Her reaction loosened the tension branching across his back. "Everything's all right?"

She clicked her mouse and checked her computer screen. "Looks to be. The officers are finishing their sweep of the center's campus."

She sank back into her chair. "But Officer Tazwell said, no matter if it's the patient's first or tenth cry-wolf call, it's their duty to come check."

Macon released the breath. So, the call *had* been a false alarm. Natalie was safe. His gut had been wrong.

He surveyed the hallways that connected to the two-story entrance. All were empty. The upstairs windows he assumed led to a meeting room didn't give him a glance at another person. Though, what he was looking for, he wasn't certain.

Wren had a smirk on her face when he turned back toward her. "Are you trying to build up the courage to walk down the hall and see her? Here I thought firefighters never ran out of bravery."

He stopped himself from dumbly asking *Her who?* By the twinkle in Wren's eyes, she knew who had brought him here. Had Natalie talked to Wren about their kiss? Or *kisses*.

He knocked his knuckles on the desk and glanced at the sign-in sheet. All the names that had been on there had been crossed out.

He'd come all the way out there; shouldn't he see her? "Is Natalie with anyone right now?" But if she wasn't busy, wouldn't she have texted him back if she wanted to talk to him?

"Only Kelsey had an early arrival but let me check." She spun in her chair. "I'd buzz down there except her phone isn't working."

Macon frowned. "Her cell phone?" Had Natalie turned off her phone because she didn't want Leon calling her anymore?

He should have pushed harder to get her a new number last night.

"Her office phone is on the fritz, but I think, based on her database schedule, you're all set. Might I suggest asking her out for lunch? She doesn't have anyone scheduled until later afternoon." Wren pressed her lips together as if trying to hold back her full smile.

Lunch. Yes, lunch was a great idea. He nodded. So, he hadn't come out for no reason. "Thanks, Wren."

She tapped her temple. "I think I'll add matchmaker to my résumé."

Macon chuckled and shook his head. He didn't know how the woman could take credit for him falling for Natalie, but if it ended up with Natalie agreeing to a date, he wouldn't argue.

A high-pitched pop echoed in the distance. Macon whipped his head around.

Wren gasped. "Was that...?"

"A gunshot." Macon sprinted toward the sound, down the hallway on the right. Natalie's office. "Call 911!" he hollered over his shoulder. "And get somewhere safe."

"The police are already here—"

Macon didn't wait for her to finish her sentence. He skidded to a stop in front of Natalie's door and twisted the handle. Locked.

She could have locked it when she heard the gunshot go off.

He thumped on the door. "Natalie, it's Macon. Are you okay?"

One breath, then two. But all he could hear were his own fears. Then another gunshot blasted from the other side of the door.

"Natalie!" Macon rammed his shoulder into the door. It shuddered but held.

"Go away, or I'll shoot them!" a man yelled from the other side.

"Macon." Natalie's calm voice had him gripping the handle tighter. "Do what he said, please."

How was he going to get her out of there?

"Is that him?" the voice growled as something scraped along the floor. The handle moved under Macon's grasp.

The shooter had barricaded the door. Where were those police?

He wanted to send his fist into the door. He had to get in there.

He closed his eyes and pictured Natalie's office. Was there a window behind her desk? He'd only been in there a moment the day her car exploded. There wasn't time to find Wren and ask her.

He ran his hands along the doorframe. Solid, heavy doors. Great during a fire, not ideal when it separated help from a hostage. Even if he had a key, the barricade would prevent entrance. Macon inspected the ceiling. A sprinkler system up to code, but not connected to tiles, which would have allowed him to enter Natalie's room from above.

But that didn't mean the connecting rooms weren't tiled.

Once in the next room, he turned on the light switch, but the well-lit area didn't offer the hope he'd prayed for. No tiled ceiling. No easy access to Natalie.

A long table took up most of the room in the center. A projection screen hung on one wall, and a cabinet filled the other. He spotted an air vent above the table, and Bryce's conversation about the training house flooded back.

Eddie crawled through the air duct and dropped into the next room.

Macon jumped onto the table. He pulled out his pocketknife and tackled the lone screw in the vent's center.

Macon poked his head into the dark hole. Tight fit, but he'd make it work. He pulled himself up. Claustrophobia had never registered in his mind during any of his training, however the metal box closed in around him quickly. He slithered forward on his stomach, unsure if his movement or his heartbeat was louder.

As he inched through the vent, he caught two muffled voices.

"Leon, why don't we go find Kelsey some bandages, and then you and I can talk." Natalie's voice had a steel edge to it. No matter what protocol he'd overstepped to be here, the fear in her voice proved he'd made the right call.

Macon switched off his flashlight app and crept closer to the vent in Natalie's office. He spotted a man through the slits. Disheveled. Pacing. One hand clenched around his unkempt hair and the other held the gun.

Natalie, however, was out of sight. So was Kelsey. Perhaps the filing cabinet blocked them?

Which meant going through the door would have likely been bad. He'd made a good choice.

What also wasn't clear was how he would get out of the air duct without Leon noticing. He prayed the cover in her room only had one screw.

The ceiling light closest to Macon's location had been shot out and dipped from the drywall. The dimness would help his entrance. If only the other officers could cause a distraction in the hallway.

Macon swiped his phone screen to text Conroy. Except his signal bar was at zero.

Why didn't God ever help him?

Macon snaked his hand back toward his pocket. He put his phone away and tugged out his pocketknife. He wedged his knife blade first on the underside of the cover and pried it up. Then he pulled it back and did the same to the top side until he pushed too hard. The metal scraped against the cover.

Leon whipped around and pointed his gun around the room. "What was that?"

“Let’s put the gun away,” Natalie said. “Why don’t you come sit by me? We’ll talk about whatever you want.”

“What I wanted was for you to love me as much as I love you!” Leon turned and punched the wall.

Macon closed his pocketknife. He locked his arms out in front and crouched back, then shoved off his feet. He shot forward and the vent cut his hand, but it flew out of the way. He dove through the air duct.

And fell.

Leon climbed back on his feet just as Macon landed on the desk. He rolled, landed on his feet, and launched himself at Leon.

Leon raised his gun.

Macon soared through the air and knocked the man’s arm down.

The gun fired. The boom echoed in Macon’s ears as he slammed against Leon.

The man fell hard, Macon on top of him. And then he heard a scream.

Macon called out, “Natalie!”

23

His shout slammed straight to Natalie's heart.

"Macon!" She squinted in the muted light. One minute she was lying over Kelsey as Leon punched the wall. The next Macon came out of nowhere and tackled him. But who had been shot?

Please, God! Let it not be Macon.

Someone groaned. Macon had Leon pinned while he shoved against Macon's chest. Who had the gun?

"Natalie, are you hit?" Macon's voice wasn't strong. He almost sounded *broken.*

"No, I'm okay, I'm okay." Natalie settled Kelsey's head down. She scrambled over the contents of her desktop, now scattered on the floor, toward Macon. "How are you here? Are you hurt?"

Macon and Leon still struggled. Sweat lined their faces. Blood was smeared on the tile. But who was bleeding? She crawled closer.

She saw a flash of Macon's gritted teeth. "Stay back, Nat!"

She should do something—there! Her stapler was in reach. She grabbed it as Leon elbowed Macon in the face.

Macon jerked back and groaned.

Leon popped free. He pushed Macon away to land on his side. Leon held the gun.

His gaze flitted back and forth between Natalie and Macon. "You are going to die." Leon raised the gun. "No one desires Natalie except me."

Natalie tightened her grip on the stapler as she hid it closer against her side. She had one shot at striking Leon. She stepped forward. "Leon, I'm right here. No one else has me."

Leon stood. Macon crouched, balancing on his feet. Blood was smeared across his shirt.

Natalie gasped. *God, we need You.* "Leon—"

Macon's leg swiped through the air and kicked the gun out of Leon's hands. The weapon discharged and skidded against the locked door.

All three of them lunged.

Bodies, hands—pain shot through her cheek. She'd taken an elbow to the face.

Someone groaned.

"Got it!" Macon rolled and pulled Natalie behind him. "Get back!"

Leon backed away. Raised his hands.

Blood. It covered her hands, her clothes. She didn't feel shot. She dropped to her knees beside Kelsey. No other wounds besides her head.

Natalie turned back to Macon. As Macon rose to his full height, all the air in the room evaporated.

Blood stained his side. Dripped from his hand. *Macon.*

"Stay back, Nat," Macon said, probably reading her mind.

"You're shot. We have to get pressure on it."

How was he still standing? He must be in shock. She moved toward him.

"Natalie. Stay. Back."

Leon's gaze stayed on Macon. "She's not yours. She's mine."

"Don't move." Macon gripped the gun in both hands. But his breaths were fractured.

Shock. He needed medical assistance, pronto. Leon must have seen it, because he crept toward Macon, almost within reach of the gun.

Macon aimed at Leon's chest. "I said—"

"Don't kill him. It won't be worth it. Leon, get on your knees."

He swayed on his feet but finally obeyed.

Natalie moved to Macon. "Where's your wound? There's blood everywhere. We have to stop it. You can't..."

She bit her quivering lip. He couldn't die because of her. Not someone else she cared about.

"I'm fine. Really."

A banging on the door rattled the room. "Last Chance PD. Open up!"

Natalie raced to the door. She removed the chair under the handle and flipped the lock.

The door opened and Officer Tazwell pushed her way in, her gun aimed at the floor.

Natalie lifted her hands. "Leon is subdued and on his knees. Macon's been hit and Kelsey's hurt. Please, they both need help."

Olivia pulled Natalie out into the hall as she and Officer Ramble entered the room.

Natalie followed them back inside.

"I need a stretcher in here. Stat." Olivia's radio crackled with a reply.

Leon grunted. His eyes rolled back, and he collapsed on the floor, his body seizing.

"Make that two stretchers."

Arms encircled Natalie. "It's okay," Macon whispered next to her ear. "You're okay."

Natalie's entire body shook as she fell into him.

He kissed the top of her forehead. "I've got you."

She fisted his shirt. Yes, yes, he did. She hated how much she needed those words.

"What do we got?" The yell came from a female EMT with brown hair and blonde highlights, guiding a stretcher into the room.

Macon moved an inch away but didn't let go. "Andi, do me a favor and get the unconscious female out first."

"Kelsey." Natalie locked eyes with Andi. "Her name's Kelsey."

Andi nodded and knelt beside Kelsey.

As another EMT entered and assessed Leon, Macon steered her out of the room.

Olivia followed. "Why don't you guys wait in the lobby? Chief Barnes said he's almost here. He'll be taking your statements."

Macon ran his palms up and down her arms. She shivered as she thought of all he'd done. She placed her hand on his heart, the beats solid and reassuring. She wanted to lean against him again. He'd risked his life for her.

"Where are you hurt?" she asked.

He pulled open his uniform where the bullet had grazed his ribs. One inch to the left and—"You shouldn't have done that, Macon."

He brushed back a piece of her hair. "Natalie, I—"

"What were you thinking?" Allen wheeled down the hall. His glare was as rough as his tone.

She pointed at herself. "What was *I* thinking?"

But his gaze fell on Macon. "It doesn't matter what you were thinking. You're on probation."

Macon's arm dropped from her. "You can't do that—"

"I can. I'm the liaison to the fire department. Until the committee and the mayor's office sorts this out, I need you to take a step back."

Natalie stepped in front of Macon. "Wait, Allen—you don't know the whole story. Macon saved our lives."

Allen held a finger up to Natalie as he returned his glower to Macon. "I want the report of the Easter egg hunt catastrophe on my desk, and then you will leave the firehouse until further notice. It's going to take a while to figure this mess out. You know the importance of protocols, and you ignored *all* of them. Including the fact that Patterson said you still haven't taken your mandatory time off this week."

Macon shook his head. "Natalie's life was in danger."

"Your desire to play hero could have gotten her killed. Did you at any point stop to think about that? Now, go find Chief Barnes."

Macon's mouth tightened.

"I'll be right behind you." Natalie watched Macon's retreat. She crossed her arms. "You're not seriously going to fire Macon over this, are you?"

"*Macon*?" Allen pulled right up against her foot. Hadn't he been trying to use his walking forearm crutches more? Physical therapy had been going well, hadn't it?

"*Chief James* didn't follow protocol for a hostage situation. Wren said she told him the police were already on campus. He shouldn't have rushed in. With one wrong move, things could have ended with body bags."

"What are you saying—that I wasn't worth saving?"

And she didn't mean it quite that like, but—well, it felt like it.

Allen's face brightened red with anger, and he white-knuckled his wheels. "What? No. Natalie—he could have gotten you and Kelsey *killed*."

Right. Yes. Of course.

She squinted down the hall and tried to get a glimpse of Macon. "He did what he thought he needed to do to save my life."

"A fire chief has to obey the police's orders." Allen lifted his chin. "No matter if there's a personal connection."

Her cousin was as stubborn as Macon. "I need to check on Kelsey."

As if on cue, Andi rolled the stretcher out of the room.

Natalie ran to her side, and Kelsey blinked up at her.

Natalie grabbed her hand. "I'm so sorry."

Kelsey lightly squeezed her fingers. "We're safe." She touched her head with her other hand and winced. "That's all that matters."

Andi cleared her throat. "We need to go."

Natalie let go of Kelsey's hand and balled hers into fists. As she watched Andi pick up speed and round the corner of the hallway, Allen wheeled up beside her.

"I'm glad you're safe." He almost seemed apologetic.

"Please don't fire Macon. He's working through stuff, but he's a good chief."

Allen stared for three heartbeats before running his palm down his face. "Then why haven't you released him yet?"

Because she was afraid to trust her gut. If she had signed the evaluation already, his job wouldn't be in jeopardy.

And maybe she wouldn't be accused of falling for a client.

Trace and Izan pounded down the hall, the stretcher from their ambulance thundering behind them. She did not want to be around when Leon left that room.

When she and Allen reached Wren's desk, Chief Barnes waved them over to one of the groups of couches. Macon stood as she approached.

Conroy flipped over a page of his notes. "I think that's about it for this round, Macon. Why don't you go get yourself cleaned up? I think one of the EMTs should take a look at that wound."

Macon's gaze went right to Natalie's. "That's okay, I'll wait and—"

She shook her head. "You should get cleaned up."

"You need a ride home."

Probably. She doubted her rental company had dropped off her car without telling her. But right now, it wouldn't look good if she took him up on the offer. "Allen can take me home."

Hurt flashed across Macon's eyes. He didn't understand she had to distance herself from him right now. She needed to prove to Allen that Macon was the perfect chief for Last Chance County.

Macon didn't move.

The last thing she wanted was a scene and Macon possibly making the situation worse.

He searched her face. But then glanced at Allen and then Conroy. Finally, he nodded. At the front doors, he stopped. He looked over his shoulder, and Natalie read his concern from across the room.

Concern for her or his job? Maybe both.

What appeared to Allen as breaking of protocols was Macon proving she was worth battling the hard stuff of life for.

Conroy cleared his throat. "He said you were brave. Knew exactly what to say to keep Leon calm."

She closed her eyes. All she had done was send out a prayer to God.

And it struck her then...He'd listened.

A wave of dizziness made Natalie bend over and lean on her knees as Leon's voice haunted her.

If I can't have you, no one will.

She'd prayed then, in that moment. Knowing she would've given her life to save Kelsey. She'd have gone with Leon if that was what it took. But she hadn't wanted to die, and God sent Macon to save her.

Something landed on her arm, and Natalie jerked back to the present.

Her leg was backed against the couch, not against her

bloodied office floor. It was Conroy blinking at her, not Leon. Allen was beside her, his hand on her arm.

"You okay?"

Not even a little. She should have defused the moment quicker with Leon. *Should* have been able to save herself and Kelsey. Instead, Macon had nearly gotten killed.

And now he might lose everything he'd worked for, because of her. No. He'd risked everything to *save* her.

What was she willing to do to save him?

24

Macon turned up his classic rock workout playlist. The drums and electric guitar in his ear buds did little to quiet his mind from the events of the day. Leon aiming a gun at Natalie. Then the way Natalie had told Macon to leave.

The open garage door dropped the temperature in the stuffy space. He pulled out the weights that had been in the corner from the first day he moved into his rental. He'd forgotten he owned a set of weights, but after finishing his Easter report, he needed this.

He adjusted the bandage on his palm. The air vent hadn't cut him too badly. And he had butterfly bandages along the tear in his side—self-administered. Save for a bruise on his thigh, he'd suffered no other physical damage. Just mental.

He blinked away the frightful look he'd seen on Natalie's face as he'd wrestled with Leon, and sat on the wobbly bench. The rusty metal dug into the soft spot between his fingers and thumbs, but he pushed through the set of arm curls.

He flipped onto his back and heaved the weights toward the ceiling. The dumbbell wasn't the only thing growing heavy. He wanted to pray that Allen would change his mind about his probation, but would it be worth the effort? He hadn't been their first choice. Why even try to stay when they didn't want him.

Macon obviously didn't have Natalie's signature on his forms yet to back up his case that he was the right candidate. Maybe he should repolish his resume. It wouldn't be too hard to find a firefighting job. But one he wanted—that would be trickier.

He wanted to stay in Last Chance County. Not to prove himself but because this finally felt like the place he wanted to be. And most importantly, Natalie was here. There would be no figuring out the feelings he had for her if they were in different areas.

His muscles burned, yet he endured another round. In order to grow stronger, there had to be pain involved. Muscles had to tear and be broken down before they could heal and grow stronger.

Finally, he set down the weights. The song "Should I Stay or Should I Go?" blasted in his ears while his lungs pulled tighter.

Natalie's face flashed in his mind. This time from when he'd carried her out of the fire.

He dragged up the bottom of his shirt and wiped his face. Something tapped him on the shoulder. Macon wrenched away, and his movement made the rickety bench tip over—and him with it. He ripped the music out of his ears to find one of the last people he expected to see in his garage.

"Houston."

His brother extended his palm. "Need a hand?"

Macon stared at the offered help. Years ago, Macon had done the same to Houston on his first anniversary of being cancer free. Houston had tripped down some steps, and the pain in his brother's hip had only gotten worse from his bone marrow procedure. But Houston had refused to take Macon's help that day. Instead, he'd blamed Macon for it all. And his mother hadn't said a word.

In a roundabout way, it *had* been Macon's fault. The pain he'd created had caused Houston to fall.

Macon shoved the bench away. "Haven't I already taken enough from you?"

Houston didn't have much left of an eyebrow, but what had regrown over the scars and the skin grafting lifted. He didn't take back his hand.

He stuck out his other one too. "I'd give you both for five minutes of your time."

Macon pushed himself up on his own. Unfortunately, he had more than five minutes. He wasn't sure what he was supposed to do with his mandatory time away. Other than look for a new job.

Macon huffed. "Follow me. I have a can of strawberry soda. But if you're here about baseball coaching, you're wasting your time."

Houston stopped at the threshold of the garage door. "Strawberry's *my* favorite. *You* hated it."

Hate was a rather strong word. "I only highly disliked it." Now, root beer, he hated.

But one day, he'd found himself by an old soda machine. He'd been thirsty, but turned out all the drinks were out except his brother's favorite. Macon discovered it wasn't as bad as he remembered. That and it reminded him of the good times with his brother.

Houston's lips twitched; however, he remained quiet as they went into the house and looked around. Probably noticing the bare walls of Macon's two-bedroom rental. He didn't need much. Just a thrift shop couch, a table, a couple chairs. "This place looks..."

Macon grabbed a strawberry soda and a water and met his brother at the wobbly table. "If you say *homey*, your five minutes is up." The only thing he'd splurged on when he returned from Australia was his mattress.

But maybe it was time to make this feel like a home.

"I was going to say it looks nothing like you. But I realized I don't really know your tastes anymore."

Macon allowed a chug of his drink to give him more time to dig through his brother's words. His family never spoke aloud what they truly felt.

It had started when his parents would try to talk to each other while he was in the hospital as if Macon wasn't there. He had known things weren't good. Could feel it in his young body. Yet his parents had treated him as if he didn't understand.

At least Houston wasn't lying to him. Just hiding his true reason for coming over. "What do you want? I'm assuming Eddie already gave you my answer about the baseball team stuff. You don't need me. You know just as much as me."

With a sigh, Houston spun the can in his hand instead of opening it.

"You don't have to drink the stupid soda. It's been a while." Since they'd had a normal conversation, let alone snacked together. "You may have outgrown it."

Just like he'd outgrown Macon.

Houston answered by opening the soda and taking a gulp. He put down the can. "Thanks. Haven't had one of those in a while." He smiled and his lips were shiny red.

Macon clenched his jaw and glanced away. Whenever their dad had taken Houston to a professional baseball game, he'd always come home with his lips stained red. While Macon was stuck in his room.

"My lips are bright red, aren't they?"

Macon grunted without looking over.

Houston put his elbows on the table, making it wobble again. It seemed like everything in his life was half broken. "How are you?"

"Peachy."

"I heard about today. You were a hero. Saved Natalie."

"Well, you heard wrong." Macon shoved away from the table. "Turns out rescuing her will probably get me fired." She obviously didn't want to tell him the bad news yet. That he was a loose cannon and she wouldn't be signing off on his evaluation. Why else would she put him at arm's length?

Macon paced the room. "After which I'm sure you'll be glad to be the only James family member back in town again."

Houston's chair scraped against the floor. "Why would I want you gone? I had the chance to leave, but I stayed *because* of your return. Macon, I'm still here because I want to fix this." He motioned between them. The disappointment on his face was one Macon hadn't seen since the first day his brother had come home from the burn unit and Macon had come to visit him.

Macon stared at the ground. "We're fine."

"You seriously believe that?" His brother pushed the soda away. "Then why won't you coach rec baseball with Eddie and me? If we're fine."

Macon rocked back against the counter. "I think your five minutes is up."

Houston did the opposite. Not with a stance ready to fight but with his palms open before him. "Macon. You should be playing baseball or at least coaching it, not putting yourself in danger. I know about the full ride you could've had—should have had. You gave up your dream of playing ball. And it was because of me."

Macon blinked at him. Swallowed.

How did Houston know that? Macon hadn't even told his parents about the scholarship offer. He shook his head. It didn't matter. "I didn't deserve to follow my dreams. It's my fault you've been through so much pain."

Not only the fire but with all the extra surgeries that came from donating bone marrow to save Macon. "You've sacrificed too much for me."

"Mac—"

"I would have been right there beside you if I hadn't been off at the batting cages, and I'd have been with you in the fire if I hadn't snuck out to see a girl that, in the end, only wanted you."

Houston just frowned at him. Then *he* shook his head. "You wouldn't have saved me from the fire that night if you were home because there *wouldn't have been a fire at all*."

"Because I would have stopped it. Yes, I know!" How many times had Macon relived the events of that night?

"No, you idiot. *I* put that note in your locker."

What?

Houston's grimace didn't make Macon understand his brother's words any better.

"Youth pastors aren't supposed to lie," Macon said. "Don't start now. Rachel told me I wasn't the one she wrote the note to. She wanted *you*." Of course.

Houston ran a hand over his bald head. "True. She wrote me a note to meet her that night, but I didn't like her." He caught Macon's gaze. "But I knew *you* did. I put the note she'd placed in my locker into yours."

"If your goal was to make me look more like a fool, it worked."

"I hoped she'd finally see how great you were." He made another face. "But I did it because I was selfish. I wanted you gone."

"Done," Macon said. He pointed to the door.

"Macon. You don't get it. My hip had started hurting again. One of the guys in my class promised he had just the thing to take the edge off. He'd gotten ahold of some weed and whiskey." Houston pushed out a breath. "I knew you'd never go for it, so I got you out of the house that night. He had a candle to light the joint... I don't know what happened exactly. I must have passed out from the shots. The next thing I remember is screaming in an ambulance."

Macon remembered arriving to find the EMTs working to save his brother's life, their house in flames. His dad had grabbed him, crying.

He'd always thought it was in grief. But maybe...what if his dad had been grateful Macon hadn't been there?

Houston tapped his chest. "I was the reason the house caught fire. The reason I got burned was me. Not you."

All he could do was stare at his brother.

"Even if the fire had been your fault, you can't fix the past, Macon. Only God can do that. I had to go through all of that in order to see what I was doing in my life was wrong. Trials suck. This sucks." Houston flipped over his hands and revealed his blotchy skin. "But it pointed me to God. He used what we view as bad for good. To turn me around."

"Giving me your bone marrow did nothing good for you. That pain was because of *me*. It's what made you want drugs and alcohol, which supposedly started the fire." It all still pointed back to Macon.

"Giving you my bone marrow let me keep my brother."

Macon raised his chin. "No, it didn't. Not really. Because you didn't do stuff with me anymore. When I was sick, I didn't get to go with you. I was stuck in the hospital. And when you visited, all you and Dad talked about was how much fun you had together."

"Dad took me to baseball games to remind us of you. The things you loved. I missed you while you were at the hospital. Dad would go to his room. Mom was with you sometimes." Houston shrugged. "Then you got better, and we had baseball again."

"As if any of you cared I was playing."

"And then you stopped playing. Why?"

"You were hurt. It wasn't fair that I could play when you couldn't."

Now Houston was the one to stare, to blink. "Wow. Okay, I get that, but life isn't fair. If it were, Christ wouldn't have had to die for things He didn't do. But He did because He loves us." His voice softened. "When I heard you went up against a gunman, I realized I've waited too long to tell you the truth. Your job is dangerous, and I could have lost you before now." He met Macon's eyes. "I was embarrassed by my past. Didn't want you to see how much of a screwup *I* was."

Macon stared at him.

Houston touched his shoulder. "It's time for me to stop hiding, wishing for what we used to have, and find it again. Even if I have to drag you down to the creek kicking and whining the entire way."

Macon snorted. "I was never the one who whined about mud in my boots."

"It felt gross between my toes."

"Never admit that out loud." Macon laughed. "Ever."

His brother's laugh joined in with Macon's. They'd used to be more than brothers. They'd been best friends. All before Macon started getting weird bruises.

Could they really have that back now? Surely too much time had passed.

"But it was fun." Houston's grin faded. "So, why might you be fired?"

Macon sighed. "It's complicated." He could hear Natalie's voice in his head. *I'm good with complicated.*

Maybe, but she was even better at getting him to be himself. And that had felt weirdly freeing.

Macon spread out his arms. "The truth is most of my crew dislikes me. I'm down a firefighter, and Natalie was supposed to have been off-limits while she evaluated the crew and myself. And, well, I'm not exactly employee of the month."

Houston put his hand on Macon's shoulder. "Rock bottom is always a good place to let God be the chief of your life."

Macon swallowed. "I don't think He'd want me."

His brother squeezed his shoulder. "Oh, He does. He even welcomed the thief hanging beside Him on the cross."

Macon closed his eyes. His favorite nurse, who had given him the handkerchief, had told him the same story.

No fancy prayer filled his mind. Just, *Lord, help. I'm all Yours.*

And it was enough in that moment.

Win or lose, Macon was ready to come home and fight to become the man he was supposed to be.

25

Natalie turned the radio up from the passenger seat in Allen's truck. *What a day.* Her earlier arguments in favor of Macon's actions to Allen and Conroy hadn't been productive. All they saw were Macon's flaws, not his strengths.

Her mood soured further when the rental company hadn't left a message about her car, forcing her to accept a ride from her hardheaded cousin.

A song she and Allen used to belt out when they were younger came on, and she flipped the volume off.

Allen stopped drumming his fingers on the center console. He took his eyes off the road and shot her a scowl. "You sure you're all right?"

She turned toward the window. "I'll be fine."

"*Fine?* Do you know how many times I used that word?"

She did. After he was hurt in the line of duty as a police officer, she'd called often. She had been stationed states away and couldn't visit as much as he'd probably needed.

Allen pressed the brake button on his modified steering wheel. "I'm surprised that word isn't banned in your line of work. You should never have been in today's situation to begin with."

"Maybe I shouldn't have taken out a restraining order against Leon. If I hadn't, maybe he wouldn't have gone to such extremes." Conroy had found out before they'd left the center that Leon had OD'd on something nasty. Apparently, he was lucky to still be alive.

Allen shook his head. "You did everything right. A restraining order is there to protect you. It can save a life, and it gives the justice system the ammo needed to put someone like Polmes away. We just hope that happens before someone is seriously hurt."

She kept her gaze on the darkening sunset. Allen hadn't once heard her argument for Macon. He more than likely wouldn't hear her on this either.

"Don't take the blame yourself," he went on. "I get that people have issues and illness that I'll never wish upon anyone, but you could have been killed. Any of the people there could have been."

Thank goodness Kelsey was okay. The memory of the last gunshot boomed in her head. The feeling of helplessness when Macon's eyes had widened. The fear that he'd been shot.

She had to step it up. Be even more alert to others' pain around her. "It's my job to see."

"You can't see it all, Natalie. You weren't made to. So before you start taking on the world's burdens, a wise counselor once told me you're not supposed to make any rash decisions in the heat of the moment."

She whipped her head around. "Does that apply to your decision about Macon's job?"

After a beat, Allen said, "He never should have gone in there. However, if it had been Pepper in there? Or Victory?" He blew out a breath. "Let's just say, I understand why Macon did what he did. But that doesn't mean he shouldn't be reprimanded…or even replaced."

Those words may as well have punched her. "He saved me at a house fire, at the training house, and today. He really is a solid chief."

"And yet, you haven't signed off on him or his crew."

She thumped her head back against the seat. She should have sent in the paperwork before they had left to go horseback riding. "Yes, Macon has issues. All people do. He's dealing with his in the proper ways. It just took me a while to see it. The firefighters under him will as well."

"So you're ready to sign off on him?"

She stared at him. "Yes." She looked out the window. Perfect. She was just making this worse. "Fine. The problem is that…he's a great chief. And I know this. But I also don't trust myself."

"Why not?" Allen said slowly.

She pressed her face into her palms. "You're going to hate me. You stuck your neck out for me to help me get this job and…I ruined everything."

"Natalie—"

"I kissed him, okay? Not once but twice!"

He said nothing, just his headlights cutting down the street in the darkness.

"I haven't told Dean yet. It only happened one time, and I was set on not letting it happen again. The evaluation is done, and they need more help, but Dean's and Kelsey's loads are so full. Still, it can't be me."

"You like him? Like, actually *like him* like him?" He looked over at her. And was…*smiling*?

"You sound like a cheesy movie line."

"And the answer is—"

"It doesn't matter if I do or don't. I doubt he'll want much to do with me after I helped get him fired."

"I never said that I wanted to fire him. Now it's up to the mayor. But rules are rules, and Macon hasn't been fully sworn in as chief yet. He knew he had to toe the line. The Easter egg hunt incident added to the fact that he didn't take his time off didn't help."

"I was at the Easter egg hunt. He handled it all by the book. But stop pointing all the blame on him. A counselor can't date their client. That's how this Leon mess all started."

"No. Leon created an imaginary relationship in his mind. I read the report. You didn't fall for Leon. You handled that appropriately."

"I didn't handle Jeremiah appropriately."

Her eyes burned.

"Nat, we're not perfect. We can never say or do all the right things all the time. There's only One who—"

"You didn't witness..." Her voice trailed off as she remembered the voice of her friend when she'd told him she couldn't meet him. "I should have seen the signs. I shouldn't have pushed off Jeremiah's desire for a coffee run."

"Even if you hadn't, you can't control people, only your own thoughts and actions. God's the perfect one. Not us. You're not responsible for the things people do...just what you do in response. God is trustworthy, Nat. Let Him have your guilt. Let Him have the brokenness that's in all of us. He's the only true Healer. No therapist can do what He can."

Was Allen right? Could she trust God to carry her past? To heal her brokenness? To save those around her?

Allen pulled into her driveway. "How about you come to Victory's play tonight with us? I'm about to go pick up Pepper. I could swing back and get you."

She opened the truck door and paused. "I think I've had enough people for the day. Can you tell Victory to break a leg for me?"

Allen nodded. "Course."

Inside her house, she set her keys and phone down and flipped on the entryway light. She hoped a bath would provide her with enough courage to call Macon and tell him she'd tried to save his job. But failed.

Allen's headlights sprinkled through the living room blinds as he pulled away and headed to his girlfriend's house. Natalie was glad he had found Pepper. She seemed to be exactly what he needed.

Through all the scary moments they'd endured earlier this year, Natalie hadn't lost hope that they would build a future. Allen, Pepper, and her niece Victory were going to make a family one day. Probably soon.

God, I want to trust You. But what about what I need?

Natalie turned on the lamp by her couch and stopped. One of her files was open on the floor, as if the heater had kicked on and blown it off. She bent down and scooped it up. Except there were two more files stacked on the floor.

What were these—

Before she could read the names, an arm snaked around her stomach and pulled her up.

She screamed and dropped the papers. All her training coursed through her. Centering her strength, she rammed her heel into the attacker's foot. Her foot met a steel-toed boot.

"Help!" Against her natural response to fight, she forced her body to go limp and arched her back at the same time.

The attacker's grip on her loosened just enough. She jabbed her elbow into his abdomen, then twisted and thrust her palm up at his nose.

He groaned and stumbled back.

She rounded the couch to get to her purse—her cell phone.

The man dove and grabbed her foot. She tripped and hit the floor. Breath whooshed from her lungs.

"Stop that! You could have broken my nose," he wailed.

He was short and stocky. Buzzed hair and a tattoo on his

neck, half blocked by the collar of his leather jacket. No one familiar.

"Help!" Natalie pushed up to her hands and knees.

Before she could stand, he yanked her toward him. "You're not going anywhere!"

She flipped over and kept her other leg tucked to her chest. She had to remain calm. Had to keep the attacker at a distance.

He tightened his hold on her one leg and rotated to pin her, but she spun on the floor and matched his move. She didn't have the upper hand in position or strength, yet she still had her mind. Her trained mind.

"What do you want?"

His teeth flashed in the dim light. "What is mine."

He lunged toward her. She kicked her free leg right into his chin.

He howled and fell back.

She heaved herself up off the floor. The front door was within five steps. No time to find her phone. She grabbed the door handle. The night's cool air hit her flushed skin.

Run!

One step out of the door, the man shoved her from behind. She tripped over the door frame, and she went flying. Her head rammed into one of her planters on the front step.

Then she landed, hard, on the path below.

Macon was in her head. *Breathe, Natalie!* She dragged in a breath and tried to find her feet. *God, I need You!*

She moved her hands under her chest, but before she could hoist her shaky arms up, two boots stepped into her vision.

She shielded against a kick. Instead, something wrapped around her mouth, muffling her.

He secured the cloth and spat, "Why can't you women do things the easy way?"

The rag in her mouth tasted like oil and sweat and her

worst nightmare. She spat it out and screamed as loud as she could.

The thumbnail moon and her burned-out porch light wouldn't alert anyone. Her head throbbed. Her chest burned. Her vision blurred.

She didn't want to die.

Before she rolled over, he picked her up and threw her over his shoulder.

She kicked her feet, but he locked down harder on her thighs, pressing them against his collarbone. She hung upside down. If only she could reach his eyes. Gouge them. He might drop her.

She clenched her stomach and reached, but her hand only got to his arms. She stretched up again. Her fingers grabbed ahold of something on the man's jacket. If he was taking her, she had to leave a clue.

With the last of her energy, she yanked.

The rip echoed in the quiet. She wished her neighbors had let their inside dog out. Maybe he would bark.

She needed help.

But Macon wasn't here this time.

Because instead of letting him take her home, she'd pushed him away, trying to save his job.

A job she shouldn't have questioned in the beginning.

"What did you do?" He spun around, and Natalie's upper half sailed through the air behind him.

She lifted her arms, but it was too late. Her head met the side of the house.

The piece of fabric fluttered from her fingers.

The last thing she heard was a callous voice whispering in her ear, "Don't you black out on me, because you are going to take me to my son."

26

Tonight, being stubborn wasn't a flaw. It helped Macon fight for what he wanted. No more running from his past. He wanted a home. Here. In Last Chance County. And he was prepared to open his heart to every question Natalie needed to know.

But he also needed to know that she was okay.

Macon pulled into Natalie's driveway.

She wasn't the only one who tried to hide her struggles. But most of all, Macon had learned he wasn't meant to carry the world. And neither was she.

Light shone from the front porch. She was home. He grabbed the Chinese takeout bag from the passenger seat.

As he got halfway down her sidewalk, he realized why the light was bright from her house. The door was cracked open. Had her lock broken again?

He knocked on the doorframe. "Natalie, it's Macon. I brought some dinner. Can we talk?"

The stillness ticked louder than a countdown to a new year. He pressed the doorbell. The chime echoed through the house, but there were no thuds of footsteps. Not even a neighbor dog barking.

He pulled up her number on his phone and hit Send. The dial tone rang in his ear, and there was also a faint ringtone inside. He nudged the door open enough to see her entryway table. It sounded like her phone was right there in her bag.

"Natalie?" He leaned inside.

The rug behind the couch was twisted. He stepped into the entryway.

Still no sounds. Another step made him grip his phone. Files lay scattered across the living room floor. She'd either gotten angry and tossed them aside, or she'd dropped them.

Or worse.

"Natalie?"

Macon ran through the house and flipped on every light. Checked every room.

Empty.

He returned to the entryway. Stilled at the moisture on the hardwood floor, not illuminated by the hall light.

Blood.

His stomach plummeted.

He shone his phone's flashlight and another drop lit up outside on the porch. A few more droplets of blood hid in the shadow beside the potted plant. She was hurt. Had Allen picked her up to take her to the doctor, and that's why she didn't have her phone?

He dialed Allen. No answer.

His gut was a fist now. A dark stain on the house made him raise his light. Blood on the siding. Had she leaned her hand against the house because she struggled to walk?

Another splotch of red along the cement walkway made him jog down the sidewalk. He followed the sprinkling as it traveled toward the driveway. This didn't look good.

Even if Leon was in police custody at the hospital and

Natalie had only cut her finger, Macon didn't want to take any chances. However, this time, he'd do it the right way.

"Nine-one-one, what's your emergency?" The female voice registered in his head.

"This is Chief James..." Was that a *footprint*? He put his boot near it. Larger than his, so no way it was Natalie's. Probably wasn't Allen's either, if he'd been in his wheelchair.

Which meant Allen hadn't picked her up.

"I'm at Natalie Atkinson's house." His chest tightened. "There's blood on the doorway and porch, and she's gone. I think something happened to her."

"Do you know the street you're on, Chief?"

He recognized her from the bit of Southern twang. "Washington Court or Circle. Verna, I think it's you. It's the subdivision by that place where your husband used to take you on your half anniversaries." Why couldn't he think?

"The Charleston. Got it."

"I know you normally stay on the line, but I need to make a few more calls." He squeezed the back of his neck.

"PD is responding. There's a patrol car two blocks from you. Do what you need to, Chief. We'll sure get it all figured out quicker than instant pudding."

"Thanks, Verna." Macon hung up and dialed Allen again. It went straight to his voice mail. "Come *on*!"

After Macon left a message, he turned back to the house. His foot slipped on something. He flipped his flashlight app back on and spotted some kind of material. He scooped it up.

The patch was purple, in the shape of a cougar's head. It was missing a section of seam, and there was blood on the back of it. Natalie's blood?

Macon fired off a text to both Allen and Conroy. He stared at the house. Then at his phone. What else could he do?

God, help.

The background photo on his phone, the one of the fire station, made Amelia's name pop into his head.

His lieutenant answered on the first ring. "Patterson."

"Call the team out—I'm at Natalie's. She's been kidnapped, and yes, the police are on their way, but...I need your help, Amelia. You and the team. And I know we have our issues, but there's blood inside and out. I need the crew here to scour the area. Pronto."

Amelia let a split second of silence hang. "On our way."

She hung up.

Macon glanced at the stars above. Houston had mentioned that God had used the trials of life to point him the right way.

He hoped that now might be one of those times.

27

Pain pulsed along Natalie's skin. Had the nurse forgotten to give her the last dose of medicine? She rolled her neck to the side. The movement didn't ease the pressure. Natalie felt for the call button, but her fingers didn't find it.

It was dim for once, and that made it hard to see. To think.

Her mouth felt like she'd been out in training without her canteen. She reached for the ice water on her tray, except couldn't lift her arm.

Someone moaned. Did she get a new hospital roommate? When the room stopped spinning, she found out why her body hurt.

She wasn't in her hospital bed, recovering from the explosion. She was in even more danger than potential infections from the burn wounds on her face.

The moan she'd heard had been her. She pushed her tongue against the soaked fabric in her mouth. It didn't budge.

She blinked again. She was in the middle of a room. Not just a room, but some kind of two-story garage or warehouse. In front of her was a workbench. Sheets of metal leaned against two of the walls. Welding masks hung on nails on the side wall, cylinder tanks lined what looked like boarded up garage doors, and there was plenty of open space.

She pushed against the tape holding her hands behind her back. Her shoulders screamed. The bruise on her back from hitting the filing cabinet earlier today had nothing on the ache on her head where it'd hit her house when the man swung her around.

She panted. Then screamed. But her voice didn't carry beyond the filthy rag in her mouth. She yanked on her arms again. The movement swiveled the chair, and it creaked under her where her feet were taped together.

Footsteps pounded behind her. Her heartbeat matched the determined steps. She whipped her head around to see who was coming. The room twirled until she came face-to-face with a stubble-faced man. Not as unkempt as Leon had been earlier today. This man wore a scowl and a beanie on his head. Short sleeves. No leather jacket. Not a bloody or broken nose either.

She clenched her fingers. Was this the same guy who'd been at her house, or was there more than one? Either way, his hazel eyes tracked her every movement.

"Where is he?" His breath smelled like peanuts.

Natalie swallowed only to gag on the fabric in her mouth.

"I'm not falling for that trick again."

Had she woken up more than once? Natalie shook her head, but it didn't help her gag reflex. The rag and the taste of oil combined with the throb of her head made her stomach churn.

The chair spun in the opposite direction, and her stomach lurched more.

"Don't you dare throw up on me." He pulled out a knife.

Natalie squeezed her eyes closed. Something cool pressed against her check, but instead of more agony, the rag loosened.

Natalie breathed in the first breath of fresh air, and her

stomach stayed where it should. She needed him to cut the tape off too. That might come soon if she could get a read on this guy. If she remembered her training.

She swallowed back her fear. "Why are you doing this?"

Her fingers shook, but she held the stranger's gaze. His eye shape looked familiar, yet she didn't think she'd ever met him.

He paced in front of her as his hand held the rag by its end, twisting it as fast as Natalie's pulse in her head.

"What's your name again?" Perhaps they'd had a session together and she'd forgotten. She didn't remember everyone she'd ever seen, and those who served often looked different in civilian life.

He stopped and narrowed his gaze. His eyes were bloodshot around the edges, similar to the way Leon's had looked except for the hate mixed with fury. Was this man on the same drugs that Leon had OD'd on?

She rotated her wrist and felt the edge of the tape restricting her. She slowly rubbed her thumbnail against the restraint. Even if it took an hour, she was getting out of here. "I'm sorry that I don't recognize you. I—"

He pointed the knife at her chest.

Natalie gasped.

"You only speak about what I need you to tell me." He ran his finger along the flat portion of the knife. "If you're any good, you might not end up like Angel."

Natalie curled her toes in her shoes. She was ninety percent sure she didn't know anyone named Angel. In the military, they mainly used last names, but that wasn't the point right now. "What didn't Angel tell you?"

"She had no right to keep him away from me. She lied to me."

What did that have to do with her? Was he placing Angel's sins, so to speak, on her?

Natalie continued to move her thumbnail back and forth against the tape. "What did she lie to you about?"

He grabbed another chair that sat beside the wall by its backrest and rolled it over. It was wobblier than the one Natalie sat on. She hoped the screws under the padded part of hers stuck out as far as the ones on his chair. She might be able to use the screws to cut herself free.

He leaned on his hands and knees and flipped his blade in and out. "She said she lost our baby." He plunged the knife into the back of the chair he sat on. "But I saw that picture once I got out, and that boy is mine. The eyes prove everything, and you're going to tell me where you put him." Spit flew from his mouth when he said *put.*

Natalie hadn't put anyone anywhere...except...

Her back stiffened.

Was he talking about Joey? That was the only boy she'd recently had contact with. If that was the case, then Angel might be...

Why can't you women do things the easy way?

The comment he'd made in her living room rang through her mind, connecting the dots. He wasn't being general. He'd compared Natalie to one other woman. Angel could also be a nickname for Angelina, Joey's mother.

"Angie," she whispered.

He jerked back around. "She was as two-faced as all her names."

Hatred settled into his gaze. This man must have had something to do with Angie's death. What if Joey had been right that his mother hadn't committed suicide?

Was he Joey's biological father? He clearly believed himself to be.

Natalie crawled her fingers farther over. She could almost reach one of the nails on her chair. "What did she do?"

"Do you know what happens to snitches?" He grabbed his knife and flung it at Natalie.

She sucked in a breath and leaned away. Her chair didn't move. The blade whistled past her ear and struck something behind her.

He stood and retrieved his knife. "They never should have turned her against me or kicked me out of the club. But I don't need them no more. My club will be stronger. Just like what they did to me made me. I'm not weak. Neither is my blood."

He kicked his chair. It landed with a crack against the workbench, and she used the noise to mask her nail tearing through part of the tape.

He whirled around. "You're going to tell me where my son is, and then him and me are going to rule Last Chance County. Willy's boys will regret voting me out. This so-called lapdog has learned some new tricks."

An inch more, and the screw tore a little away. Natalie coughed to cover the noise. Her head buzzed and the room spun. "I don't know where your son is."

He lowered his nose right beside hers, and she froze.

"Yes. You. *Do.*" He didn't blink.

Breathe in. Out. Think about the problem.

This man wanted to see his son. She'd never give him Joey or the Cunninghams' address, but he didn't need to know that.

She arched her wrist and loosened the tape on her right hand. "I'm sure we can get a meeting arranged. How about tomorrow for breakfast? We can have chocolate chip pancakes. Do you like—"

He lifted her chin with his knife.

Natalie locked her teeth together.

"You're a smart woman. Smarter than Angel." His hot breath brushed her skin. "Prettier too."

He put the tip of the knife to her cheek. "I'm not dumb. Your files have helped point me in the right direction. But I'm tired of hunting and waiting."

Files. In her house and at her office. Probably why only Peter's file went missing. He was trying to locate Joey. There had been a motorcycle once in the camera feed. Maybe Leon hadn't cut off the center's surveillance cameras. Unless he and this maniac had been working together?

He pulled the knife away, and Natalie drew in a lungful...

"Joseph's 'father'"—he used his fingers as quotation marks—"can't even care for him right now. There's no point in having strangers keep him when his own blood can have him. Is he at the gray house on Meridian or the brick one?"

He was too close to finding out where Joey was. If she didn't give him something, who would this man hurt next? Mrs. Cunningham?

"He was on Meridian." She licked her chapped lips. "They moved him."

He finally blinked. Once.

Natalie swallowed. She couldn't let this man hurt Tosha, either. Where could Natalie say Joey was?

Allen's horse barn was the first place that came into her head. Her cousin wouldn't be there. They were at Victory's play. It seemed like the safest address.

He stomped toward her, knife out.

"Okay, okay!" She overplayed her breathing, like she'd relented. "He's outside of town, up in the hills. It's called Pine Creek."

She stared at the knife in his hand. "There's an old barn at the front of the property." Natalie found his interested gaze. "If you untie me, I can show you."

The man used the tip of his knife to lift up her sleeve and then put the cool metal against her skin. He dragged the blade down her arm, leaving behind a trail of fire. She whimpered and tried to move away.

There was no pretending fear.

He pulled his knife back. Her blood dripped onto the concrete and sprinkled through her sleeve. "If my son is there, then maybe I'll let you live. After all, Joey needs a new momma."

Natalie bit her cheek and squeezed her numbing fingers. She would not allow this man to feed off her terror. She didn't move until he grabbed his leather coat off the workbench. The one she'd torn the patch from.

The door slammed behind him.

Using the toes of her shoes, she rotated her chair. The shop was empty, which meant she needed to work fast.

She rolled her chair over to the workbench. It was too high to reach anything. She spotted a lower nail holding a welding helmet. Once she made it over there, she gritted her teeth and positioned her hands below the nail and used it to break the tape.

Sweat dripped down her forehead and stung where her head throbbed. With a grimace, she yanked her arms forward, pulling tape and hairs off her skin. Then she ripped the tape off her legs. Finally, freedom.

She stood. Her legs tingled. Her head and arm throbbed. Natalie braced a hand and steadied herself against the workbench.

When the dark spots clouding her vision cleared, she ran toward the door. She turned the handle. It didn't move, and there was no visible lock to flip. A keypad blinked beside the door.

Her lungs pulled tight. The dizzy room made it hard to think. She checked the nearest window. Metal bars blocked her exit. Behind her was another door, but it proved to be a small bathroom. No window.

There was no phone on the walls anywhere.

She inspected her knife wound. It wasn't too deep. Her sleeve would have to serve as a bandage.

She glanced around, then up. There was a tiny vent at the joint of the roof. She spotted something else in the open ceiling. Hope. Her fire training was paying off.

The welding garage had been wired with First Call sprinklers.

A half laugh, half cry bubbled from her lips. The kind of sprinklers that automatically called the fire department. With all the welding equipment, surely there was a way to make some kind of fire. A lighter lay on another worktable beside a roll of blue shop towels.

Natalie climbed on top of the workbench, lit the towel roll, and held it near the sprinkler unit.

"Come on." She moved to the next unit.

Shouldn't water come out, or an alarm? She waved the lit roll toward the next sprinkler.

Why wasn't this working?

"Please." *God, can You hear me?*

The door slammed. Natalie leaned too far. Her foot slipped off the edge and she cried out. Her hip clipped the bench as she fell. The fiery towels dropped onto the floor and rolled.

"Someone is too smart for their own good." Joey's assumed father kicked the lit paper towel roll. It sailed across the room like a field goal, straight into a stack of cardboard boxes. "You should have stayed put."

She scooted away.

He lunged and grabbed her by her hair.

Natalie screamed as she clawed at him.

The roll of paper towels ignited the cardboard.

She arched her back and kicked her feet. "We have to get out!"

"Shut up!" He dragged her along the floor. "Guess it was a good thing Angel's old truck didn't start. I can't have you getting away until I figure out if you're telling the truth, can I? Or have you running for the cops."

She growled and dug her fingernails into his skin.

With a howl, he pinned her arms down and shoved her into the tiny bathroom, slamming the door closed.

Darkness washed over her. She swallowed down a whimper and felt for the door handle. She pushed her good arm against the door. Nothing.

"Let me out!" She banged her fists against the wood. Her hip and head throbbed. She hit it again.

The door cracked open an inch. She gritted her teeth and shoved harder.

Something sharp poked her shoulder. Natalie cried out and rubbed her newest wound. Outside, something made a banging sound. Not a shot, but an echo—

Oh no.

He was nailing the door shut.

"No!" She jimmied the handle again.

Natalie panted and lowered to her knees. She peeked under the door to see his boots. When the hammering stopped, his feet no longer blocked her view.

Another slammed door. Then a motorcycle rumbled outside. Joey's father had actually left this time.

But the roar and the crackle from behind the door came straight from her nightmares.

28

Patience. It was not a virtue. Not now.

Macon shone his flashlight along the grass where he'd found the clue. "This is where I found the patch." He glanced at Conroy dressed in his off-duty clothes with his gun belt over his jeans.

Before the first patrol car arrived, Macon had scrutinized the house twice and texted Conroy a picture of the fabric he'd found.

The police chief flipped the fabric over in his hand. "This is an old Demon Kats patch, a prominent motorcycle gang on the east side of Last Chance County. However, it disbanded about five years ago. Some of the previous members are now in a group called the Redeemables."

Conroy clicked off his flashlight. "Good news is the Redeemables are much more willing to help us than their counterparts. Most of them have burned that old patch, but their former leader, Willy, says if he had to guess, this patch could belong to an old crew member."

"You have names?"

Conroy eyed him. "Rumors hold that Spencer Brooks, who

also went by the name Spades, was recently released from prison. There's definitely some bad blood surrounding the Demon Kats and Brooks, but that's from way back when Alan Ridgeman was the chief of police."

Conroy's radio beeped, and he answered someone at the station before focusing back on Macon. "It's hard to know for certain if we got an actual tip or we're just a way for them to seek revenge."

"What do we know about Brooks?" Macon asked. "How do we know he's the one who took Natalie?"

"We don't have much on him beyond his rap sheet." He sighed. "What we need is time. I've got a call out to his parole officer, and I'm waiting to hear back. Hopefully that'll give us an idea where to find him."

"That's time we don't have. C'mon, Conroy—you have to have something."

"Willy gave us a list of old hideouts and associates of Brooks's during his stint with the Demon Kats. My guys are combing through those now, but you have to know the information is years old."

Another set of flashing lights joined in with the police cars. First, his command vehicle pulled in. Followed by Truck 14. He could guess who was manning his vehicle. But it didn't matter if Amelia was gunning for power. For his job. He'd surrender the position to just about anyone if it helped find Natalie.

"My crew can help."

Zack jumped out and jogged over first. "You found her?"

Macon had to shake his head.

The kid winced. "What can we do?"

As Ridge and Amelia rushed over, Conroy eyed each of the crew members and then motioned for them to follow. He led them to his police car, where Olivia handed over a tablet. Conroy said, "Here is the list of addresses and past businesses, including their covers. Until Brooks's PO tells us where to find him, this is where we search for leads."

Amelia grabbed ahold of the tablet. "Let's assign who goes to what premises."

Olivia frowned.

"You have more locations than men," Amelia pointed out. "And time is ticking." She scanned the screen. "This one's a bar. Natalie could have been taken there, but at this hour, there would be lots of witnesses."

"Which he probably wouldn't want." Ridge nodded along with Amelia.

"Good, fresh eyes." Conroy crossed his arms. "Give me your best guesses, and I'll pair your crew with my people. Hopefully, we'll find her quick."

Amelia scrolled. Ridge and Zack looked up some addresses on their phones. Macon read over her shoulder, but nothing popped out at him.

The radio on Amelia's belt squawked.

Macon bit back a groan. So much for more able bodies—he was about to lose his truck squad. Because yes, he'd called them out, but the search had consumed more than an hour of time.

And if there was a fire somewhere…

"Chief." Ridge put his hand on Macon's shoulder.

Macon's hope fell with his heart. Was this all the aid God would provide, or was this the part where Macon had to surrender to Him? "I know."

"Sorry, Chief." Zack twisted his mouth to the side.

But Amelia stepped up. "What was the address for the call again?"

Ridge repeated what had been said over the radio.

"That's on this list," Amelia said. "Lincoln Ave."

"What are the chances that a call came in for one of the

listed addresses?" Macon headed straight into the middle of the police circle. "I know where she is."

Olivia stepped in front of him. "Chief James, you can't possibly—"

Amelia stalked past her. "We know where she is."

Every cop turned.

Macon said, "We just got a callout for Lincoln Ave, one of the possible old hangouts for the Demon Kats. I know you told us to narrow it down. But what if she's there? We're responding to a fire. Come with us, or don't."

Zack held up his phone with a street view. "It's an old welding shop. See?"

Macon's heart thumped as his mind worked out the pieces. "They could have First Call sprinklers."

Amelia shifted on Macon's other side. "He specifically spoke to Natalie about those kinds of sprinklers during her firefighter training. This could be her sending us an SOS."

As they turned and ran for the trucks, Macon prayed this was only God's way of letting them know where she was.

Not an actual fire.

29

Natalie was alive. At least, presently. Smoke filtered into the room, but the air remained breathable. Still manageable. Thinkable. Nothing on her body was burning. She wasn't tied up or being threatened. She had to focus on the positive truths.

Brighter light filtered through the gap under the door. The fire ablaze on the opposite side had to be growing. And since the sprinklers had never kicked on, that meant no one knew she was here.

No one except God.

First step, get out of the locked bathroom.

She rose and let out a cry. Her hip throbbed and the cut on her arm stung. But for the moment, they muted the wound on her head. She bit her lip and felt along the wall. She knocked her knuckles against a sink. Her fingers brushed against a bar of soap, a mirror, and a roll of toilet paper.

The tiny space grew darker as smoke trickled beneath the door. Her firefighter training had taught her that most fire deaths were caused by smoke inhalation. If only this were a drill.

She grabbed the toilet paper. There would be enough to stop some of the smoke from filling up the room. She shoved a wad under the door, all the way along the air gap.

Her throat itched, and coughs rattled through her. She felt for the faucet and turned on the sink, gulped down water, then splashed some on her warm neck and cheeks. As the water dripped down the back of her shirt and her trembling fingertips, an idea hit. *Water.* Fire hated water.

If she plugged up the drain and overflowed the sink, would the water travel under the door all the way to the fire?

She pushed the stopper down and allowed the stream of water to help slow down her heart rate. After another breath in and out, she pushed the toilet paper from under the door. Water pooled under her shoes. She used her foot like a guide to hurry it out of the bathroom. But if the ground was uneven, it may never reach the fire.

She dropped to her hands and knees. Water soaked her pants. She swished the water toward the door with her hands, cupping and scooping. She pushed the soaked toilet paper out of the way.

Another cough pricked stars at the edges of her vision. Her chest tightened. She leaned back on her heels. She steadied her trembling hand against the wall. She was alone. *But God, aren't You always supposed to be here?*

Fire had rumbled through Joey's room, leaving no path out. And like now, she'd thought no one was coming to rescue her.

She might be right this time.

She shook her head. Fire had not surrounded her in the bathroom yet. There had to be another way out. Could she break the mirror and use the pieces to cut through the wood and drywall?

A noise came from behind the door. A pop followed by some muffled sounds. She gasped and put her ear to the door. Had someone else entered the building?

She banged on the wood. "Help!" Her voice cracked. "Someone help me!"

Nothing. She banged again.

She must have imagined the sound, because she heard nothing but the roar of the fire.

Strength sapped from her body, and she slumped against the wall, her breathing ragged. *Help.*

She would die alone.

She sank to the floor and water seeped into her pants. Her arm knocked against something that scooted away from her. A trash can. She felt around for anything else on the floor.

Nothing around the sink, but by the toilet was a long handle. She pulled it out and realized it was a toilet brush. At any other moment, she might have gagged at how the other end of the stick looked. Instead, she was briefly thankful for the darkness, save the glow under the door.

She squeezed her palm around the handle and used it to stand. She stuck the end of the brush into the crack in the side of the door and put her weight against it like a prybar.

More light bled into the bathroom. "Please open!" Natalie's arms shook, but she pushed harder. The nails in the blocked door groaned.

She got her foot almost wedged in between the door and the wall. Only a few more inches and she could squeeze through. She gritted her teeth, placed one foot on the wall, and braced her good shoulder against the door. But instead of the door opening, the toilet brush snapped.

The pop echoed, and Natalie fell onto the puddled floor. With the water on the floor soaking into her clothes, she couldn't tell if anything else was bleeding.

She growled and threw the broken piece of brush that remained in her hand onto the floor. It smacked against the trashcan.

Her hands covered her face. Oh, she didn't want to die

beside a pile of trash. She didn't like the lies that sprang to her mind. Ones she had believed years ago.

After her father had been counseled through his depression, Natalie went back to living with him instead of her aunt and cousins. There had still been so many questions and emotions fluttering in her young mind. Why would her dad want to leave her orphaned? Was Natalie not enough to live for?

Then her father remarried a woman who already had kids. Younger ones that he seemed to spend more time with than Natalie.

Joining the army hadn't made her father proud of her like she'd hoped.

Natalie had tried to become more like her mother instead. The person her father had loved the most. But he never even came to Natalie's basic training graduation. Never visited her at her first permanent duty station. He never came until she graduated from her online university.

The memory of her father giving her a one-arm hug afterward as she held her counseling diploma clouded her mind.

He pulled something from behind his back. None of her step siblings nor her stepmother had bothered to make the trip. "Here."

Natalie stared at the dangling keys. "You want me to drive you back to the airport?" Was he only staying one hour?

Her father had pointed to a white Volkswagen Beetle in the parking lot. "Your mother and I talked before..." His lip quivered. "Before she left for that last deployment, we stayed up talking about...everything."

Tears blocked her vision. She shook her head. "Dad, I can't."

"You're going to keep it. Amy bought her kids way more expensive first cars. It's only fair that I finally give you this."

She really didn't want a memory of her mother to become a guilt offering.

"But there's something else your mother and I talked about that last night. Fought over." A tear rolled down his cheek, and he wiped it away. "She said that the new chaplain had been having lunch with her, that they'd become friends. Your mother said he was starting to make sense. I'm not sure how it happened exactly, but it started an argument. The last night we had together, I said things I never meant."

"Is that why you..." Even after all she'd studied and learned, it remained painful to talk about her dad's suicide attempt.

"I was so lost, sweetheart. I was so twisted on the inside for so many years that I believed you'd be better off without me. But your mother was right. That chaplain? He came and visited me not long ago. He shared the true hope—Christ. I just, I'm sorry for it all. I hope you can forgive me one day."

Natalie opened her eyes and lifted her gaze at the ceiling, the closest thing to heaven.

Had she not forgiven her dad? Maybe, maybe not, but right now, yes. Because she got it—the weight of regrets.

No more. Time to ask for forgiveness. Instead of feeling broken. Instead of the bitterness and the pain of all she'd endured, she needed to focus on and trust someone else. On the true hope.

Inside her gifted car's glove box had been a little Bible with circled verses and notes from her father. Ones that promised joy and peace—the very things she was trying to share with her clients. Except she kept falling short on her own. Because, like Allen had said, she wasn't meant to be their healer.

God, it's been about You this whole time, not me.

Smoke had multiplied inside the bathroom. She blinked her watery eyes as a cloud of smoke twirled up in the shadows toward her prayers and escaped through what looked like a small gap in the ceiling.

A gap...

Natalie sprang up from the wet floor. If the ceiling was tiled with the same stuff as her aunt's laundry room had been, she could slide the rectangular sections out of the way. The metal frames holding the tile in place would be wide enough for her to climb through—the way Macon had done with the vents at the Ridgeman Center.

Natalie hopped onto the toilet seat and reached up, but her fingers didn't even graze the ceiling.

She let out a grunt of frustration and stomped through the puddled water. She swiped off the faucet and wiped the water off the counter. She held her breath and shimmied her knees up onto the wobbly sink.

As she stood to her feet, her cut arm brushed against the wall. She winced and grabbed ahold of the mirror to keep steady. She reached and pushed up on the ceiling. The tile gave way, and a happy cry escaped her lips.

She slid the tile out of its frame and gripped the metal ceiling support. Something scraped her fingers, but she didn't let go. Couldn't. She wasn't ready to give up.

With a jump, she pulled herself up and dangled from the groaning metal.

"I'm sorry I ate that piece of cake the other day," she panted. "Please hold me."

She wanted to live. Not only to help others, but for God. To tell her father she forgave him. To study the Bible and learn about joy and peace. She wanted all of it. Her way of trying to save everyone from the pain of life wasn't working.

And if she could see Macon again, she wanted to fall against his chest and thank him.

"One. Two." She grunted and swung her feet up onto the metal support. Her arms quaked, but the metal held, and she got her entire body higher. Nothing but insulation and gray smoke surrounded her. Fire training said to stay low, but low wasn't going to help her.

She inched forward until the edge of the bathroom ceiling

disappeared. The bathroom's ceiling had been blocked off so it wouldn't be open to the rest of the building. Smoke watered her eyes and made her cough. The flames had reached the arch in the roof.

Spiderwebs tickled her face. She twisted around and held her stomach against the edge of the bathroom. With nothing beneath her, she had to trust and let go.

She landed back on the cement floor with a thud. Her knees buckled, sending her onto her backside. She was tired of hurting. But thankfully, nothing was completely broken.

When she stood, her vision grew hazy. It was harder to see where the fire was in all the smoke. Except the heat wasn't hard to miss. Or forget. The flames had climbed from the boxes to lick up two walls.

Natalie crawled for the exit. The roar of the fire urged her faster. She grabbed the door handle. Once again, it was locked.

No. She had escaped the confines of the bathroom, and she wasn't going to stay locked in the fiery building.

She coughed and pulled her blouse over her nose, put her foot on the door frame, and yanked. Her grip slipped and she stumbled. Her shoulder hit something that fell over with a bang.

She blinked at a welding gas cylinder as it rolled against her foot. She jerked her eyes up. There were half a dozen others behind her.

Her firefighter training had been a blessing and curse. Her legs locked beneath her. If the fire reached those canisters, the building would be done for.

And so would she.

How could she put the fire out and get outside when all the water was locked inside the bathroom?

The fire had lit the third wall of the building. She stared at the last remaining wall beside her and spotted a window peeking from behind stacked metal sheets. Squeezing behind the metal, she opened the window, then rested her forehead against the iron bars on the outside. She gulped in the fresh air.

"Help!" She wheezed. "Someone help me!"

Lord, save me!

Her throat felt like it was lined with sand. She squinted out into the night, but her vision blurred.

She pressed her head farther against the bars. "Please." She sputtered into a cough.

And behind her, the fire roared.

30

Hope. A double-edged sword. An easy word to roll off the tongue, but harder to live. Especially as they pulled up to the old welding shop on Lincoln Ave and Macon spotted the inferno. In truth, he'd spotted it blocks away but had held out hope...

Please, God, don't let her be in there.

Zack nudged Macon's arm from his seat in the back. "The First Call sprinklers should have done the hard work for us."

Ridge kept his gaze on the road. But Macon figured the twitch in his brow meant he was thinking the same thing Macon was. *What if they hadn't?*

Amelia had hopped into his command vehicle before Macon claimed what should be his, but he didn't care. The ambo was two minutes behind them. Rescue was five. Now as Ridge pulled the fire truck around the corner, smoke saturated the air. He hit the brakes and pulled over close to the hydrant.

"Not what I was hoping for," Zack said.

Macon either.

A two-story metal building that had bars on its few windows. Even without the fire engulfing one side of it, the structure had seen better days. Hard to tell if the roof sagged from the heat or from age. Gray smoke poured from the right side of the building.

Please let Natalie *not* be inside.

If the main door wouldn't budge, then the massive garage door on the left could be their way in. They would just have to go around the stack of metal barrels blocking the path.

Macon ran to the door and tapped the top of his hand against the handle. It was lukewarm. He grabbed the knob, but it didn't budge. He rammed his shoulder against it. "Natalie!"

"Chief." Ridge grabbed Macon by the arm. "You need gear on."

He spun back. "We're going to have to find a way in. What about the garage bays?"

"They've been walled up from the inside."

Macon nodded and ran around the building as the crew hooked up the hoses and began to spray down the building. Water saturated his skin.

He came back and found Ridge getting the cutters from the truck. Macon sprinted over. "I need turnout gear."

"Chief, do you want mine?"

Macon stopped.

Ridge shrugged. "We can switch right now, and I'll find the extra on the truck."

He watched Ridge's expression. His jaw was clenched, and his shoulders pushed back. "But you don't want to switch?"

"Honestly?"

"Absolutely."

"I think you're needed out here." Ridge shook his head. "You're gifted at seeing the fire, the situation, as a whole. Where to send everyone." He made a face. "But you're the chief. It's your call."

Ridge's words stilled him. Yes, Natalie needed a rescuer, but it didn't have to be Macon.

It could be all of them.

And ultimately, God, as their real chief.

The sound of another fire truck siren spurred Macon into motion. He took the cutters. "Keep your pants on. I need you going in. But for now, help Stephens on the hose. Patterson!" Macon waved her over as Ridge took her place helping Zack. "Get a ladder on that roof, and see if we can find a way in."

"The best way in I saw is through the front door." She wasn't arguing. She was suggesting.

The metal door. The one they'd have to cut open. "Good call, Lieutenant."

"We could try and pry off the bars on one of the windows. Smoke is pouring out of one cracked window. My TIC showed temperature by it."

"Natalie."

"If she's in there, that's my best guess for her location." Amelia motioned for Rescue's truck as it came in.

Macon took in the building again. Smoke had turned black. The opened window that potentially was keeping Natalie alive was also feeding the fire oxygen that it craved. Fuel to burn. Eat. Destroy.

Macon turned to Amelia. "Which can you do faster?"

"The door."

He handed over the cutters. "Get on it." Macon turned to Jayson Owens. "Vent the roof."

"Yes, sir." Bryce's guy ran for the ladder.

Amelia dashed for her crew. Bryce, along with Charlie and Eddie, got the cutters revved up and attacked the metal hinges.

Zack and Ridge knelt, the hose blasting away at the flames that had crusted the metal roof.

Macon grabbed the extra gear from the truck and pulled it on.

He took a walkie from the truck and called all his men. "Listen up. As soon as the door opens, I want Benning and Rice on a second hose, spraying it down. Patterson and Crawford, go in."

The fire grew higher in the sky. They needed to get the water through the door. Hit the fire at its core.

"Rescue, ETA on your hose?"

"Thirty seconds," Charlie answered as he worked it from their truck.

Macon gripped the radio. "Stephens, get your hose and attack that left side."

"Copy that." Zack and Ridge dragged the hose around the side of the building.

Macon pulled up the truck's TIC, then the radio. Jayson was already coming back down the ladder from the roof. "Patterson, if I say get out, I mean immediately. Run. This place could go up if there are still any welding cylinders inside."

"We're in." Amelia's voice rattled over the radio.

"Benning?"

"Water," Charlie said.

Macon split his focus between the smoke and the truck's TIC. The most lit area was on the left, while his crew's dots moved toward a faint warm temperature on the right.

Charlie and Eddie swept inside, their hose snaking in after. The heated area on the left dimmed for a second until the front door fell completely away. The rush of oxygen fed the fire, and the temperature rose.

He checked on Amelia and Bryce's progress. "Crawford, are there any tanks?"

"Found her!" Amelia answered instead. "Might need a backboard at the door when we come out."

"On it," Ridge said, and when Macon looked up, the man was running for the rescue vehicle.

The crew shuffled to adjust before Macon had to do it for them.

Jayson took Ridge's place on the other hose with Zack.

Macon squeezed the TIC in his hands. Oh, he wanted to go in there, but his crew had this.

He needed to trust them, despite their flaws. Their mistakes.

His job was to train them...and let them do their job. And frankly, Ridge would probably think clearer than Macon if he went in there and found Natalie hurt or not breathing. His crew had Natalie. Everything was going to be okay.

God, thank You.

He pulled out his phone and dialed Conroy.

"Did you find her?" the police chief asked without a greeting.

"I think so. My crew is battling a fire to get to her."

"Anyone else there?"

Macon stared down at his TIC. He counted the warm areas. "Doesn't look like it."

"Sending someone your way." He hung up and Macon watched the smoke change direction.

As Ridge entered the building with the backboard, a flame jumped from the roof and sparked a low-hanging tree branch. It would die out sooner than the fire inside. All their focus needed to remain on the core.

"Chief, do you want us to get on the ladder and blast it from the top down?" Zack called.

Macon kept his eyes on the roof. "Stay where you are."

"Okay, Chief."

The radio crackled. "The fire is at the tanks."

At the temperature the fire was still climbing to, those gas cylinders would explode. Had they loaded Natalie yet? *Please—*

Macon braced. "Everyone out!"

He couldn't breathe in the three heartbeats it took for his first firefighter to appear. Ridge crested the doorway, holding the end of backboard with a body on it. Amelia appeared at the other end. They headed straight for the ambulance. Trace and Izan opened the back and ran toward them.

Macon forced himself not to run over yet. He turned around in time to see Charlie and Eddie pull the hose through the door. Five were out safe. Only one left.

Amelia and Ridge leaned over, hands on their knees, panting. Charlie and Eddie had their hose on the outside, battling alongside Zack and Jayson without needing guidance.

Macon rechecked the TIC. Bryce should crest the exit any moment. Except Bryce's heat dot wasn't moving.

"Crawford!" Macon radioed. "Get out."

The fire popped and roared while the gush of the water spray hammered the building, yet no other sound filled his ears.

Amelia straightened and her eyes widened. Macon predicted what she was about to do a second before she rushed toward the door.

Macon beat her there. "Hold up."

She was worn, and he was fresh. It wasn't about a power struggle here but who was the right firefighter for this moment.

And this time, it was Macon. "Guide me to him."

He waited for her to argue, but relief washed over her face. "Yes, Chief."

He pulled on his face shield. He wanted to ask her if Natalie was all right, but there wasn't time.

Based on the smoke color curling from the roof, if he didn't move now, Bryce wasn't coming out alive.

31

"Easy there." A man's voice broke through Natalie's spell of dizziness. Another wave of pain crashed right behind it. She bit back a moan and reached for her head. Her fingers landed on a bandage covering her wound.

"Slowly," the voice commanded again.

Not her kidnapper, so that was a win. This voice sounded soothing.

She forced her eyes open and found bright lights directly over her. No smoke. No burning walls around her. Just medical supplies. She was in an ambulance. Through the open back doors, the night sky was filled with flashing red and blue lights, and flames. So many flames.

"The fire—"

"Shh. You're safe."

She blinked. It wasn't the man who'd terrorized her or Macon only inches from her face. Trace shone a flashlight into her eyes.

The sprinklers had worked. Or God had performed a miracle for her. Both, probably.

She reached for her cut arm. Another bandage. She

turned her head. Something tightened around her cheeks and nose. Her fingers crawled up her face and grabbed ahold of tubes.

"Better leave that be." Another male voice came from beside her. Izan. "Oxygen is your friend."

Trace moved his flashlight to shine on one of the wounds on her forehead. But not the bandaged ones from tonight. Her past ones. Ones she didn't need to hide.

"Those aren't from this." She gulped for her next breath. Fresh air hit her lungs. So much she'd taken for granted.

Izan handed her a cup of water. Her hands shook, but she chugged it down. As she tipped it back for more, he gave her a stern expression. "Let's go slow."

The water cleared the chaos from her mind. There was no time for slow. She needed to warn the police of where she'd sent that man to make sure Joey was safe. Tosha, Mrs. Cunningham, and Peter too.

She looked past Izan into the flames and firefighters running around. She wished Macon was somewhere she could see him. "Macon—"

"The chief is busy with the fire." Izan's gaze went to Trace, who grimaced.

Something wasn't right.

Trace leaned in closer to her old burns and blocked her view of outside.

Natalie batted him away. She ignored the pain and scooted toward the end of the gurney she sat on. "Those are old wounds." The past that kept clawing its way toward the future she was ready to fight for. "I need to get up."

"Whoa, hold up." Izan came to the end of the gurney. "There are some fresh wounds too. We've bandaged you, but you need to get fully checked. You're also probably dehydrated and have smoke—"

She tore the oxygen mask off her face. "The man who did

this is heading up to Allen's barn. I've got to give the information to the police."

Izan glanced over his shoulder, and when he did, Natalie removed the oxygen mask from over her head and slid the rest of the way off the gurney.

She slid onto the step, but Trace caught her good arm. Instead of stopping her, he held out his hands to help her.

She bit the inside of her cheek to hide the wince from the throbbing that coursed through her. "Thank you."

"Promise you'll stay right by me." Trace gave her a glare. "Give your info, and then you get checked out. Fully."

Natalie answered by tightening her grip on his offered arm. Her head and cut ached less than her hip. They must have put numbing ointment on the bandages. Her lungs battled for each draw of air. Only five steps and her body panted like she'd run a mile.

"Get back in the ambulance." Trace frowned. "I can run and get one of the officers."

"I'll make it," she huffed.

The blue and red lights brightened. They finally rounded the first police car, and she spotted Lieutenant Basuto. His gaze hardened when he spotted them. "The victim is walking around, Bently? Really?"

She held up her hand. "He said he was Joey Johnson's biological father—" Her lungs pinched, but she kept going. "He's the one who took me. I sent him to Allen's horse barn. Hopefully, you'll find him there. But Joey is in temporary foster care at the Cunninghams'. You need to get someone there and keep them safe."

Natalie gasped. "The man wants him. He told me he killed Angelina Johnson, Angie. Her accident wasn't a suicide."

Something clogged up her lungs. Trace steadied her as she hunched over and coughed. When she could breathe once more, she glanced around.

Fire hoses were teamed on the building, two great arcs of water spraying the flames, the firefighters working in pairs.

The flames arched over the building, the entire shop practically engulfed, smoke pouring out of the windows, the door.

She'd be dead if she were still inside.

She glanced around. No Macon. Had he not come because of his probation? But Izan had said he was busy fighting the fire.

She sagged, and Trace widened his stance beside her.

"I'll get men enroute to Allen Frees's house." Lieutenant Basuto grabbed his walkie and gave directions. He paused and spun back to her. "Natalie, I'm sorry life keeps throwing curve balls. Rest up and get checked out, but I'll need to take your statement while it's fresh." He lifted his hand as if to lay it on her shoulder, but apparently thought better of it.

In the flashing lights, she noticed why. Blood stained her shirt sleeve. Her pants were still a little damp from the bathroom flood.

Trace led her back to the ambulance.

"Do you have your phone?" Natalie asked. "In case the lieutenant doesn't let Allen know what's coming toward his barn. I'm ninety-nine percent sure he won't be there, but I can't chance it."

As Trace's free hand went to his pocket, he said, "Do you have his number memorized?"

Natalie frowned. Allen's number ended with a three, or maybe a two?

They walked past a motionless Amelia, whose attention was glued to the TIC. She held her walkie only inches from her mouth. A statue of an active firefighter except for her furrowed eyebrows. "Come on. Come on."

Why was she acting as chief? Where was Macon—

Oh. No.

"Amelia?" Natalie swerved away from Trace, but he held on tight and veered with her.

Trace motioned toward Izan. "We should get you back to the bus."

"No." She ran up to Amelia, hoping she was wrong. Please—because one look at the inferno and...*No*. "What's going on, Lieutenant?"

Amelia didn't have to say it. Natalie's gaze searched each firefighter. Eddie and Charlie manned one hose. Jayson had teamed up with Zack. Ridge ran back from the truck. She counted again. Two were missing.

Bryce and Macon.

Natalie whipped around and faced the fire. Numbness dulled the pain and seeped into her fingers. Her legs. She wobbled.

"Macon?"

Amelia leaned the TIC in front of Natalie. "They're so close. See."

So close to what? Escape? Or so close to disaster?

"There." Ridge pointed over Amelia's shoulder.

Natalie blinked and saw two images on the screen. They were practically on top of one another, which probably meant one was carrying the other.

Which one was Macon?

Amelia spoke into her walkie. "You're right on him, Chief."

Amelia had called Macon *Chief*. Interesting. Except, "Why isn't he answering?"

Trace stared at the doorway, tapping one hand on his leg. Like he was trying to convince himself to stay put. "He's probably busy helping Bryce."

Amelia glanced at the EMT. "He ordered us out, Bently."

"C'mon, Chief," Ridge said.

"They're both coming this way." Amelia reattached her radio to her uniform. "They're going to make it."

Natalie squeezed Trace's hand on her arm.

Before Macon or Bryce appeared at the door, a thick smoke cloud drifted out of the building—

"Chief!" Amelia yelled, looking up.

An explosion shook the air, thundering into the night. The ground rumbled beneath her, and Natalie fell.

"Get down!"

Something was pressed on top of her, but this time, it wasn't burning debris. She lifted her head and found the something on her was actually a *someone*. Trace shielded her.

"I'm fine—I'm fine!" She pushed him away, and he rolled off her.

The fire had plumed, now lighting nearby trees.

"Get water on those trees!" Amelia yelled, running for the building. She still carried the TIC.

But the doorway that Macon and Bryce had been racing toward was gone, flames roiling out of it.

They were gone.

Natalie's legs buckled.

Trace barely caught her. Lowered her to the ground as she stared, everything in her hollow.

Zack and Jayson aimed their hose on the newest flames. Ridge ran toward them.

Tears swam in her eyes.

There was no way anyone could be in the building and survive.

Two lives taken way too soon. All because of one man's evil decisions.

Now she would never get to approve Macon's crew. She would never get to tell him that she did care for him.

No, that she was falling in love with the man who saw her weaknesses and kept by her side anyway.

She drew up her knees to her chest. *Lord, I need Your help getting through this.*

Someone yelled. Natalie looked up.

Amelia started for the fire in a run. Ridge pointed his hose at the burning debris. Natalie shielded her eyes. Did that piece of wood move?

Trace started to move away from her, but Natalie stopped him with a hand on his arm. "I know you want to help, but you'll just get hurt. You need gear."

But yeah, she wanted to run too when Amelia and the rest of the crew shoved off the door and metal pieces.

Natalie was on her feet beside Trace when she heard, "They're here!"

Two still bodies lay on the ground.

"Macon!" Natalie shouted, but the flames and spray of water overpowered her voice.

Trace's hand tightened on *her* arm.

Jayson broke off his position to aid Amelia. The two of them hauled Bryce on a backboard to the ambulance. As Ridge raced to his chief, Macon twisted and sat up.

Natalie pressed her hand to her chest.

Ridge got under Macon's shoulder. Amelia ran back to them. She mirrored his actions on Macon's other side.

They moved him to the ambulance.

Natalie took off toward them. Trace beside her.

Bryce had taken her space in the ambulance. Trace climbed in, and he and Izan set up his care, moving around each other in a rhythm.

Natalie stood behind them. Out of the way.

"Get his gear off him," Macon hollered with a rasp as he leaned against the ambulance.

His helmet was missing, and his turnout gear was now blackened. Macon turned toward Amelia, grabbing her arm. "Is Natalie already on the way to the hospital?"

Amelia just stared at Bryce, unmoving.

Natalie stepped forward. "I'm here."

He spun around. Blood dripped from somewhere on his head. It was hard to tell where the cut was. He was covered in soot. He blinked. His eyes soaked up her every movement as he met her halfway.

He opened his arms, and she collapsed into him. She couldn't hear his heartbeat through his layers of gear. Did that mean this was only a dream?

She pulled back and put her hands on his cheeks. His five-o'clock stubble scratched her palm. This wasn't a dream. It wasn't the past either. It was the future she'd been scared to dream of.

Macon lowered his forehead to hers. "Going into that fire without knowing if you were alive was one of the hardest things I've ever had to do."

Instead of letting her words explain all that flowed through her, Natalie rose on her tiptoes and planted her lips on his.

There would be time to talk about what had happened in the past. Right now, she let her feelings do the talking. Because she was ready to start thinking about the future.

He tugged her tighter against him, and she'd never felt like she belonged anywhere more than she did right here. Right now.

"Chief!"

Macon pulled away, and Amelia had zeroed in on Macon.

Natalie stepped in front of Macon, separating Amelia from the man she had more than likely been trying to get replaced.

Natalie wouldn't let Macon take the fall for their kiss. "Amelia, Macon and I—"

Amelia shook her head and held up her radio. "Chief Barnes says they have Spencer Brooks surrounded in a standoff."

Her eyes went from Macon back to Natalie. "But they can't find the boy."

32

Macon's entire body buzzed underneath his turnout gear. Or maybe it was only his heartbeat. When he had located Bryce covered by a burning beam, he'd wondered if God might only allow Macon to survive so he could endure what Houston had lived through. But in that moment, it had been about saving Bryce regardless of what happened to Macon.

Amelia looked at him. "What do you want to do, Chief?"

Macon rubbed his palm along his head. Was his title coming from Amelia's mouth? Maybe he'd hit the ground harder than he thought. The ringing in his ears didn't help, but based on Amelia's expression, she hadn't misspoken.

Natalie turned to him. She was safe. He wanted nothing else but to draw her back into his arms. But instead of this being over, a child was in danger. "How does Brooks have Joey?"

Amelia grimaced and looked at Macon. "I'm sorry, I don't know. It was difficult to hear exactly on the radio."

Something vibrated his leg. Through all the heat and flames, apparently his phone still worked. He took off his turnout gear as fast as he'd put it on and reached into his gym shorts pocket, but it was too late. He'd missed the call.

Missed five calls. Three from Frees, and two from Conroy.

Macon hit Call Back.

"Did you find Brooks?" Macon asked.

Conroy spoke at the same time. "Did you find Natalie?"

Macon locked eyes with Natalie. "She's safe."

"Can I talk to her?"

"Here." Macon handed his phone to her.

Natalie's hands shook, and he wrapped his soot-covered fingers around hers.

"Hello...do you need me to..." Natalie put her finger in her other ear. "Say again." She swayed on her feet and Macon caught her.

He rubbed his hands along her arms, and she shut her eyes. He searched for his EMTs, but the ambulance had closed its doors.

Was Bryce in that bad a shape? But if he were, wouldn't they be heading to the hospital?

He'd barely had that thought when the lights came on and the ambulance pulled away. Izan wasted no time picking up speed.

Every firefighter and Natalie watched them leave, and Macon said a silent prayer for his rescue lieutenant.

"Correct. Yes. Well...I...no, that's not good." Natalie frowned. "Okay. Thanks, Conroy." Natalie handed the phone back to Macon.

"So?" Amelia prompted, but without the disapproving glare this time.

"They have Brooks surrounded at Allen's barn. But when the other officers went to check on Joey at the foster house"—Natalie met Macon's gaze—"he wasn't there."

"So, they think he's somewhere at the barn?" Amelia asked.

Natalie tucked a piece of hair behind her ear. "Mrs.

Cunningham found a note in Joey's backpack. I guess Brooks had communicated with him, asking Joey to meet up. It said if he refused to meet, he'd hurt everyone around him. Like he did his mom."

The look Natalie sent his way simply stripped him.

"If the cops don't know where he is, then there's a chance Joey is at the arranged meeting place, right? Or on his way there. Perhaps Brooks hadn't caught up with him yet," Macon said.

Natalie shook her head. "He acted like he didn't know exactly where Joey was. Had been going through my notes. I think Joey ran away. If someone threatened to hurt the people around him, I think he'd try to be by himself. He's a thoughtful kid, and Brooks killed his mom. He must be out of his mind with grief."

"Okay. If Joey's not with him, where would Joey go?" Where would Macon have gone as a kid?

He probably would have headed to the ballfield dugout. "Does he play any sports or—"

"Or have a clubhouse or treehouse?" Amelia chimed in. "Something familiar. A safe place."

"His house." Natalie grabbed on to Macon's T-shirt. "He would go to his home. His closet."

"His closet?" Amelia frowned. "This is the kid with the burnt house, correct?"

"It might be the safest place that he can think of with no one around."

"But he can't be in that house. It's not safe. And besides, there may not be a closet to hide in." Amelia stole the phone out of Natalie's hand. "We have to call Barnes to send someone over there before he goes inside."

"I don't want Barnes sending one of his men inside an unsafe structure." Macon held Amelia's gaze. "I need you to take charge here. Can you do that? I know you can handle the crew. Get the fire put out and this place cleaned up."

For the first time, Amelia looked haunted. "I should have noticed that Crawford wasn't moving."

Macon put his hands on Amelia's shoulders. "When could you have done that? When you were carrying Natalie out to safety? It was no one's fault. This is the job we do."

She didn't appear convinced.

"I'm sure we'll get the full details out of Crawford later, but my guess is something fell on his head and disoriented him. Then he got trapped. This isn't your burden to carry, Lieutenant."

And just like that, he saw it. A burden lifted. *Mickey's* burden. That's what she'd needed.

Healing. Forgiveness. Just like everybody else.

She nodded, took a breath. "It would be an honor, Chief."

The lieutenant swung her attention to the dwindling flames inside the building, which were more than manageable for one squad, let alone two. They could get this done.

He called Conroy and asked his opinion about the plan to head to Peter's house in case Joey had gone there. Conroy agreed that Macon was the best one to search the unstable structure.

After he hung up, Macon took in Natalie's condition. Her old burn scars were visible beneath her mussed hair. She had a bandage on her arm and two butterfly bandage strips on the side of her head. He'd have to commend Trace and Izan for bandaging Natalie up so quickly.

"You coming with me, or am I swinging by the hospital to drop you off on the way?"

Natalie's smile was small, but it was everything to him. "I thought I might have to win an argument in order to come along."

She wasn't the kind to rest if there was work to do. Much like himself. But together they were stronger.

"Come on. But promise you'll get fully checked out as soon as we find Joey." He motioned toward his command vehicle. "If Joey is there, he might need help dealing with things. Talking things out. You're the best at that."

Natalie dropped her gaze and worry creased her brow. The opposite effect he'd meant for his words. "I'm not so sure anymore." She went to the other side of the command vehicle and hopped in.

He shoved his jacket into the back of the truck. "I'm sure enough for the both of us. He knows you."

Macon closed the door and started the truck. She had her head turned toward her window. Macon pulled out quick, lights and sirens. Had she not heard him?

He rested his hand on her leg, and she put her hand over his as he drove as fast as he could safely. "I knew Leon. I wasn't enough for him."

He looked at her.

She cleared her throat. "Joey's house is off Wellington. The subdivision by the purple-colored building."

She might know Joey's house location, but she wasn't correct about her comment.

"Natalie, when I was in the air vent listening, you were calm. So professional." He glanced at her. "The man had a gun. He could have shot you, or me, or anyone. Rational thinking doesn't always prevail, but you're a great counselor. I was wrong about therapists. They are useful and needed. You help people. And you are enough. For Joey and..." He took a breath. "For me."

She stared at him. "No. It's God who is enough."

"You're right." God was enough. "But He does use us." Houston had said how God even used the burns to point his brother to Christ.

His headlights bounced off a purple building, and he turned into the subdivision. It wasn't hard to spot the caution-taped house. He pulled up to the driveway and left his truck lights flashing. Maybe Joey would see them and know he had protection.

Natalie hopped onto the sidewalk with a grunt. "Joey!"

Macon grabbed his helmet and flashlight. Natalie ducked under the caution tape, and he spotted her wince at the movement.

"Wait, Natalie!"

She slowed, and he jogged toward her. He handed over his phone. "Stay out here. If something happens, call Patterson. Not dispatch. She'll get here faster."

"I want to come with you."

"The structure isn't safe. Stay here, please." He wiggled the phone. "I'll be able to think clearer if you're out here. I only have one helmet in the truck." He shone the flashlight around the burnt edges of the missing section of roof. "Let me see if he's in there first. Then we'll worry about how you can talk to him if he needs it."

She took the phone. Her blue eyes widened enough the moon reflected off them. She took in the structure of the house like there would be a quiz later. "What if the stairs are missing?"

"Then he probably didn't make it up to his closet. He could be downstairs."

She lifted herself up and gave him a quick kiss. "Come back to me."

"Absolutely."

The first room of the house appeared stable. Ash covered the floors and the furniture. Moonlight drifted inside a hole near the far portion of the wall.

The floor creaked but didn't groan beneath him. Papers and books on the dining room table had been eaten by the heat and flames. What looked like a briefcase had been opened. Not only was it wiped clean, but the contents were oddly untouched by the fire.

"That's my briefcase."

Macon whipped around to shine his light on Natalie's face. "Thought you were staying outside."

She pointed at the doorframe. "I am outside. Technically."

"Outside. Not on the porch." He closed the briefcase, crossed the room, and handed it over to Natalie. "Please."

She rubbed her fingers over its leather. Soot stained her cheeks. "How are the stairs? Is Joey here?"

"I'm heading up there now."

"Right." She hooked her thumb over her shoulder. "I'm backing up."

When she was back on the grass, Macon found the stairs. He shone his light up and down. The ceiling was coated black, but a trail of small footsteps headed up. No discarded shoes this time. "Joey, it's Fire Chief James."

"And Ms. Natalie," she yelled from outside.

"And Ms. Natalie." Macon tested the first step, and a bird flew down at him.

He sidestepped and landed on steps two and three. Both held his weight.

With no other creatures lurking, he reached the bedroom he thought was the one where he'd had to push over a loaded bookcase. The bookcase wasn't where he'd left it on the floor. It had been shoved over to the front of the closet. The books, however, were all missing.

"Joey?" He aimed his flashlight on the once-hidden closet door.

It opened much easier than last time. "Joey?"

A scream resounded off the walls, and a swinging baseball bat knocked the flashlight from Macon's hand. It hit the floor and lit the legs of a terrified boy.

Another swing collided with Macon's helmet.

He stumbled back, wincing. "Hey, buddy. It's okay."

In the dim light, Macon reached for control of the bat. Joey screamed again. "Let me go! Let me go!"

Macon half expected Natalie to race up the stairs and join them in the room. He pulled the bat from the kid's hands.

The flashlight spun around on the floor, highlighting Joey's closed eyes and headphones on his ears. Macon yanked them off. "Joey, it's Chief James. The fire chief."

The boy struggled. Macon wrapped his arms around Joey. "It's okay. It's okay."

"Macon!" Natalie's voice sounded much too close.

"Stop, Natalie. We're coming out."

"Ms. Natalie?" Joey shouted, and Macon grabbed the flashlight from the floor. He lifted it so they could both see each other. The light sprinkled behind Joey and revealed where all the books had gone. Joey had apparently used them to block in the other side of the closet. The shoes once on the stairs were shoved at the top of the book pile.

"It's okay. You're safe."

Natalie called out again. "Joey, it's okay!"

The kid's breaths huffed out like he was exhausted. "Ms. Natalie's here?"

"She is, and if we don't hurry down, she's going to come up here. It's not safe."

"I know." Joey shook his head. "She can't come up. He said he would hurt them." He pressed his lips together and tears filled his eyes.

Macon squatted in front of him. "Did someone tell you they'd hurt your family?"

Joey wiped at his cheeks. Moisture remained on his freckles. "Like he did my mom." He sniffed. "Anyone around me. But no one can hurt superheroes, right?" The boy looked Macon right in the eyes. "Can I stay with you?"

Once upon a time, he would have loved to be compared to a superhero, but now, he wasn't after saving himself.

But for Joey's sake… "Let's get outside with Natalie, and we'll get it figured out."

This time down the steps, the boy walked right beside Macon.

Outside, Natalie waited with open arms, and Joey launched himself at her. She caught him. Then held him. "I'm so glad you're safe."

Joey wiped his wet cheek on Natalie's shirt and grabbed her hand. He then took ahold of Macon's with his free one. "He's a superhero, isn't he, Ms. Natalie?"

Natalie reached out her hand and caught Macon's. "He's a hero all right."

Macon nodded. "Ms. Natalie's the hero. We wouldn't have known where to find you, but she knew right where you'd be."

"Macon, no. I'm not a hero."

Joey frowned at her. "My teacher says heroes are people who help. And you always brought me special pretzels when me or dad were having a bad day. That's helping. That's being like a hero."

Macon gave her a told-you-so look.

Joey's face started to crumple then. "I want to go see my dad. My real one. No matter what that other one said. He's not my dad."

"He's not going to be taking you anywhere." Natalie engulfed Joey in another hug. "However, you can't be leaving Mrs. Cunningham's house. She's very worried about you. And I'm sure Benjamin is too."

Joey's shoulders drooped. "I didn't want anyone to get hurt because of me."

Macon understood that feeling. "Sometimes it's better if we allow the people around us to help."

As if on cue, flashes of blue light filled the air beside his command vehicle's red.

Natalie wrinkled her nose. "I sort of called the cavalry when I heard the screams."

"Can I ride in the police car?" Joey let go of their hands and ran toward the road.

"Stay on the grass, Joey."

Macon circled his arm around Natalie. The spot on his bicep where Joey had nailed him with the baseball bat twinged. "Hey, Natalie."

She nestled into his side. "Yeah?"

"When this is all over, remind me to ask Peter if Joey wants to play rec baseball."

Natalie smiled as Truck 14 rumbled toward them.

"You really did call the cavalry." A truck pulled in right behind the fire truck, and Macon's back stiffened.

Allen. The boss who had sent him on probation.

Yeah. Macon needed another miracle.

33

It was now or never. And unfortunately, never wasn't an option. Natalie sat in one of the folding chairs in the bay of the fire station.

She pressed Macon's phone to her ear. There was no easy way to tell Dean what had happened. But hiding helped no one.

She took in a deep breath. "And…we kissed…more than once. But only after I'd made my decision about the evaluation, and I made it clear that was a mistake."

Silence hummed over the phone and across the near-empty fire station bays. Only the command truck and Ambo 21 had returned to Eastside so far tonight.

After saying goodnight to a reunited Joey and Mrs. Cunningham, Natalie had talked Macon into taking her to the firehouse instead of the hospital. She'd only won the argument since all her wounds had been cleaned in the ambulance. He needed to be waiting for his crew, not beside her hospital bed.

She squeezed her eyes shut. "And if you have to let me go from the Ridgeman Center because of my unprofessionalism, I understand. However, even if that hadn't happened, especially after tonight, I believe Macon and his crew—"

"Natalie." Dean's voice rose. "I've only heard bits and rumors so far about the evening and even this afternoon."

Natalie dug her fingers into the blanket on her lap and held her breath.

"But I couldn't be prouder to have you as one of our counselors. Yes, we'll need to address your relationship with Macon, after you've had time to rest and cope with what you went through. But I've been looking over everything you've turned in about the firefighters so far. I trust your work. No, Mr. King...wait!" There was a noise and then Dean was back. "Natalie, I'm sorry. I need to take care of this."

"Duty calls."

"In a couple of days, we'll talk. Until then, rest. Boss's orders."

She ended the call to find Macon holding out a plate. The sight of two perfectly browned grilled cheese sandwiches made her stomach growl—and her eyes fill with tears. The last day she'd spent with her mother, they had made grilled cheese for lunch.

Sometimes it was the little things that triggered reminiscences, and other times the memories hit her like a wrecking ball.

She leaned back. Her hip pressed against the backrest of the chair and she grimaced.

Macon's brow knitted together as he knelt before her. "Are you sure you don't want me to take you to the hospital?"

She smiled. "I'll be fine." This time, her words weren't hiding. She would be okay. "Remember, you already had Trace and Izan recheck me after they dropped off Bryce at the hospital."

The only thing left to do was to heal. Physically and mentally. Spiritually.

And after talking to Dean, she was already feeling a little better. Macon slid onto the seat on her other side and took a bite of his own sandwich. "Sorry, I couldn't find much in the fridge for you to eat."

He had been in the kitchen for a while, but people dealt with stress differently. Izan had secluded himself in the ambulance, checking supplies. Trace was in the weight room. She had thought it best to write down anything she remembered about today's events, especially since Conroy would eventually need her complete statement.

Macon had been quiet. And apparently, resourceful.

"Thank you." She made herself take a bite. "This is good."

"Just don't look on the backside of your sandwich." He twisted his own sandwich and revealed a blackened crust.

She peeked at the back of hers, but he'd given her the better sandwich.

He'd been attuned to all her needs even before she had known them. He'd already gotten her his phone and a water.

She wiped a crumb off the blanket on her lap—another thing Macon had been thoughtful about since they'd arrived at the station from the Cunninghams' house.

He hadn't said much since Allen told him they'd meet up at Macon's office for another discussion.

She kept praying her cousin would change his mind about Macon's job.

Swallowing the last of her food, she picked up her briefcase from the chair beside her and combed through the belongings she'd assumed were lost in the fire at Peter's house. She flipped through each file. But Peter's original file wasn't there.

"What's wrong?" Macon turned toward her.

"I know I had one of Peter Johnson's files in here when I went to his house." She frowned. "When I redid his file, that also went missing from my office, and then at my house, the files there were on the ground."

Macon clenched his jaw. "Brooks?"

She closed her briefcase and hugged it to her chest. "He'd been after information about Joey. He could have even been watching Peter's house the day of the fire. If that was the case, the fire was—"

"A blessing in disguise." Macon leaned his shoulder against hers. "Without it, Brooks could have taken Joey."

The last bay door opened, and Truck 14 pulled in. Finally back from cleaning up at the welding shop.

Amelia hopped out and jogged toward them. "Anything?"

Macon shook his head. "Bryce's parents and his sister are waiting at the hospital to hear word. They'll call if there's an update."

Ridge came up beside Amelia. "We'll recharge our gear and park at the hospital."

"Better not," Macon said. "I talked to Logan. He thinks our nervous energy wouldn't be helpful to his parents or sister. And as much as I want to be there too, I agree."

Amelia opened her mouth but simply crossed her arms.

"Why don't you guys get yourselves a sandwich? There's a few left in the kitchen. They may be half burnt and cold, but..." Macon shook his head. "Never mind, let me order in from Backdraft. Everyone's worked so hard. I could never repay you for what you did tonight."

"I need to pay." Natalie rested her palm on her chest. "Seriously. Thank you."

Amelia shook her head at Natalie and pushed back her shoulders. "We don't require special treatment for doing our jobs, Chief."

She called him *Chief* again. Natalie sent a grin in Macon's direction.

After Amelia walked away and grabbed her gear from the truck, Ridge leaned beside Macon. "One day I'm going to be your lieutenant, and I can promise you I'll take you up on any food you want to order, Chief."

Macon offered Ridge a half smile. "Sounds good."

Zack rubbed his belly. "Burnt and cold. Just how Grandma used to serve it."

Ridge slung his arm over Zack's shoulder. "Let me show you how it's done." He steered him toward the kitchen. "First you peel apart two separate half-burnt sandwiches. Then you put back together the two good sides—"

Macon's phone interrupted the explanation, the sound echoing off the arched ceiling. Before he could pull it out of his pocket, Ridge and Zack moved in.

Logan's name lit up the screen.

Amelia ran over. "Answer it."

Natalie placed her hand on Macon's knee. He laced his fingers with hers while he answered the phone with his other.

"Yeah?" Macon stared at his shoes. "I see."

Natalie couldn't get a read on his face.

"I'll let you know." He paused. "Okay, thanks." Macon set his phone on his leg and swallowed. Not even Amelia rushed him.

As Macon squeezed Natalie's fingers, he lifted his head. "Logan's on his way to the airport in Australia, but he got word from his mother already. Miraculously, Bryce sustained no burns, but there is a problem with his leg. Apparently, Bently and Collins need medals for their quick work. And according to a well-medicated Crawford, the doctor is wrong—he won't need eight weeks to recover. And he'll be in bright and early tomorrow morning."

Amelia rapidly blinked at the wall.

Ridge snapped his fingers and hit his palm with his fist. He released a low whistle. "Honestly, I've never been that scared."

Zack's grin fell. "Thought it was Mickey all over again." He ran his hand through his hair. "But I knew whatever happened"—his focus bounced from Macon to Ridge to Amelia—"we'd get through it. Together."

Ridge patted Zack on the back. "Because we're a family."

Amelia sniffed.

Natalie placed her other hand on top of Macon's arm. They had finally become a team. Or, like Zack had said, a family.

A family wasn't without hardships, but a healthy one worked as a unit.

Any of her professional concerns about the crew were erased.

Each new call from dispatch would bring new emotions. Hurdles of life to jump through. They would each deal with Bryce's close call in different but healthy ways, whether that meant admitting to being afraid, or the hope of working together for a long time to come. Amelia's show of emotion was more than okay. It was real. These firefighters weren't robots who swept everything away until stress piled up and they exploded.

They had learned to communicate.

Amelia cleared her throat. "I'll have the report on your desk as soon as I can. There were no rekindling spots tonight. Everything was squared away at the welding shop."

"If it takes a day or two, that's fine. Give yourselves some grace, but don't skip the important stuff."

Ridge took off for the hallway. "Important stuff, like getting the best grilled cheese."

Zack sprinted after him until Amelia yelled, "Stop!"

Ridge and Zack gave her a dirty look but listened to their lieutenant without a snarky comment.

A rare grin crossed Amelia's face before she raced past the boys. "Last one there has toilet duty."

Macon's laugh rumbled in his chest, and it was a welcome sound.

His arm brushed up against Natalie's, and she shivered.

He let go of her hand and moved the blanket that had drifted to the ground back to cover her lap. "You're cold."

She took off the blanket and draped it over the chair with her briefcase. "I'm not cold." She covered a yawn.

"But you are tired. Do you want me to take you home?" He shook his head. "I'd have to call Barnes. They may not be finished with your house. You're welcome to stay here in the girls' bunk room. Or I could take you to Allen's or Hope Mansion."

It felt like déjà vu. The spark from Macon's touch. His thoughtfulness. Except this time around, she understood his kindness wasn't based on trying to get her to sign off on his crew. It was the real Macon.

She shrugged. "I'll stay anywhere that has a clean bed and a pen."

Macon bent down in front of her and inspected her eyes. He held out his finger and moved it horizontally. His face pulled in compassion and worry. "A pen? You sure Bently and Collins checked you over fully?"

She batted away his finger. "I promise I don't have a concussion."

Natalie rose. She rested her palms on his shoulders. Shoulders that were far better at handling life's heavy burdens than she'd originally assumed. Plus he'd learned he wasn't required to be a superhero. "I need a pen to sign off on your evaluation."

Instead of leading her straight to his office, he crossed his arms. "Is it wise to sign now? When there are feelings...unless for you there aren't." His gaze drank her in, but she saw the edge of worry in his eyes.

She squeezed those strong shoulders. "Feelings are definitely involved, but I'm not signing off on your paperwork because I'd like to start a different kind of relationship with you."

Macon's shoulders drooped underneath her touch. "Oh."

She bent her head and caught his lowered gaze. "I'm doing it because you and your crew proved back at the training house incident that you can work as a team and deal with stress. Everything you firefighters are up against every single day. Though the evaluation will now also need Dean's signature due to my feelings for a certain fire chief."

He grinned. Natalie leaned her cheek against his chest, but when her bandage touched his T-shirt, she jerked back. "Ouch."

He inspected her face and her wound. "I'm so sorry, Natalie."

"Me too." But Jesus loved her despite her wounds and brokenness. She no longer had to hide her own pain but trust the One who had endured everything for her.

Macon pushed a section of her hair gently behind her ear. "I'm here for you."

"Good." She smiled.

He shifted his feet. "Should I wait to kiss you again until after you and Dean sign everything? I don't want to jump the gun when we're so close."

Her arms wound around his neck. Macon tucked her tight against him. She rose on her toes as Macon dipped his head.

Their lips met. Soft yet firm. A spark ignited in her stomach. One she was no longer afraid of. How had she ever thought she could forget his kiss?

She sighed and leaned further against him. She felt him smile against her mouth before he deepened the kiss.

A throat cleared behind them.

They broke apart. Natalie expected to see Amelia, or Zack with a mouth full of grilled cheese.

Not an angry-looking Allen. Perhaps the future wasn't as bright as she'd hoped.

34

Macon fisted his empty hands. He already missed Natalie, and she'd only moved a few feet away from him, like she had after the incident with Leon. His gut clenched, and he locked his knees. No doubt this was what it felt like to be fired. Or he would soon find out.

Natalie reached over and slid her fingers around his. Ran her thumb over his skin. No matter what the next few minutes or days held, it was nice not to feel like he had to do everything on his own.

God, whatever happens, help me to remember You're in control.

Frees didn't open his mouth. He didn't ask why Macon had ignored his order and been at the welding fire. He didn't yell. He just looked at them.

"Frees." Amelia jogged toward them, a half-eaten sandwich in her hand. "Sorry to interrupt, but I've got to speak with you." She put the food behind her back as if she wasn't allowed to be caught eating. "It's urgent."

Allen wheeled his wheelchair back. "This isn't over." He pointed at Natalie and then to Macon before following Amelia out of the bay area.

Natalie bit her lip. "What if you can't be the chief anymore?" Her blue eyes watched him with something that looked like hope. "But say they let you take an open firefighter position instead? Would that be enough, or would you need to search for a higher position?"

She crossed her arms. Despite saying she wasn't cold earlier, she shivered once more. "I know that's probably not what you want. And it might prove too difficult to be under the people you previously had seniority over."

He stepped forward. "If they offered for me to stay, no matter the position, at least I'd be here."

"It'd mean Amelia bossing you."

Macon sighed. Being under Amelia wouldn't be easy, but he'd had worse bosses. Maybe he could talk Logan into applying for the chief position instead. "She's a good firefighter. Even if we don't see eye to eye on every detail, she and I share the same common goal. We both want Eastside to be the best fire station in Last Chance County."

Natalie shivered again. "You'd stay?"

He rubbed his palms along her arms. "When I first applied to be chief, I didn't know if I really wanted the job. To stay. Really, I wanted it for the wrong reasons. Then I overheard one of the committee members say they didn't actually choose me. That they wanted someone else."

"That doesn't mean you're not a great chief."

"I know that now. But back then, I wanted to prove myself to them. To Houston. To the town who I thought only ever saw me as the cancer kid or the kid with the brother he should have rescued from a fire. And then you came along."

"Macon, I'm sorry if I caused you any grief."

"I'm not. By trying to prove myself to you, I finally figured out it wasn't about me. This job. The crew. Even this station. I thought I needed to be in control. A hero to earn my way to a better future." Macon looked away. "My brother helped me see the past for what it was."

"Something you can't change?"

"It wasn't supposed to be my burden. Whether things were my fault or not. That's God's business. Forgiveness. I'm ready to look only toward the future."

"You're a natural leader, Macon. You could get another chief job somewhere else. It sounds like you'd give up too much if you stayed here." Her voice and gaze dropped.

He inched closer. "Do you want me to stick around?"

She licked her lips, and Macon had to fight not to follow the movement instead of focusing on her answer. "I'm not sure I'm worth staying at a job where you've been demoted."

He cupped her face. When his pinkie brushed her neck, she trembled. "I'd be a rookie again if it meant another date with you. I'm thinking fresh air. Actual fresh air."

Her arms draped around him. "Why would we ever hike when we could ride?"

"I didn't hate the company." He leaned closer. "What do you say? Will you go on an official date with me, Natalie?"

It didn't seem possible that they'd never been on an official date. They had spent so much time together. Having her by his side had already become a habit, one he wasn't interested in breaking.

She lifted on her tiptoes and pressed her lips to his. It was the perfect way to answer.

Until someone cleared their throat again.

Of course, it was her cousin.

Macon moved in between Natalie and Allen. "I take full responsibility for my actions earlier today. Also tonight, with my being at the fire despite you telling me otherwise. However, my crew had a tough call, and Crawford is at the hospital recovering. We do have some good news on that end. But if you request my resignation, I can have it on your desk by the end of the night."

Natalie squeezed her fingers between his, and Macon knew he wanted to stay. No matter what position that led him to. "I'd be grateful if you'd consider me potentially taking one of the open firefighter spots. Since we're technically down three men, including myself. At least temporarily. And I have a recommendation for the chief position."

Allen didn't have his hands on his wheels but crossed them over his chest. "That won't be happening."

The air in the room seemed to rush out.

This time, Natalie stepped in front of Macon. "Allen, you can't be serious. Macon was a hero. Twice today."

"Which is one of the reasons why we'd like him to keep being the chief."

Macon blinked. "You're not firing me?"

"Unofficially, no. The rumors the mayor is hearing are that you didn't follow protocol with the gunman, but you're new to the station, and the people of Last Chance County see you as a hero. No matter how you look at it, your quick actions saved lives."

Allen rested his hands on his legs. "Not only that, but someone recorded you from a nearby roof going in after Bryce. They also caught you coming out at the same time as the explosion. Your team is alive because of your swift decisions. And every one of your people in there"—he pointed to where he'd gone with Amelia—"backed you as their chief."

"Everyone?" Macon asked in disbelief.

"What do you think Lieutenant Patterson wanted to talk to me about?" Allen said. "I'll be following up with Natalie and Dean about your evaluations. We might have to extend the counseling sessions if Dean wants someone you aren't in a habit of kissing to sign off on your paperwork."

A beat, and Macon stared at Allen, glanced at Natalie, then back to Allen.

Who smiled.

"I might have told him," Natalie said.

"Not to mention I just caught you twice."

Right. He looked at Allen. "Understood. And totally doable." Macon couldn't stop his grin.

Except Natalie wasn't smiling. "I'm sorry. I know how much you hate therapy sessions."

Macon sent her a wink. "You were worth it."

"On that note"—Allen rolled his wheelchair around—"I'm heading home, and Natalie? We're so glad you're okay. Pepper and Victory were worried about you." He glanced at Macon. "I apologize for not answering the phone. I wasn't screening out your calls. I honestly didn't see them during Victory's play."

Natalie reached down and hugged her cousin. "I'm sorry I sent a crazed man to your horse barn."

"I'm just glad they caught him. I take it you don't need a ride home?"

Natalie shook her head. "I think I'm going to hang out here for a while."

After Allen said his goodbyes, Amelia came up to them. "Sir? I mean, Chief, can I talk to you?"

Macon motioned for his office, but Amelia shook her head.

"This kind of affects both of you." She glanced between Natalie and Macon. "That report? The evaluation. It was because of me."

The only sound came from Zack's voice rumbling down the hall, more than likely from the kitchen.

She lifted her head. "I didn't think you were the right person for the chief position. I complained to Allen and the committee. That was the main reason they made us do the counseling sessions. Though I didn't realize they'd make us all subject to evaluations and talk about our feelings and stuff."

Tears filled her eyes. "I blamed you for Mickey's death. I couldn't handle the pain of being responsible for losing him. I'm sorry."

"Patterson," Macon said gently, "it was an accident. And even if Mickey's death was someone's fault, we'd figure it out. Together."

Amelia wiped away a tear. "I was wrong. You are the right fit for this firehouse."

Natalie nudged her shoulder against his, and Macon closed his gaping mouth.

"Thank you, Patterson. It sounds like neither one of us wanted to talk about our feelings, but I think it was best for our crew."

Her gaze snapped back to his. "Ours?"

Macon narrowed his eyes. "Please don't tell me you're leaving Eastside."

She made a face.

"Patterson, I want us to be a team. A family. I may be the front leader, but you're a leader too."

She smiled. "A family. I'd like that very much."

"Good, because I'd hate to lose you. You're a great firefighter, Lieutenant. And speaking of our team, with Greene fired and Crawford injured, I'm going to talk to Frees about—at the minimum—hiring Logan as an emergency fill-in as rescue squad lieutenant."

Her scowl was back. "You want to hire Logan Crawford, Bryce's brother?"

He didn't know how it was possible, but her eyebrows dipped even further. Their agreement had been good while it'd lasted.

"Are you sure that's the best idea? Having two members from..."

Macon raised his brow.

Amelia pushed out a deep breath. "You know what? It's

your call who to hire. I'll try to trust your judgment...Chief James."

She stuck out her hand to Macon. Then to Natalie.

"Thanks for putting up with us, Natalie." Amelia stepped back. "You're a great therapist...and friend."

"The best." Macon smiled down at Natalie.

He was still the chief. Except now, it was for the right reasons. Who would have thought the day he'd literally almost lost his life would be the day he fully started living again?

EPILOGUE

Three weeks later, Natalie peeked into Allen's office. The team—as Macon currently referred to the crew—was out on a call. Not at all convenient for the chief ceremony that was now postponed, and yet ironic.

She snuck into the empty room, her hip no longer bothering her. She lifted the lid of the box sitting on Allen's desk beside a picture of Pepper and Victory, which reminded Natalie how Macon's desk had changed from the first day she'd seen it. Along with his files, he now had a picture of himself and Natalie horseback riding right next to the framed handkerchief with the three crosses on it.

"Hey now." Her cousin's voice made her stop.

Natalie froze. *Busted.* Goosebumps raced up her arms.

His office was cooler than she'd like, and she wore a sleeveless dress. She rubbed away her chill. Her fingers brushed over the spot where Brooks's knife had cut. The wounds and scars on her body were proof that God had not only restored her physically but also continued to heal her mentally and spiritually.

She stared down at the perfectly creased tissue paper. Not the plaque she was after.

"Put the lid down slowly and step away from the desk." He used his police officer voice. "Why don't you use your nervous energy for something good?"

As Natalie let her arms drop to her sides, she tightened her grip on the lid. She'd tried and failed at that already.

She'd sent invitations to all of Macon's family to attend today. His parents had never responded, but Houston had promised to be here. Except, even one hour after Macon's ceremony was supposed to have started, Houston hadn't arrived. And he probably wouldn't appreciate a seventh missed call. Hence her need for stealth, sneaking into her cousin's office down from Macon's.

She had even called her dad to fill the time. After forgiving him and realizing her feelings of worthlessness and abandonment might always be a struggle, she had to rest in the fact God could help them heal together. His biblical truth was the only source of true peace.

Natalie didn't meet Allen's eyes. "I'm just going to take a peek, and then I'm open to suggestions."

Allen positioned his walking forearm crutches through the door. His braced legs wobbled but got him to his desk. He may be faster in his wheelchair, yet she was thrilled to see him working hard at physical therapy. Going through the tough stuff would be rewarding for him in the end. Just like in life.

He didn't take the lid out of her hands. "Natalie, I thought you wanted to wait until the ceremony."

She shoved the lid back on the box. "You're right."

A piece of her grown-out bangs swung into her eyes, and she brushed them behind her ears. She may never go back to the hairstyle she had before her burn wounds, but hearing Macon tell her how beautiful she was inside and out, with or without bangs, helped her not be so self-conscious.

He was correct about how she'd been hiding for a long time. It was okay if her clients saw that their counselor had her own hurdles. She'd believed that she had to display this perfect life in order to help people, but she couldn't have been more wrong. God used people's weaknesses too.

Maybe especially.

Allen studied her from his seat. "How are you doing? Any triggers lately?"

"Do I need to be worried about my job?" Natalie crossed her arms. "Are you tired of the firehouse or wanting to get an office with a forest view instead?"

Allen rolled his eyes. "That answer is called avoidance. I don't have to be a therapist to ask about my favorite cousin."

"About time I reach that position. I don't know why you put your cousin Wyatt there instead of me for all those years. But yes, I'm doing—" She swallowed back the word *fine*. "I'm managing well."

Brooks had confessed to the police that he was responsible for exploding her car to scare her and breaking into the Ridgeman Center and stealing Peter's files, as well as threatening Joey and kidnapping her. He'd also confessed on record to killing Angie and explained how he had ended up with her old truck. Leon had recovered from his overdose and was now behind bars. Yet his sentence might get shortened if Leon shared who he'd scored the newest mixture of hallucinogens and PCP from that was still causing trouble around the streets of Last Chance County.

After Peter had gotten out of the hospital, he'd been adamant about not only continuing his sessions with Natalie but also adding therapy for Joey. Together, they were all dealing with what they'd been through. For an almost-seven-year-old, Joey had endured so much, and yet it was clear to her there wasn't the bitterness in him that Natalie had felt as a child—and buried.

Allen's phone chimed. "It's show time."

"They're back?" She picked up the box and hurried out, nearly running into the back of a man in the hallway.

Peter turned around.

"Hey." Natalie shuffled the box. "When did you guys get here? I'm so sorry I wasn't here to greet you."

He'd added a few more worry lines around his eyes, but his gaze sparked with a joy that hadn't been there before. "No problem." Peter smiled at the fire receptionist next to him. "Meredith has been very kind in showing us where to go."

Meredith's blush made Natalie bite her tongue. Peter's gray hair made him appear older than Meredith, but if Natalie had to guess, they weren't too far apart in age. The receptionist had never acted interested in any of the firefighters that hung around her constantly. Apparently, a veteran was more to her liking.

Joey stepped around the pair and lifted the lid on the box. "Pretzels?"

"Sorry, bud. I didn't bring any with me."

"That's okay. I don't need them. Plus, Meredith says there's gonna be cake."

"Want to go take a peek at the cake?" Natalie turned toward the conference room, and Joey kept up with her. "School going okay?"

He glanced back at his dad, who walked beside Meredith. "Some kids in my class haven't been the nicest lately. Simon makes jokes about the stuff that happened. But Dad's bringing me to a play date with Mrs. Cunningham and Benjamin this weekend. She's going to teach me how to make homemade chocolate-covered pretzels just like Mom used to make me."

Her heart tugged. If she hadn't been carrying the box, Natalie would have offered Joey a hug. No wonder the boy liked pretzels so much.

She prayed that Peter would remember the good of his

former wife and forgive the rest. It took a humble approach as a parent for someone like Peter to allow a foster parent like Mrs. Cunningham, who loved his kiddo, to remain invested in his future.

Being a family was more than blood. Peter could have gotten mad that Joey had to be placed in foster care while he was ill. Or after he got out of the hospital, when he'd been asked to show legal proof that he was Joey's guardian. Instead, he had thanked Tosha for taking Joey to such a loving home while he was healing.

In the conference room, Allen picked up a microphone off the round table in the front corner. "Ladies and Gentlemen, thank you for being so patient. The team is finishing up their checklists, and then they'll be right in to start the ceremony."

Natalie nudged Peter's arm. "Why don't you guys come on down and sit in the front with me? Meredith, you're welcome, also."

The receptionist fiddled with her fingers until Peter whispered something. Then she agreed.

Natalie set the box on the round table and took her seat beside Joey. It wasn't hard to figure out when the ceremony would begin. Clapping started as soon as the first firefighters entered the room.

Zack came in next. He clapped, chanting, "Chief. Chief. Chief."

The crew members of Truck 14, Rescue Squad 5, and Ambo 21 marched to their seats.

Finally, Macon entered. His gaze searched the room. When his eyes landed on Natalie, his face lit with a smile.

She sent him a wink. She hoped that despite her trying to get his family here for his big day, she and his fire family would be enough.

Allen tapped the microphone. "Macon, why don't you come on up front here. I hope you know how much your team respects you. And it's on this day that Last Chance County Fire Department inducts you officially as the chief of Eastside Firehouse."

The mayor stepped forward and handed Macon his official badge. "Congratulations, Chief."

Each committee member in attendance made their way forward and offered their congratulations, shaking Macon's hand.

Mr. Greene, Dave's grandpa, was the last to come up to Macon. The balding man wore a grimace on his face until he stuck out his hand. "Welcome, Chief James. Last Chance County is lucky to have you."

Macon grinned, such warmth in his eyes it made her want to tear up.

"Before we get to the cake, we have one more presentation." Allen pulled on his ear, which was the signal.

Natalie tapped Joey. "It's show time. Sure you can you handle it?"

Joey scooted his chair back. "If Chief James can carry you out of a fire, I can go up there and give him a hug."

Peter also rose. He laid his hand on Natalie's shoulder. "Thanks for letting us be a part of this."

She smiled. He'd said that to her twice already this week. He'd admitted in their last session how this gesture was something positive that he and Joey could talk about. Something good from the mess.

Joey and his father walked up beside Allen as he spoke about leadership and what it took to be a hero.

Peter lifted the plaque out of the box and held it up for the crowd. Natalie wanted to see, but her eyes swam with tears.

"So today, we'd like to introduce an award. A new tradition for our fire family at Eastside Firehouse." Allen smiled at Natalie. "One that has special meaning to my own family. It's named after my aunt, Natalie's mom. She may not have been a firefighter, but she was a leader in extraordinary conditions. We recognize Chief James as the first recipient of the Ruth Atkinson Award for excelling at the true meaning of being a hero. A brave heart set on helping others."

Natalie put her hand on her chest, and one of the crew members catcall whistled across the crowded room. Then someone bumped into her chair. "Sorry," the man whispered.

Natalie scooted up to the table, but he didn't move farther down. He sat in the chair right next to her.

The room filled with people applauding and rising to their feet. Finally, she realized who was beside her.

Houston leaned toward her. "I'm so glad I didn't miss it all."

Allen handed Macon the microphone, but Macon waved him off. The clapping stopped.

Macon sent a wink to Natalie. Then he nodded toward his crew. "Thanks, everyone. I'm grateful to be at this station, and a part of this team...our family." He lifted both of the items in his hands. "I hope to make you all proud. Leading you is an honor."

His entire crew circled Macon.

Houston turned in his chair. "Sorry I was late. And for not calling you back, Natalie. There was an emergency with one of the kids from our baseball team. Eddie asked me to go to the boy's house since he or Macon couldn't." He rubbed the back of his neck. "Anyway, I made it. Sort of. I just hope Macon knows how proud I am of him."

Macon came over, and Houston stuck out his hand. Macon took it and they pulled each other into a hug. "Congrats, man."

Macon thumped his brother's back. "Thanks for coming. It means a lot." He held up the plaque Natalie had been trying to get a peek at since Allen had ordered it.

A rich chestnut stain. The golden font glinted in the light. Macon smiled at her. "Thank you."

She went into his open arms and gave him a quick kiss.

"You deserve it." She pointed at the words she'd agreed upon with Allen.

Excelling in leadership under pressure. Bravery. A hero.

Not only had he gotten his crew to work as a team, but he'd rescued one of their own. Just like her mother had in combat.

Macon moved her finger with his to where her mother's name was engraved.

Tears sprang to her eyes.

Macon squeezed her against his side. The very place where she fit. "I'm beyond humbled. I'm glad God showed me I didn't need to be a hero but to focus my heart on what truly matters."

On You, Lord.

"Happy for you, bro," Houston said.

Macon kissed Natalie on her forehead. She didn't cringe. It no longer bothered her that he might touch her scars. Houston was helping with that, during Natalie and Macon's Bible studies.

His brother's lips twitched. "I think that's my cue to head out."

"You're leaving already?" Natalie pulled her attention from Macon. "Can't you at least take some cake with you? I got enough to feed the entire firehouse times three."

Zack paused by them. "Only three?" He backpedaled and pointed his fork at his plate. "This is my fourth piece. Should I put it back?"

Macon only shook his head at the half-eaten slice. "Do I even want to know how you've managed that much in two minutes?"

"Probably not." Zack stuffed his face with another bite. "I will neither confirm nor deny that it might have something to do with a contest and toilet duty."

Macon laughed. "Be careful or Patterson will make you run drills to work off all that sugar energy."

"Stephens!" Amelia's voice overpowered the room from the

group next to them. “You were supposed to let the chief cut his own cake.”

Zack gulped his latest bite with guilt clouding his expression. “Thought you said don’t touch his name...like the actual lettering of *Chief James* on the cake.”

Amelia folded her arms, but a smirk crossed her lips.

“You might want to leave the scene while you still can,” Macon stage-whispered.

Zack saluted his fork to Macon. “Congrats, Chief. Thanks for the cake, Mrs. Chief.”

“Stephens!” Amelia reprimanded.

“What I’d do now?”

“They’re not married.”

“Not yet.” Zack flashed his teeth at Amelia and ducked out of the room.

Macon gazed down at Natalie. They might have only had four official dates outside their moments at the fire station, but as she reached up on her toes toward the chief she’d fallen for, she knew one thing.

The hope of more to come.

WHAT HAPPENS NEXT...

Macon grinned against Natalie's goodbye kiss.

Amelia hadn't been wrong yesterday when she'd said Natalie wasn't Mrs. Chief. It was far too early to put a ring on her finger. However, the urge to forget his team watched them and deepen the kiss was only one of the many reasons Macon had started saving for a diamond. He wanted the forever kind of future with his favorite counselor.

A catcall came from behind them in the station's bay. At present, he'd have to settle for lunch and a quick kiss.

"If I hear one more whistle"—Amelia's voice rose over the boys' kissing sounds—" I'm going to get the cones out and you'll be running sprints."

Natalie's eyes twinkled as she stared up at Macon. It was quite different having Amelia on his side. Especially when she couldn't make him run.

"Macon and Natalie sitting in a tree—"

"Crawford!" Amelia's footsteps stomped somewhere by the fire truck. "I expected more out of you."

Logan poked his head out from around the fire truck.

"Come on, Amelia. Macon would be disappointed in our friendship if I didn't give him a hard time."

"Friendship or not, you better give him the respect he deserves by calling him *Chief*, and for that matter, you can call me—"

"Chief," Logan whined, "my new sister is being bossy."

"That's her way of making you feel at home," Ridge added.

Logan had fit in perfectly with the team, as Macon had prayed would be the case.

Macon kissed Natalie one more time before pulling back. "Sure I can't tempt you into taking a longer lunch?"

"I'd love to suit up again and hit the smoke house." Natalie sighed. "But I can't. Duty calls on the west side of town. The address is on my desk if it's needed."

She ran her finger across his newly pinned chief badge. He occasionally had nightmares about the night Spencer Brooks had taken her, and since Macon had admitted that to her, she'd tended to keep him updated on her daily plans. "This guy's a repeat client. Dean has his information. Afterward I'm going to check on Joey. Meet you at the horse stables at five?"

"As long as these guys get their work done."

She pointed her finger at Logan, who smirked and held up his hands. As Natalie left out the bay's open door, Logan's actual sister marched inside. Andi Crawford stared at them all with a pinched expression.

"Speaking of siblings," Logan said as if he'd read Macon's mind. He opened his arms. "Come in here, sis. My favorite Westside Firehouse EMT. Don't be mad. I was gonna take the trash out before I left."

Amelia rolled her eyes.

But Andi Crawford didn't accept the offered hug from Logan. She didn't even blink his way. Instead of going to her brother, she came all the way over and stood toe to toe with Macon. "I need to talk to you."

Logan chuckled. "You're too little, too late, little sis. He's already got a woman."

Andi fired a scowl at Logan that rivaled Amelia's death glares toward Macon only a few weeks ago.

Andi shuffled her feet. "Please, Chief. Can I talk to you in your office? I can wait, if now's not an ideal time."

There was a plea in her eyes that Macon couldn't quite figure out. He motioned for her to head down the hall.

Once inside his office, Macon gestured to the two chairs in front of his desk.

She leaned on the back of one. "I want a shot at the open position on your crew."

Macon blinked. "I don't have any ambulance spots open. You're a great EMT, but I already have all my shifts covered."

"No, I mean on your firefighting crew."

His mouth opened. "Andi..."

"I can be a fantastic firefighter. I only need a chance. Please."

Macon was glad he was close to his desk. "You want to be a firefighter? You understand there's training involved? You really want to do that with your brothers watching?"

"I'm all set, and I don't care who is watching." Andi lifted her chin. "I've done all the qualifications and passed the test. I just need a shot, and yours is the only firehouse with an open slot."

Her determined expression didn't change.

He had a spot open while Bryce was healing. After that, would Logan settle for being on Truck under Amelia? Only time would tell.

Macon uncrossed his arms and picked up his phone beside the picture frames on his desk. "Hey, Meredith, will you page Amelia Patterson and Logan Crawford to come to my office, please? Thanks."

Without saying a word, Andi took a seat in one of the open chairs.

Logan was the first to enter. He raised his brow but took the seat next to his sister.

Amelia jogged in and shut the door. “Yes, Chief?” A whistle hanging around her neck swayed like a pendulum. Someone was about to do drills.

Macon took in two of the best firefighters he knew and then Andi’s determined gaze. He did need another firefighter to round out his teams. “Pending ironing out some of the finer details and approval by Frees, it seems our solution while Bryce is recovering has found us.”

Amelia stomped forward. “You can’t seriously be thinking about giving Greene another chance. I understand his grandfather was nice to you during the ceremony, but don’t fall for it.”

Macon held up his hand, and this time, Amelia stopped. “While Bryce is recovering, Logan continues as Rescue’s lieutenant, and Andi will be temporarily assigned to Truck.”

Logan pointed to her. “This Andi?” He shook his head. “No way. I know you said you wanted my help with things around here, but no.” He crossed his arms. “Sorry, sis, but you can’t be on Truck. You’re a paramedic, not a firefighter.”

Macon saw the flash of hurt on her face.

A second later it was gone, and Andi leaned into her brother’s space. “I can do this. I know I can. I just need a chance.”

Macon didn’t need a sibling argument, and Logan was gearing up.

Before he could speak, Amelia said, “Your sister wants a shot, Crawford. And I happen to have been one of her references when she applied for the EMT job. I have no reason to say no to having her on my team.”

Silence hung over the room like a cloud before a thunderstorm.

Amelia stepped forward, her game face on as she sized up Andi. "I like the idea."

"Really?" Andi blinked.

Amelia nodded. "Let's make a firefighter out of you."

"What is even happening here?" Logan scratched his head. "She's just an EMT."

Macon got the idea Andi Crawford wasn't "just" anything.

Andi turned. Not toward Logan but to him. "Chief, I won't let you down. I promise."

Macon wished Natalie were still here observing his team. For a lot of reasons. Most of them had to do with seeing her more. But right now, there was something brewing in this room, and it all centered around Andi's promise.

The same one he would make with Natalie.

A promise to do the best he could, and let God take care of the rest.

Macon sat back in his chair. "Let's do this."

A NOTE FROM MEGAN

Dear Reader,

Honestly, I wasn't sure if I wanted to write this story. Wasn't sure if I actually could. Suicide has devastated my extended family. Twice. And I know how gut wrenching the effects are on those left behind. I was afraid I wouldn't use the right words. Terrified of triggering a reader. Of making a mess of such a serious topic.

But then I realized where my hope was resting—in my own abilities. Instead of Christ. So I prayed. For the story. For you, the reader. For all. The. Things. Did it make the journey of writing easier? Nope. It was the most challenging story I've ever written to date. However, remembering that my best (and worst) is nothing without God was humbling. Yet needed. And the peace that only the Lord provides began quieting my fears of failure.

If you are like my heroine Natalie and you're left wondering why you weren't enough to live for or you constantly play out a cycle of "if only" and "what-ifs" in your mind, I only have one word of wisdom: Jesus. We may never get all the answers we seek on this earth, but the Creator of the universe cares about *us*. 1 Peter 5:7 tells us to "cast your cares on Him." He wants us to run to Him. With the good. The bad. With our brokenness.

And dearest reader, if you are struggling with depression, please seek help. You are loved. Romans 5:8 says, "While we were yet sinners, Christ died for us." Not *after* we got ourselves put together. But *before*. We aren't required to offer anything but our imperfect selves.

You and I are loved that much.

When we trust in the Lord, life doesn't magically become filled with unicorns and cotton candy. Problems are still there. Our feelings are still very real. Yet the only trustworthy thing in this world is that Christ alone provides the only true Hope.

He is the missing piece.

With love and prayers,
Megan Besing

Turn the page for a sneak peek at the next Last Chance Fire and Rescue novel, *Expired Promise*...

EXPIRED PROMISE SNEAK PEEK

LAST CHANCE FIRE AND RESCUE #3

CHAPTER 1

The scent of salt and sweat hung in the air as ATF Special Agent Jude Brooks waited, breath held, at the edge of the gated Sosa Compound. He could just catch the repetitive sound of crashing waves not more than three hundred feet beyond the cliff the massive villa perched on.

His team surrounded him, guns drawn and waiting for his go-command, but he hesitated. The op was clear. A quiet breach of the villa's perimeter, thanks to disabled security sensors and cameras. Four teams at infiltration points ready to go on his signal. His main command team focused on finding and capturing cartel leader Diego Ruiz Sosa.

Thanks to countless scenarios he'd run on paper and in his mind, the op would involve quick engagement of Sosa's security team and minimal danger to all involved. It was by-the-book perfect, but there was one piece of information he was waiting for confirmation on. He wanted to know where the tip had originated from. The one that had first alerted the San Diego ATF field office of Sosa's presence in their area.

No matter that his team's surveillance had the drug lord on camera numerous times since the tip had come in a week before. Jude didn't like open ends. They got people hurt. Best to dot your i's and cross your t's.

"Sir?" His earpiece crackled to life. The team was waiting for his signal.

"Hold."

He wiped away a bead of sweat slipping from beneath his helmet. The heavy tac gear made the warm evening temperatures seem desert-like. He had to make the call. One last check of his phone showed no reply from the agent researching the tip. A bit of a gut punch, but the info would only be a redundancy of the work he'd already done.

An untraceable call from the greater Denver, Colorado, area—a location Sosa was known to frequent for its proximity to I-70. No identification on the person who left the tip. No credible leads.

He'd run the risk assessments. He'd checked every box. The intel was credible. He could see Sosa with his own eyes. It was go time.

"All units ready," Jude subvocalized.

He did a visual check of the line. His team intermingled with SWAT, guns ready and eyes out.

"Cameras off at my command." Jude resisted the urge to clear his throat.

"Copy," came the disembodied reply.

It was now or never. No way would Jude let Diego Ruiz Sosa slip through their fingers. While the cartel leader's enterprise had been hit significantly over the last several years thanks to an informant they'd successfully embedded, the agent had been injured six months ago and opted to take the out. End the operation.

Jude couldn't blame him. The Sosa cartel spent money faster than it could move product, but that hadn't taken Sosa out of the game. It did, however, provide a perfect opportunity to catch him unaware.

"On my count." Jude flexed his fingers around the grip of his M-4 and settled his mind. "Cut cameras."

"Copy that, sir. And...we're dark."

He kept his voice low and counted off, "Three. Two. One. Go go go!"

The team rushed ahead like a tidal wave of black tactical gear. The breacher took care of the locked gates, and Jude's unit headed toward the left side of the villa. Accent lighting glowed everywhere, politely showing them the way toward their entry point.

Surveillance had reported that every night, around eight, Sosa liked to smoke a cigar on the patio overlooking the ocean. After fifteen minutes or so, he would retire inside to watch a telenovela. Sometimes with a woman, sometimes alone. Their intel said he would be alone tonight. Jude hoped that was accurate. He didn't want any collateral damage.

He paused where the edge of the house and the clear glass barrier narrowed before expanding to the patio. Jude's back pressed against the rough stucco of the house, stored heat radiating back at him, and he carefully peered around the corner.

Signaling his line of sight was clear, he made hand motions to direct his team. He would make his way straight to a rocky pillar as his cover while agents Jackson and Perry kept under the windows. He signaled for Vanessa, or "Wiley" as they called her, to hang back for cover. The minute he gave the order, he saw her anger flare.

"Jude," came her hushed whisper.

He didn't have time for this. "Wiley, channel three."

Vanessa was headstrong with a hero-complex she needed to curtail sooner rather than later. Despite what she thought, his directives weren't about gender. It was about leadership, and he needed her on their six.

Her reply was instantaneous. "Sir, I think I can—"

"I gave the order. You follow it. That's how we're playing this. Or do I need to send you out?"

She waited a beat. "Copy."

Their eyes met for a fraction of a second, and he saw the rebellion bubble beneath the surface. He'd be having a talk with her about proper conduct during an infiltration the minute they were on the other side of this.

"Unit three in position."

Jude shifted back to the window. He repeated the motion for her to stay, then clicked his mic to signal his response to Unit 3. He looked back at his agents, pointedly not holding Vanessa's gaze, then counted down with his fingers.

They rushed ahead in ducked position to clear the windows, and Jude reached the pillar without incident. His breaths came heavy now, more from anticipation than exertion. A snatched look around the pillar showed a glass-fronted view of Sosa with his feet propped up on a mahogany coffee table. He had a glass of wine in one hand and the remote in the other. He was alone.

Relief flooded through Jude. It didn't make this easy, since Sosa always had dangerous guests in addition to an in-house security team, but it meant an innocent woman wouldn't end up in the crossfire.

"Unit two in position." The unit leader's voice was barely above a whisper. "I've got visual on two armed hostiles in the poolroom."

Jude played through the positions in his head. Unit 3 was on the northernmost side of the estate. Two was ready to breach from the front to the east. Four flanked them all, and he was in charge of Unit 1, with the sole focus of capturing Sosa. Everything was in place.

Jude readied his mic. "On three." He took one more deep breath. "Three. Two. One. Go go go!"

A flurry of activity hit all at once. Wood splintered. Gunshots filled the night.

He moved from his position to the glass-fronted side door. Jackson and Perry reached it just before him. They were preparing to break in when shots exploded the wall near his head.

Jude whipped around to see a tall man wearing black and wielding an automatic weapon. Where was Vanessa? His gut clenched. Had this goon blindsided her?

He aimed and took three shots. They hit center mass and the man went down hard. Jude waited, but no one else came around the corner.

"Wiley, report." Jude spun back to the task at hand, awaiting her reply. Nothing.

Intel indicated all glass in the house was shatter- and bulletproof, so Perry used thermite to break the door lock.

The door swung inward. On count, Perry went in first, followed by Jackson, then Jude.

"ATF. Warrant. Hands up!" Jackson roared.

The couch was empty, the wine glass spilled on the floor.

"He's gone." Perry's reply came out muffled by his black balaclava.

"Come on." Jude motioned to the hallway he knew led toward the rest of the house from the media room.

Jude led with his gun out. He paused at one doorway—a bathroom—to check. Empty.

"Book, where's Wiley?" Perry ran down the carpeted hallway.

Jude wondered the same thing. Why hadn't she responded? He tried again. "Wiley, report?"

"Back of house," came a soft, staticky reply.

Jude held back a curse. She'd gone off on her own? He was

going to throw the literal book at her. His agents would love that—adding kindling to the flame of their favorite nickname for him. "Book" because he did things by the book. They could tease him all they wanted, but he'd learned that sticking to the rules provided guidance and saved lives.

"Hold your position, Wiley. I repeat, *hold*."

There was no reply. He motioned for the men to stop with his hand held up flat. He replayed the map of the sprawling estate in his mind. They needed to go left, then straight to reach the back.

Jude took off at a fast jog, and they cleared rooms as they went until they hit a long hallway that ended in a circular room with a glass-fronted door. That had to be the one leading to the back deck.

"I've got him!" Vanessa said over the coms, her channel clear now that they were in proximity.

"Hold your position. I repeat, hold." Jude motioned for his agents to follow, and they raced toward the door. Just as the hall ended, a shot rang out.

Jude slid to a stop. Had that been over the coms or in the house? "Wiley?"

Her silence pushed him toward the door.

He left the cover of the hallway, and a shot echoed in the small space.

A thudding pain sent Jude reeling back. The bullet lodged in his vest above his left shoulder. Jackson grasped Jude's vest and hauled him back behind the wall. Every movement increased the thundering pain.

"You okay?" Perry's face swam into view.

"Yeah." Jude gasped. His left arm had gone numb. "Wiley?" He shouted over the com.

More bullets ate into the wall opposite him. Why wasn't she answering?

They needed another plan. He looked around and caught

his reflection in a mirror. A quick explanation, and Jackson and Perry had the mirror ready to go.

"On my signal." Jude stood. Both men looked at him like he'd grown a second head, but he was regaining feeling in his arm. He'd be bruised, but nothing worse. Jude swapped out his M4 for his Glock. "Go."

Jude kept his back to the wall. The mirror went out, and he spotted a man positioned behind a waist-high bar before more gunfire shattered the glass. Jude nodded to the other agents as he pulled a flash-bang from his vest.

The explosion of sound and light disoriented the shooter, and Jude took him out with well-practiced shots to center mass. Jackson used the distraction to reach the back door. "Book!"

The note of panic in his teammate's voice was unusual.

Jude rushed to the open door. Vanessa lay in a pool of blood. Her eyes were open, staring. Sightless.

The sound of an engine erupted into the night air.

"Check her." Jude rushed to a steep set of stairs at the edge of the deck. He took several steps down but slowed. Below him, illuminated by orange dock lights, a black-and-red cigarette boat jetted off into the dark ocean waters. He could make out the figures of four men. One in particular.

Diego Ruiz Sosa had just gotten away.

"This is Unit Command. I need air and water support stat. Sosa is escaping by boat."

"Copy that. Dispatching now. Over."

"Sir...Vanessa..." Jackson's voice came over the coms.

Jude took the steps three at a time. He burst onto the deck, his left arm anchored to his side to minimize the pain. The sight before him churned his stomach. Vanessa.

One look from Perry and he knew there was no hope.

"Call it in." He swallowed hard.

"Brooks, we need you in here." The voice of the Unit 2 leader came over their command channel.

Everything inside of him wanted to break down. Vanessa, only twenty-six, and with so much life left to live. Vanessa, who bucked the system at every turn. Vanessa, sweet and funny.

"Brooks?" His coms barked again.

As much as he needed to process, now was not the time. "On my way."

The air inside the villa was warm, scented with alcohol where they'd shot up the bar. He rushed past and followed the directions of the Unit 2 leader until he came into a room on the third floor set up like an office.

An agent stood behind the desk.

"What is it, Owens?"

The agent looked up. "We think this might be a clue to what Sosa is up to next. You're the most familiar with his recent actions. Do you recognize anyone?"

Jude stepped past the tall man to look at the images scattered across the desk. Black-and-white photos. Clearly surveillance images. A woman and—

His sharp intake of breath caused the agent to spin around. "Everything okay, Book?"

"Yeah. I just..." He lifted a photo and his gaze traced the soft, feminine lines of a face years older than he remembered. "Yeah."

The agent moved back to the computer he was attempting to hack, and Jude shuffled through more of the images. *Andi.* Her mother. Her brothers. Her father.

The faces, all in various candid states, yanked him to the past. To summers spent at his grandfather's house. Cookouts with friends, playing guitar on the back porch, fishing the river, and spending time with her.

His first kiss.

Jude blinked and stepped back.

Not all of those memories were pleasant. It was a good

reminder to take in the full picture—not just her beauty or the blue eyes that were once so familiar.

Cartel lord Diego Ruiz Sosa had pictures of Jude's first love, the girl who got away, and her family. There were too many questions, but his biggest one eclipsed all the others.

How in the world was Andi Crawford involved in his case?

ACKNOWLEDGMENTS

To my husband. My Love, thank you for never complaining about what's for dinner. For working so hard for our family. For listening to my plot issues and then not getting too upset when I don't like your suggestions. For your encouragement, even when it's: "If you want to keep writing and making yourself crazy on a deadline, that's fine with me as long as you're happy doing it." I am happy, and you're a big part of that reason. I love you.

To my daughter and son. Thanks for not complaining when I say I have to go work out in the writing shed. And for eating more leftovers than you prefer. I hope you know that if I had to choose between you and writing, hands down, I will always choose you. I love having the privilege of being your mom. You both are a gift.

Huge thanks to Abigail Wilson. I never want to imagine this writing adventure without you. You are more than an awesome critique partner; you are my best friend. God so richly blessed me with you. #iheartyou #wemeshforever #justkeepswimming (And thanks to your family for letting me steal your time via Marco Polo. But seriously, you all live too far away.)

A great big thank-you to all the Sunrise team for all that you do, and specifically for taking a chance on a writer who hadn't ever really written suspense before. Especially Lisa Phillips. You are rocking this mentor thing. Emilie Haney and Laura Conaway, I wasn't sure what I was getting myself into, but I was blown away by your and Lisa's friendships. Making these stories with you all has been a treasure.

To my parents. A thank-you for *everything* never feels like enough. But thanks lately especially for Tuesday night dinners with you and for watching my kiddos once a week so I can work a bit more efficiently. Mom, I love getting to talk writing with you, and Dad, thanks for always being so patient with us while we're in author mode.

Thanks to my in-law family—yes, the entire crew. For Sunday lunches and making sure life is never too quiet or boring, providing me with lots of fodder for writing. For reading my books and for simply loving me. I wish all were as lucky as me when they married into a family.

Rachel Kent. Thank you for being a truly fabulous agent.

Erin Smithers. I bet you didn't expect to see your name here, huh? You don't generally read fiction and yet you consistently ask how my writing is going. Thanks for your listening ear, your prayers, friendship, and biblical wisdom. I appreciate you greatly. And a thanks also needs to go to Sarah Warner for reminding me of how muscles work.

Thanks to all I'm forgetting who have read, supported, and loved me throughout this journey. Ah! I'm so sorry! Please tell me if I forgot you, and I will put it in bold next time. Writing this acknowledgement section is bit like having stage fright. My brain is mush, but I do know that I'm so grateful for you.

To my Lord and Savior. Whether this books flops or not, You are so good. Thank You for taking a story that I thought was for my readers and using it to mold me. Without You, I am truly NOTHING. And I'm so thankful that life is dependent on You and not anything I do.

Thank you, readers, for taking a chance on Macon and Natalie's story. Thanks ahead of time for your reviews, thoughts, and messages about your favorite character or scene.

It's those little things that bring encouragement and makes my writer heart smile. And as always, I'd love to connect with you on social media and at www.meganbesing.com.

CONNECT WITH SUNRISE

Thank you so much for reading *Expired Hope*. We hope you enjoyed the story. If you did, would you be willing to do us a favor and leave a review? It doesn't have to be long- just a few words to help other readers know what they're getting. (But no spoilers! We don't want to wreck the fun!) Thank you again for reading!

We'd love to hear from you- not only about this story, but about any characters or stories you'd like to read in the future. Contact us at www.sunrisepublishing.com/contact.

We also have a monthly update that contains sneak peeks, reviews, upcoming releases, and fun stuff for our reader friends. Sign up at www.sunrisepublishing.com

ABOUT THE AUTHORS

Lisa Phillips is a USA Today and top ten Publishers Weekly bestselling author of over 50 books that span Harlequin's Love Inspired Suspense line, independently published series romantic suspense, and thriller novels. She's discovered a penchant for high-stakes stories of mayhem and disaster where you can find made-for-each-other love that always ends in happily ever after.

Lisa is a British ex-pat who grew up an hour outside of London and attended Calvary Chapel Bible College, where she met her husband. He's from California, but nobody's perfect. It wasn't until her Bible College graduation that she figured out she was a writer (someone told her). As a worship leader for Calvary Chapel churches in her local area, Lisa has discovered a love for mentoring new ministry members and youth worship musicians.

Visit Lisa's Website to sign up for her mailing list to get FREE books and be the first to learn about new releases and other exciting updates!

https://www.authorlisaphillips.com/sunrise

Despite adoring happily-ever-afters, **Megan Besing** didn't unlock a love for reading until her mid-twenties, which quickly expanded into writing. Her stories have won many awards, but her most cherished achievements are being a wife and mother. She lives in a pocket-size Indiana town, centered around extended family. She's always planning a road trip with a view, yet her favorite place may just be on her front porch drinking tea.

Connect with Megan at meganbesing.com

OTHER LAST CHANCE COUNTY NOVELS

Last Chance Fire and Rescue Collection

Expired Return

Expired Hope

Expired Promise (May, 2023)

Expired Vows (September, 2023)

Last Chance County Series

Expired Refuge

Expired Secrets

Expired Cache

Expired Hero

Expired Game

Expired Plot

Expired Getaway

Expired Betrayal

Expired Flight

Expired End

Expired Hope: A Last Chance County Novel
Published by Sunrise Media Group LLC

For more information about Lisa Phillips and Megan Being please access the authors' websites at the following addresses:
https://www.authorlisaphillips.com
https://www.meganbesing.com

Published in the United States of America.
Cover Design: Ryan Schwarz, thecoverdesigner.com

www.ingramcontent.com/pod-product-compliance
Lightning Source LLC
Chambersburg PA
CBHW030606310726
48979CB00003B/589

* 9 7 8 1 9 6 3 3 7 2 7 2 4 *